POLAR BEARS ARE FOREVER

BOOK ONE: SUPERNATURAL ENFORCERS AGENCY

ELIZABETH ANN PRICE

Also by Elizabeth Ann Price

Grey Wolf Pack Romance

1. A Mate for the Beta
2. The Alpha's Mate
3. The Librarian and the Wolf
4. Into the Arms of the Wolf
5. Wolves for the Bears
6. The Witch, the Wolf and the Snowstorm
7. Patient Mates
8. The Omega's Mate
9. The Wolf and the Bobcat
   - Short Stories Collection One
10. Mating the Red Wolf
11. Valentine's Wolf
    - Short Stories Collection Two
12. The Tiger's Mate
13. The Reluctant Mate
14. One Night with the Wolf

Supernatural Bounty Hunters

1. Foxy on the Run
2. Dead Man Running
3. To Catch a Snake
4. Bears in Flight
5. Flamingo Fugitive
6. Gorilla in the Wind

Supernatural Enforcers Agency

1. Polar Bears are Forever
2. For Your Paws Only
3. You Only Live Nine Times

One Shot Shifter Romances

- Loving the Tiger
- Keeping the Wolf

Monsters

- Monster Love (short stories)

CONTENTS

As part of the Supernatural Enforcers Agency, polar bear shifter Gunner Christiansen can handle just about anything thrown at him. He wasn't thrilled to have a human foisted onto his team, but he could deal with it. What he couldn't deal with was the fact that he couldn't keep his paws off her.

Psychic Erin Jameson is thrilled to be promoted to the Agency's Alpha team. She's spent years as the oddball that nobody gave a second thought to – talking to ghosts that no one else can see isn't exactly great for your reputation – but now it's her chance to prove how useful she can be. There's just one little problem – her smoking hot polar bear boss. Just a look from him has the power to turn her into a quivering mess.

Shifters are going missing, and one of the shifters has just turned up dead with his heart cut out, but can they keep their minds off each other long enough to catch the killer?

PROLOGUE

"How much?" rasped Tom 'the hammer' Murphy into the phone.

"Five hundred grand." The answer was given to him nonchalantly by a bored, yet steely voice.

"What?! Half a million? That's ridiculous! I'm just trying to stay alive, not buy a fucking private island in the Caribbean."

Forty years of shaking people down, building up his empire, and making himself one of the most feared shifters on the east side of Los Lobos, and he was getting screwed by a fucking nobody!

"It's your decision."

"No, wait! Don't hang up, can't we, I don't know, negotiate?"

Tom bristled at the malicious chuckle that reached his ears. *Apparently, they didn't negotiate.* "I don't need the business bad enough. My talents are in great demand."

"How soon could you do it?"

"You give me your details, and I could find a match within a week. I'd need the money before then."

Tom felt a wave of excitement course through him that quickly devolved into a coughing fit. He sipped at a glass of water offered to him by his

1

nurse. Finally, calming, he waved her away impatiently.

"I don't know if I can get the money that quickly," he lied, still trying to negotiate. *Fat chance.*

"Then call me when you can."

"No, wait, I can… I can maybe move some things around…"

"Mmmm hmmm."

Tom growled at the smug tone. "So what do you need?"

"Your medical file, and a five percent deposit; that's non-negotiable and non-refundable - in case you suddenly grow a conscience and decide you don't want to go through with it."

"Not an issue with me," he sneered.

"Fine, then it's non-refundable in case you die in the interim. Do we have a deal?"

Tom hesitated, not from any qualms about what they were about to do, but because he really resented handing over an extortionate sum of money to someone who was obviously weaker than he was.

However, his annoyances were quickly overruled. "Deal."

"I'll call you back with details on where to send the money."

They hung up and Tom stared at the receiver in distaste. *Nobody had ever dared to hang up on him!* Maybe he'd teach them a lesson. If he played this just right, he could get what he needed, and keep all the money.

Yep, soon, Tom would be back on top of the world. With that, he lapsed into another coughing fit, and slapped at the weary nurse as she tried to help him. Soon, he'd be back to his old self and all of this would be a bad memory.

CHAPTER ONE

Erin fidgeted in her seat. The bright lights, the hard, unforgiving seat, and the tight, itchy pantyhose all conspired to make an uncomfortable situation downright unbearable.

Unobtrusively, she tried to shift in her seat, and the leather against the cheap fabric of her suit created a loud fart-like noise. She cringed, and her cheeks duly turned to raspberry pink.

The director looked up from the file and raised an unimpressed eyebrow. The slight movement spoke volumes. *Why am I wasting my valuable time talking to someone as inconsequential as you?*

She looked down, immediately feeling guilty for even daring to step into his office, never mind for actually having the gall to ask for a job. Erin worked for the SEA or Supernatural Enforcers Agency. They were basically cops who dealt with crimes committed by supernatural creatures. The Agency was created by the Council of Supernaturals, who oversaw all matters pertaining to the supernatural world.

She focused on her shoes, a stylish pair of pumps that had set her back more than the monthly budget she allowed herself. *But they were worth it.* They were comfortable, yet hinted at sexuality, and gave her confidence where before she had none. *They were super shoes.* Looking at them made her realize she had nothing to be ashamed of. She had every right to be here, and just as much right as any of the other applicants. *She just wished that she hadn't spotted a ladder in her pantyhose…*

"Hmmm, so you've never been out in the field."

Erin started. It was the first words he'd said since he told her to sit down – ten minutes ago. And was that a question or a statement? *Crap, he was looking at her with an irritated expression.*

"No," she squeaked, "no, I haven't."

He pursed his lips and lowered his eyes back to the file.

She pinched the skin on her hand. Why couldn't she have come up with something clever? She could have extolled her virtues, and persuaded him that it didn't matter. She could have told him about the many times she had supported the field agents, and explained how much of an asset she would have been to them if she had been allowed to go out into the field with them. Yep, she could have done all that, but, instead, she chose to parrot back what he'd told her.

Lord, there was no way he was going to give her the job. She could barely even make it through an interview without falling to pieces; there was no way he was going to allow her out with a team of investigators. He wasn't going to trust her to interview potential suspects.

Erin licked her lips. *Hell, why was it so hot in there?* She felt beads of sweat prickle over her forehead.

"So, why do you want this transfer?"

She sucked in a breath. It was a question she'd been asking herself over and over, and she still wasn't entirely sure of her motivations. She wanted to do field work. She couldn't say why exactly, but she did. She had a yearning to push herself and do more. It was all very well sitting at a desk touching objects in the hope of getting some kind of clue, but she wanted to be in the thick of it.

Not waiting for an answer, he continued, "I mean, you seem to be doing well in the Playa Lunar division. Why would you want to give that up to come here? Most of my agents would love to go to Playa Lunar." He raised an eyebrow at her.

Erin shrugged. "I'm not from there, and I don't have any family or…" She was about to say friends and caught herself at the inquisitive look he flashed her. She *wasn't in the mood to throw herself a pity party.* "One city isn't much different from another to me."

"I think the appeal of Playa Lunar rests in its high percentage of shifter residents; shifter agents find it easier to fit in and work undercover," he mused.

"I'm not a shifter." *And I don't fit in anywhere, anyway…*

"No, you're not," he said placidly.

She wasn't sure whether that was supposed to be an insult or not so she ignored it. Not that she would have said anything if it were. *She was far too chicken.*

"There were no openings for a field agent in Playa Lunar, and you have the highest closure rate of any of the SEA offices in the whole country. I figure I could learn a lot."

The director leaned forward, resting his elbows on the desk, and capturing her with a deadly serious gaze. "Are you trying to kiss my ass?"

Erin almost barked out a laugh at the unexpectedly casual words, but his countenance certainly didn't court humor. "No, sir. Simply stating a fact."

He stared at her with unrelentingly cold eyes, and unknowing what to do, she held that gaze until he looked away. *Crud.* Maybe she should have averted her eyes to show that he was dominant to her. If she were a shifter, she would have instinctively known to do so.

The majority of the Agency Enforcers were shifters, with a few witches and some vampires peppered in. They did employ a few humans, but generally only as analysts, and rarely as field agents. *Erin was human.*

She knew the director was some kind of shifter, but she didn't know which species. It wasn't something that was talked about. Probably, other shifters could tell each other's species, and never needed to ask. Erin was too embarrassed to ask. She couldn't be sure whether it would be crossing a line or not.

He sighed and closed her file. His fingers tapped the cover, and he looked pensive. Anxiously, she wondered whether that was a good sign or not.

He snapped his eyes to her. "When did you realize... I mean when did you start..."

Erin was surprised at the sudden discomfort in the stoic man; he was curious about her abilities, but feared whether she would be offended by his questions. She quickly put him out of his misery.

"When I was five."

The director gave her a grateful smile and nodded encouragement at her to continue talking. Erin felt buoyed by the first sign of friendliness he had shown.

"I didn't exactly realize at first. I met a girl called Eloise, and we used to play together. It took a few weeks for my parents to figure out that she was actually a ghost and, not just in my imagination. It was a girl who had been killed by her uncle about ten years before. She wasn't able to move on.

"The visions started when I was ten. I was, ah, living somewhere else then, and a friend of mine, her cat went missing. She had some cat hair on her sweater, and when I touched it, I saw her neighbor, ah, killing it." *More like torturing and eviscerating it – that had given her nightmares for weeks.* "Apparently, they were having an argument over the height of the hedge between their properties."

He blinked at her. "You had a vision from a single cat hair?"

Erin nodded and rubbed her lips together. It used to annoy the heck out of her having to tell people that story over and over. Mostly, they burst out laughing, while others just thought she was a freak.

She thought she saw sympathy flicker over the director's face, but it was quickly masked by a look of indifference. *The sympathy was new.*

He quickly changed the subject. "I was impressed by the reports I heard about the Carradine case."

A flicker of pride burned within her, but she wasn't about to let it get out of control. "I got lucky; I got a vision that showed he just faked the fire, and that really he was running to Mexico."

"Your supervisor informed me that you pushed yourself hard to get that vision, and that the team wouldn't have found him if it weren't for you."

Alright, that was enough with the praise. She wasn't used to it, and it was creeping her out. "She's too kind."

Her eyes widened as he actually let out a chuckle and shook his head. "Fran Elway is not kind. She was furious when I called her to get an oral report on you."

Erin prickled. "She knew I was applying here."

He nodded and smiled. "She admitted that, but, forgive me for saying so, she never actually expected for me to take it seriously. She was livid when I talked to her."

Erin shuddered. Fran's temper tantrums were legendary, and the one she threw when Erin informed her she wanted to make a move to Los Lobos was a doozy. When screaming didn't work, Fran had tried wheedling. But, ultimately, Fran would never give her what she wanted – to be a field agent, so Erin had insisted she apply elsewhere. Of course, Fran had calmed down when she realized that Erin was exclusively applying to be a field agent. Her supervisor had never even considered that she would get past the application stage.

Well, at least she made it further than anyone anticipated.

"So," he interrupted her reverie crisply, "we have two openings for field agents. One is in our Delta team, who deal with fraud and identity theft, and the other is with the Alpha team. They deal with our top priority cases, such as serial and ritual killings."

Erin bit her lip to stop herself from smiling. It sounded like he was actually offering her a job. It sounded like he was actually giving her a chance! Yes, the Delta team would be right up her street. Would it be too much to give the director a kiss to say thank you? *Hmmm, probably.*

"I'd like to offer you a place on the Alpha team."

Her jaw actually dropped at that. *The Alpha team?* Was he kidding? If Los Lobos was anything like Playa Lunar, every career minded agent in the building would be vying for that spot. They dealt with the toughest cases, and being on that team was the quickest way to get into the upper echelons of the Agency. The director himself had once led that team personally.

He furrowed his brow. "Are you okay?"

She opened and closed her mouth a couple of times. "Just surprised," she spluttered. "I kind of assumed that you would want someone with experience…"

The director waved his hand at her. "All field agents have to start somewhere, and in spite of what some people in this building may believe, there is no more or no less prestige from working in any of my teams. I put people where I think they are best suited, and where their talents would be most beneficial, and I think, for you, that would be the Alpha team."

"Well… I… uh…"

Come on Erin, use your words. Just one problem, she had no idea what she wanted to say. She was just making sounds to cover the fact that she was actually speechless.

Okay, maybe she was being a little contrary, but when she envisioned being a field agent, it was starting off doing something a little prosaic like credit card fraud, or maybe someone selling bootleg DVDs. She just didn't imagine they'd want her to tackle anything major straight away. *Not with her only managing to scrape through the physical, and having no practical weapons experience.*

"You can take a few days to decide, if you'd like," he told her, not unkindly.

No, this was it. This was her opportunity to prove that she was just as capable as the rest. Once and for all, she'd show that she was special, that she was worth something. She'd put to rest all the things everyone had ever said about her. *Crazy. Fruit loop. Nutter. Freak.* She'd show them, the other kids, her siblings, her parents… *She could do this.*

"I don't need a few days," she said decisively, "I'll take the job."

He beamed at her and stood up, holding out his hand for her to shake. She followed suit, and almost managed to cover up her embarrassment at the loud fart sound the chair made as she stood up. *Almost.*

*

"Gerry, are you fucking kidding me with this latest recruit?!"

The director didn't look up from his computer. "Watch your language," he said placidly.

Gunner gave him a sour look and slammed the office door.

The director's eyebrow twitched. "By all means, come in."

The huge polar bear shifter strode across the room and leaned over the desk. Anyone other than the director might have cowered at the hulking form, but you had to try real hard to scare a python shifter.

The bear thumped a massive paw on the desk. "She has no experience of fighting or using a gun, no experience with interviewing, and she flunked the Agency physical six times. Why am I even wasting my time yelling about this?"

The director leaned back in his chair and looked at Gunner impassively. "I don't know; why are you wasting your time? I've already told you that she's your new teammate. You should be preparing her training rather than pointlessly getting angry with me."

"Don't I get a say in…"

"No," the director coldly interrupted him.

Gunner sank down into the chair facing the desk and growled at the loud fart-like noise. "Why her?" he demanded.

"She has potential."

"It took her seven goes to pass the physical!" he scoffed.

"But she did pass it."

"Probably because the instructor took pity on her. Old Sarge is losing his touch."

The director's face remained stony. Sarge had been the lead instructor at the Agency Training Center for over twenty years, and he was proud to say he had made more recruits cry and flunk out than all the other instructors combined. *Erin Jameson, however…* Yes, Sarge had a sweet spot for her after she helped him communicate with his late wife. In turn, Sarge might have fudged a couple of her times in the training exercises. Feeling remorseful, he had confessed everything to the director. He felt he had let himself and the whole Agency down. The director had easily smoothed his worries away. Without admitting it, he wanted Erin on the team no matter what. *Even if she didn't meet the high standards of the physical.* The director had enough people who could run around waving their firearms at people; he didn't have anyone like Erin Jameson, though.

The director took a small sip of water. "According to her file, she passed. That is enough."

"But she'll slow us down – she's human for crissakes!" *The director was clearly losing it.*

"We cannot be *speciesist*. A number of our employees are human."

"But they're either witches who can defend themselves, or they work in the office. Look, I have nothing against this… this… girl, but if you want her to work with me, then keep her here as a consultant." *Out of harm's way.*

The director leaned forward and tented his fingers. "She will have a weapon."

Gunner bared his fangs. "Oh! You mean a gun. Do you actually trust her to run around with a gun? It took her eight goes to pass the weapons training. She missed the target completely her first three attempts."

The director looked at him through narrowed eyes. "That wasn't in her file."

The bear had the good grace to look a little sheepish. Okay, so when he found out he had been lumbered with an untested human, he might have put in a few calls to the Playa Lunar field office and the SEA training facility. He couldn't get a bad word out of Sarge, but others had been more than pleased to co-operate. *Bumbling, timid, weird – they were just a few words that were thrown around about the human woman.* And the guy he spoke to couldn't stop laughing at her inept attempts at shooting a gun, *apparently she kept aiming with her eyes closed…*

"Fine, I might have done some checking on her."

"I'd expect nothing less from a conscientious team leader," the director said, patiently.

Gunner watched him for a few beats. Hmmm, he wasn't going to touch that comment, it seemed like a trap. Instead, he focused on his many objections to his new recruit.

"Plus, the only gun training she has is from a shooting range; she hasn't even gone through the simulator. By all means, if all the bad guys are paper silhouettes who don't move while you're trying to shoot them, she'll be fine. But, in the real world, she won't handle it."

The director gave him a ghost of a smile. "Then it's lucky she will have you as a mentor."

"So, my team and I are supposed to pick up the slack for her?"

"Your team has a sufficient number of agents who can rely on their natural speed, strength and agility to catch people. I don't expect Ms. Jameson to chase an elephant shifter down Main Street, and proceed to cause thousands of dollars of damage to city property, nor do I expect her to pose as an underground boxer and try to beat a rhino shifter half to death."

Gunner winced; he wasn't particularly proud of either of those things.

"She will be useful in other ways," continued the director smoothly. "Like I

11

said, she has potential."

"Potential? For what? If you want my advice, she should quit the Agency and marry a school teacher. She doesn't sound like she could handle anything more exciting than that."

The python shifter gave him a look that could freeze an active volcano. "I don't want your advice."

"It's my team…"

"Of which I am your supervisor, and I don't want another problem like we had with Zane."

Gunner blanched at the mention of his former teammate, but he felt a stirring of loyalty to his former colleague. "Zane was a good guy at the start."

"I'm focusing on what he did at the end," hissed the director.

"So, because you're worried about getting another Zane, you've given me a girl scout?"

The director smirked. "Don't worry, you don't have to buy any of her cookies. And like I said, she has potential."

"She's spent her life at a desk…" *The bear had a bad feeling that he wasn't going to get his way on this.*

"And now is her opportunity to get out into the field. She has to start somewhere. The teams she worked with have an extremely high success rate, better than any of my teams…"

Gunner bristled as his bear roared in consternation. *They did just fine!*

The director ignored his look of fury. "Not enough to make Playa Lunar's success rate higher than ours, of course, but enough for me to notice. I'd like some of that success too."

"Fine, then hire her as a consultant." *Why was this even an issue?*

"I think she can be more helpful as a field agent. You've read her file, you know what she can do."

"So what? Psychics are a dime a dozen."

The director curled his lips. "No, angry polar bear shifters are a dime a dozen. Psychics who can actually produce helpful and insightful visions are rare. Not to mention, she can communicate with the deceased. We're lucky she chose to work for us. I imagine she could make a lot more money in the private sector."

Gunner scoffed. "Oh, so you're pandering to her. You're afraid she might run off and take her psychic powers with her if she doesn't get her own way."

"Not at all. I don't believe she would do that. She's not a short-tempered shifter; she has more sense. If I hadn't offered her this job, I believe she would have returned to Playa Lunar and awaited the next opportunity."

The bear growled impatiently. He didn't want a human female on his team. *Fine, call him speciesist, call him sexist, but he could give a crap.* If she were there, he'd be constantly worrying about her, and he couldn't afford that. He needed team members who could be trusted to take care of themselves. And just one read of her file proved that he couldn't trust this girl even to put on a Kevlar vest without falling flat on her face.

He snapped his fingers together when a thought occurred to him. "Delta team needs a new field agent too."

He knew because a she-bear on their team was going on maternity leave. He'd dated her casually until she gave up on waiting for a commitment and mated with a lion shifter from the tech division. They were still friends.

"Why don't you palm her off on them?"

The director stared at him with all the warmth of an icicle; Gunner had the good grace to squirm a little.

"One month," declared the python.

"What?"

"One month probation, and if she doesn't come up to scratch then I'll reassign her."

Gunner breathed in and out heavily. He didn't like the sound of that at all, but he doubted it was going to get any better than this.

"Fine," he said through gritted teeth.

The director chuckled. "Oh, that wasn't a question, that was me telling you what I've already told Ms. Jameson. Don't think for one second that you have any say in the matter, because you don't."

Gunner fought back a snarl. *The guy was his boss after all.*

The python leaned forward and softened ever so slightly. "To be clear, I want Ms. Jameson here. But, if for any reason she doesn't work out, then the blame is mine. It's my decision, so the consequences – both good and bad – are all on me."

The bear rolled his eyes. *Whatever.* "Are we done?"

His boss pursed his lips to keep from smiling. "As I recall, you burst into my office, you're free to leave anytime you want."

Gunner grunted and made as if to do just that.

The director coughed. "Just to keep you in the loop, Zeta team have reported four missing shifters in the past two months."

The polar bear turned back. "That's not unusual? You know how shifters are."

A number of shifters tended to be quite flighty, and not given to take commitments like jobs and rent contracts seriously. They tended to let their animals make the decisions, and so when their beasts told them to travel south for the winter – off they went. Zeta team handled missing persons, and Gunner did not envy them one bit.

"Indeed I do," replied the director smoothly. "However, they have raised concerns over four as they all seem to have left a similar note, and a couple of them had strong ties to their clan and packs. Zeta are concerned and are investigating. I'm keeping you in the loop should the case come to you."

Meaning should the missing shifters turn up dead. Gunner grunted in acknowledgment and headed to the door.

"Give her a chance," called the director in a steely voice. "I'm sure she has a lot to offer."

The big bear huffed, and slammed the door behind him with as much ferocity as he dared. *The last time he broke the director's door he had to pay for it, after all.*

He stomped through the halls of the Agency offices. Everyone knew him well enough to get the heck out of his way. *Shame.* He could have done with a nice, juicy fight at that moment.

He'd go to the gym and work out. He'd pound the faces of some of the other agents, and that would make him feel better. Besides, he needed to be in tip-top shape. After all, he now had a human to chase after.

CHAPTER TWO

A week later

If Tom 'the hammer' Murphy didn't despise this person so much, he would be tempted to reach down the phone and give them a huge kiss. "Say it again," he croaked.

"I've found what you need," replied the voice disdainfully.

Tom didn't care; they could be the biggest asshole on the planet at the moment, but he didn't care. This was it; this was finally his chance at a real life again.

"How soon can I have it?" he demanded impatiently.

"I can make arrangements for tomorrow night, however, if you need more time to get the money…"

Tom felt a sharp stab of pain to his heart; his face twisted in agony, and his bored nurse rolled her eyes before making her way to him. He waved her away.

"No, tomorrow night is fine. I'll bring the money with me."

"Good, I'll call back with the time and address. I'm sure I don't have to tell you about the risks…"

"I'm not a fucking amateur," snapped Tom, prickling in anger.

"For your sake, I hope so."

They hung up on him. *Again!* Oh what he would like to do to them…

His beast, his poor, suffering beast raised his head and let out a small hiss of annoyance. It was the most animated he had been in weeks, and Tom cheered a little at that. Soon, he soothed his animal. *Soon everything would be back to normal.*

*

Erin smiled sweetly at the security guards. One remained stony and uninterested, while the other leered at her. She could have sworn he was looking at her like he wanted to gobble her up, and it was actually starting to worry her. He must be some kind of shifter, nearly everyone in the building was, and most shifters didn't tend to cover up their more, *ahem*, lascivious urges. No, most put them out there for the world to see. Not that she had experience in that area. *At Playa Lunar, her co-workers steered clear of her.*

She wasn't used to garnering attention of the opposite sex. She looked okay enough, if a little forgettable, with long brown hair, unremarkable brown eyes and cheeks that tended toward the pink. It was a source of annoyance to her that she was a little on the curvy side, and at five-foot-six, her legs were a little short. Both factors she was sure contributed to her numerous failed attempts to pass the physical. Although, it didn't help when she kept getting visions that caused her to topple off the monkey bars, and those ghosts that kept appearing when she was trying to climb the rope were no darn help either. Still, she got through it eventually. Ultimately, she was just a non-descript young woman who men rarely gave a second glance to. *For the best, most likely.* Those who did give second glances usually regretted it.

A tall, gorgeous woman glided into the lobby and the security guards, even stone face, immediately took notice. *Took notice? They were virtually drooling!* Not that Erin was surprised. The woman was a vision. She was lithe but toned, and moved with the easy grace of a dominant predator, and *holy crap*, she was making her way over to Erin.

Erin gulped at the woman towering over her, and a gurgle came out.

The woman wrinkled her brow. "Erin Jameson?"

"Uh-huh."

The woman gave her a toothy smile. All white teeth that looked like they ripped into innocent prey on a regular basis. "I'm Avery Jones; I'm a member of the Alpha team, it's nice to meet you."

Erin staggered to her feet in a very uncoordinated fashion. *Think of a dog on roller skates.* "It's nice to meet you," she squeaked.

Why was Avery so perfect? Tall without being lumbering. Fit without being too buff. Blonde and blue eyed without it taking away an ounce of her predatory nature. She was undoubtedly a shifter, but what kind?

Avery looked her up and down, but kept her face neutral. It was worse than if she had sneered; at least Erin would have known what she was dealing with. Avery cocked her head on the side. "Come on, let's get you sorted, and then I'll introduce you to the rest of the team."

Erin plastered on her fakest smile. "Great."

*

Avery was nothing if not thorough. She gave Erin a tour of the building, introducing her to everyone she came across. Erin was mostly glad she wouldn't remember all of their names, most of them had gaped at her in disbelief, while others sneered. *No doubt the agents who had been gunning for her job.* One female in particular had looked at her with out and out hatred. *Jeez, get over it.* Some just seemed like they were in a hurry, and couldn't care less who or what she was. Erin liked those people.

She had a badge made; she was given a new cell phone, and then she was given her gun. Avery saw the trepidation on her face but carefully ignored it.

Finally, Avery led her into a bullpen.

"Here's your desk," she motioned to a tiny cubicle. "You can do whatever you want with it, but we don't spend too much time here anyway. You're opposite me," she told Erin with a smile.

Erin returned the smile and sat down, trying to forget the gun she had stowed in her purse. Her desk back in Playa Lunar was twice as big, but then she hadn't really been allowed to leave it. Now, she would rarely be here. She thought of Fran's words as she cleaned out her old desk – 'you're welcome to come back here anytime.' *Comforting and nerve-wracking.* Fran expected her to fail. Well, she wasn't going to. *Hopefully, she wasn't going to.*

"All us grunts get a cubicle, and the team leaders get offices."

Avery nodded in the direction of a row of doors. Judging by how close together the doors were, not very big offices. No, you had to make it to director level before you got something cushy. She seriously doubted that was ever in her future, not that she wanted that. She wasn't really ambitious. Maybe it sounded lame, but she just wanted to help people.

"The BBB is in the end office."

Erin raised her eyebrows. "BBB?"

Avery grinned, showing an unnerving amount of teeth again. "Big Bad Bossman."

"Oh." *She wasn't sure she liked the sound of that.*

To distract herself, Erin pulled out a ratty and worn stuffed cat. It was only small, about the size of her palm, but she'd got it in an Hola Sunshine kids meal when she was four-years-old, and it had a place in her heart. She thought of it as her good luck charm, even though there had been periods of her life that could be described as anything but lucky. But, she countered, they could always have been much worse.

Avery stood up and peered over the cubicle, mirth dancing over her lovely face. Oh, Erin wasn't used to feeling jealousy toward other women for their looks; in general she didn't notice things like that, but Avery was disgustingly attractive, and it bothered her. When they were walking around the building, Erin might as well have been invisible next to the goddess-like charms of Avery. But, she suspected, that also might have been due to the fact that she was human. She knew that some shifters and witches mated with humans, but the majority stuck to supernatural creatures.

"Nice kitty," smirked Avery, "but I doubt the BBB will approve of that. He doesn't even like us having family pictures on our desks; he says it distracts us."

Erin felt a flash of irritation at this Big Bad Bossman, or whatever he was called. People were allowed to have family pictures for heaven's sake. "Well, it's not hurting anyone so he'll just have to get over it," said Erin primly.

She almost slapped her hand over her mouth when she said that. *Where the heck had that come from?*

Avery chuckled. "Couldn't agree more."

Erin blushed and decided to change the subject. "So, uh, when do I meet the rest of the team and the, ah, BBB?"

Something flicked over Avery's face, but it came and went too quickly for Erin to identify it. *Concern, maybe.* "Soon, the BBB is in with the director upstairs, can't you hear that?" Avery cupped her ear exaggeratedly.

"Hear what?" whispered Erin, her eyes rolling upwards, imagining the director's office.

Erin frowned; there was a slight, sporadic banging noise.

Avery nodded. "Yep, that's him."

"What are they doing? Playing racquetball?"

The blonde shifter let out a bark of laughter, and actually had to wipe her eyes. "No, the BBB is banging his fists and stamping his feet over you being on the team."

Erin felt the blood drain out of her face. "Me?"

"Yep, the BBB doesn't want a human on the team, and he's making a last-ditch attempt to get the director to change his mind. Fat chance; the director isn't budging on this."

"Oh." Erin looked down at her feet. *Hello super shoes — you're no comfort right now!*

Avery sighed and came around to her side of the cubicle. She perched her graceful frame on the edge of the desk. "Hey, I didn't tell you that to be mean, I told you so you know what you're dealing with. The rest of the team won't be clamoring to be your best friend either, but they'll get over it. No matter who got the job, the BBB would have found some objection to them. And, hey, I like you."

Avery gave her a playful punch on the shoulder and Erin forced herself not to yelp. *Playful for shifters was painful for small, human females.*

Feeling a surge of friendliness towards the blonde shifter, Erin also felt courage. "Do you mind if I ask what kind of shifter you are?"

Avery threw her head back and laughed; a number of the other occupants of the bullpen looked up. "Of course I don't mind; I'm a lioness."

Erin's eyes widened. "Really?"

The lioness waggled her eyebrows. "Don't worry, I won't eat you, unless you ask me nicely. I'm sorry; that came out weirder and more sexual than I intended."

But if Avery felt any discomfort, she didn't show it. *No, Erin was plenty embarrassed for both of them.* Thank god for the interruption.

A gruff voice called out, "Hey, Avery, conference room. Bring the newbie."

She nodded in the direction of the voice. All the glee was gone from her face, and she was all business. "Time to meet the team."

*

Avery strode into the conference room with all the confidence that befitted a beautiful lion shifter. Erin scuttled after her.

The lioness took a seat and patted the one next to her for Erin, which she gladly slipped into. Avery pointed to the two rough looking males staring at them.

"Erin, this is Cutter and Wayne. Guys, meet our new team member, Erin Jameson."

"Nice to meet you," she trembled.

They looked her up and down before bestowing her with matching grunts.

"Oh, and so you don't have to ask, Cutter's a wolf shifter and Wayne's a gator." Avery beamed at the three of them. "Erin's human," she told the males.

Wayne rolled his eyes. "We know."

Cutter narrowed his own. "So is it true that you see ghosts?"

Erin shuffled in her seat. "Some ghosts. Most have already crossed over."

Wayne looked around the room suspiciously. "Are there any in here right now?"

Erin bit back a giggle. "No, and even if there were, they'd have to want to show themselves."

Sometimes, she just wished so many didn't want to. As much as she'd liked her ghostly roommate, Gina at her last apartment, sometimes all she wanted to do was sleep – not stay up until 2am consoling her about how unfair it was to have been killed by a falling bathtub from the apartment above.

Cutter crossed his arms and looked at her doubtfully. "And you have visions?"

"Sometimes." *Oh, she knew where this was going.*

"But you don't know when or where you're going to get them?"

"No," she admitted quietly.

"So, if we come to a dead-end in a case, we can't even rely on you to give us some kind of miracle vision?"

"Well, I…"

Cutter scoffed. "So, you can't run as fast as us, you're not as strong as us, and you can barely even shoot a gun. And the one thing you can do is actually just a random fluke?"

The wolf shifter sneered at her in disgust.

Avery let out a low snarl. "Stop it, wolfy, unless you want to feel my fangs in your hairy backside."

Erin shook her head. She'd been there a couple of hours and already she was causing problems. "No, it's fine, he's right. Physically, I'm not like you, and I can't promise that I can get visions on demand."

Cutter threw up his arms. "So what good are you?"

"Enough," rumbled a soft but deadly voice.

Erin leaped out of her seat in surprise, and spun to find herself face to chest with an absolutely enormous man. She craned her neck to see him looking down on her with interest. *Oh, holy hell, he was unbelievably handsome.*

Erin immediately looked away and gave herself a mental kick for that thought. *So unprofessional.* She'd never responded to a man like that before. It was the darnedest thing. Tingles of awareness swept through her body, and her heart rate started racing like a damn motor vehicle. Not a good thing in a room full of natural born predators. And yes, she was certain that this mountain of a man was a predator. *Well, he wasn't likely to be a fluffy bunny shifter!*

Lord, he must have been at least seven-feet tall, and he was the beefiest man she'd ever seen. His t-shirt was stretched so tightly over his bulging muscles that she feared, *or should that be hoped,* that one flex would have him bursting out of it - Incredible Hulk style. But, no, it wasn't just his body, *which was outstanding,* it was his face. It was finely sculpted and set off by a pair of dazzling, pale blue eyes. *Oh, those lips, the things she wanted those lips to do to her...*

Erin blushed seven shades of embarrassed. *She had to stop — that instant.* Shifters could scent arousal, and she must have been lit up like the Aurora Borealis. She thought back to her visions — the ones that haunted her at night – and soon she was back on home territory, trying not to gag at eviscerated cats and people stabbing one another.

He opened those magnificent lips to speak, but was cut off by the director walking into the room with a huge scowl on his face that melted at seeing her. The snake shifter actually smiled. Had she done something to make him like her? If she had, it was completely unintentional. Usually, people started off smiling and then scowled when they saw her.

"Ms. Jameson, Erin."

The director walked toward her and carefully nudged the giant out of the way, who seemed disinclined to move. The snake shifter took her hand and shook it. She was very aware of the giant watching them closely.

"So, Erin, how are you getting settled in?"

"Umm, very well, thank you. Everyone's been very helpful."

She glanced at Avery and the lioness preened and beamed at the director.

"And you had no trouble finding an apartment and moving up here?"

Erin felt a little uncomfortable at his solicitousness. She wasn't exactly accustomed to people caring about her wellbeing, or even pretending to care about it, which is what she was sure the director was doing. She murmured that everything was fine.

He nodded shortly. "Good. I'm sure you've met your other team members, but I want to introduce you to your team leader."

He motioned to the big guy who stepped forward, never taking his eyes off hers. Even when she averted her gaze, she was sure his eyes were searching for hers. It was unsettling and yet disturbingly arousing.

"Gunner Christiansen, this is Erin Jameson, and Erin, this is Gunner."

Wordlessly Gunner reached out and took her hand. The heat of his large hand engulfing her tiny one immediately warmed her all over. *Just holding his hand was a heavenly feeling.*

What the heck was wrong with her? She never had this kind of reaction. Actually, she'd never had much of any kind of sexual reaction to a man. She wasn't accustomed to feelings of lust or desire; she could only go so far as to say that she endured curiosity as far as the opposite sex was concerned.

"Nice to meet you," he said lowly.

Great, even his voice was sexy – like the smoothest chocolate. Now she was hungry, and her stomach chose that moment to make a very loud gurgling noise. If he heard, he didn't react, thank goodness. Nope, he was still staring at her with those inscrutable eyes.

She muttered about how nice it was to meet him too. After a few seconds, she realized he still hadn't let go of her hand, and it didn't seem like he was about to. Not that she was complaining. No, she raised her eyes to meet his, and he caught her in a look. *Why did she feel like she was prey to his beast?*

The director clapped his hands together, and the spell was broken. Gunner looked away, and at once, dropped her limp hand. He strode around to the other side of the table – as far away from her as possible - and smoothly sank into a chair. Before her legs gave out, Erin slithered back into hers.

She pinched the skin on her hand, and the pain gave her some modicum of control over her body again.

Don't look at Gunner, don't look at Gunner. Crap, she couldn't help herself; her eyes drifted to him, but thankfully he wasn't looking her way.

The director opened his mouth but groaned as the door was flung open and a, *no other word could describe her,* bubbly woman erupted into the room.

"Sorry, sorry, sorry," she chanted while twitching her nose.

The director sighed. "Thank you for joining us, Jessie," he hissed.

She smiled at him, and was that a flutter of her extended eyelashes? "My pleasure," she said, apparently ignorant of the snake shifter's heavy sarcasm.

He rolled his eyes. "Jessie, this is our new recruit, Erin. Erin, this is the team's tech consultant, Jessie."

Jessie's eyes lit up, and she bounded over to a seat next to Erin. "It's lovely to meet you," gushed Jessie.

Erin was dumbfounded by the first person who actually did seem to be thrilled that Erin was there. *Other than the director, maybe.* She was also a little surprised by the woman in front of her. She looked like she belonged there even less than Erin did. She was shorter than her, but exceedingly curvy, and her colorful clothes and hair were in stark contrast to the muted blacks, blues and combat gear of the other team members.

"Umm, lovely to meet you too," garbled Erin.

Jessie mouthed that they would talk later, and Erin could do nothing but nod. She felt a sudden twinge, and looked up to find Gunner watching her again. She held his gaze, unsure of what to do, until the director cleared his throat, and Gunner finally looked away.

What was that about?

The director gave them all hard looks and passed them some files. "We have a new case, referred to us by the Los Lobos police force. Over the past two months, three female shifters have been attacked with the same MO, and last night the latest victim was murdered in her home."

Cutter, Wayne, and Avery let out matching snarls of disgust, making Erin jump. Gunner simply tightened his lips and took the file.

Jessie frowned. "I usually monitor all the news stations, how come this hasn't come up?"

"The victims were all wealthy, and their families made sure it stayed quiet."

"Why weren't we told about this sooner?" snarled Cutter.

The snake shifter shrugged, but it was obvious he was unhappy about the situation. "The cops thought that they could handle it."

"Fucking humans," muttered Cutter.

"There are plenty of shifters on the police force, too," murmured Jessie in a singsong voice.

"Do they have any leads?" asked Wayne putting an end to Cutter's growl.

"No, the perp was careful about covering his scent, and his DNA isn't on file. None of the victims were sexually assaulted, but they were beaten up, and the perp licked their cheeks."

Avery pursed her lips in distaste. "So what changed with victim number four?"

The director let out a long breath. "They were all attacked in their homes, but the others seemed to have been planned out in advance. The perp brought duct tape with him, but victim four was restrained by a telephone cord. Plus victims one to three were in their early twenties, and they were the daughters of males high up in their respective clans. Victim four was a housekeeper. It seems to have been a spur of the moment thing."

"Or the other attacks were leading up to this. Are we certain it's the same guy?"

They were the first words Gunner had said since he told her it was nice to meet her, and Erin almost fell off her chair. It was disgusting the way his sinfully, sexy voice affected her. No, she had to focus. *Her lust wasn't important right now.*

"The cops think so, but it might be best if we look at each attack separately so that we don't make any assumptions."

"Agreed," rumbled Gunner. "Jessie, get me all the info you can on the victims. We'll start with the most recent attack. Avery, you go and talk to the cop in charge of the case, get all their files and notes. Cutter, go to the morgue, I want the autopsy report. Wayne, I want you to talk to victim four's neighbors. I'm sure the cops have already spoken to them, but I want to know if there were any issues with her being a shifter. New girl, you're with me."

Erin's eyes widened as they were met by Gunner's steely look.

"Keep me in the loop," said the director as he swiftly made his way to the door. "Oh, and Erin, welcome aboard."

CHAPTER THREE

Erin flicked a glance at the massive man next to her. He hadn't said a word to her since they left the conference room, and honestly, that was fine with her. The less she spoke, the less she could make a fool out of herself.

He didn't look at her; if anything, his attention was resolutely directed in front of him as he drove them to their destination. *Wherever that was, he still hadn't deigned to tell her.* But, was it her imagination, or was the tension between them crackling?

The big guy was tense; there was no mistaking that, but wasn't it going a bit overboard? According to Avery, he didn't want her there, which was fine - admittedly she kind of expected that. But, he was giving her the silent treatment, and his body seemed to be repulsed just by her nearness. *Wasn't that a bit much?*

She was his new teammate, and although she was sure she was a disappointment, shouldn't he just be professional about it?

"When we get there, let me do the talking," he ordered gruffly.

The words were so unexpected, she started and hit her head on the passenger window. Finally, he did glance at her. *Probably wondering how he managed to get trapped in a vehicle with such a lunatic.*

"Okay?"

Erin nodded quickly, "Of course, you'll do the talking."

"No, I meant is your head okay."

Too much to hope that he'd missed that. "It's nothing, you just… umm… startled me."

He grunted. "You should think about wearing flat shoes."

"Oh!" Her cheeks burned bright red. "I'm sorry."

Gunner rolled his massive shoulders. "Not a big deal, but you're likely to do a lot of walking, and maybe some running."

"Yes, of course, I wasn't thinking." *Oh hell, running.*

"You don't have a problem with that, right?"

"No, not at all, I can… run." *She looked like a giraffe attempting a three-legged race when she did, but she could run.*

"Well, uh, we'll take things slowly. Right now, we're going to the crime scene. Maybe you can get, I don't know…"

"A vision?"

He let out a long breath. "Yeah, a vision. Don't worry, the body's already gone."

Erin let out a snort of laughter but sobered at his raised eyebrow. *Why couldn't she behave normally?* "Sorry, I'm not laughing at the situation. It's just that I've been having visions of dead bodies since I was a kid; they don't freak me out anymore."

"I'm sorry to hear that," he murmured.

Erin scrunched her forehead. "That they don't freak me out?"

The corner of his mouth twitched in an almost smile. "No, about you having visions, I wouldn't wish that on any kid."

She looked out the window. "You can get used to anything," she muttered.

They continued on in silence. She clenched her thighs together, trying to quench the burning need that had decided to assail her the moment she met the reserved man-mountain sat next to her. Even his indifference didn't do anything to cool her down. *Jeez, twenty-eight years old and she had to choose this moment to grow a sexual appetite.* She had the worst timing.

Erin spun around to look at him; the motion didn't go unnoticed by him. A question occurred to her, and her first instinct was to blurt it out at him, but when faced with his cold, questioning face, she lost her nerve and bit her lip.

"What?" he demanded impatiently.

Crud. "I… umm… I just wanted to ask you something."

"So ask," he hissed but then relaxed a little. "I won't bite."

His words reminded her of Avery's earlier, only she wouldn't mind if he wanted to bite her. No, stop it, she had to do something about that overactive imagination.

"I just wondered what species you were."

He burst out laughing, and she tried to sink down in her seat. *Way to make her feel an inch tall.*

"It's not funny," she grumbled. She didn't know if there were rules about that sort of thing!

"No, it's not," he said, but his shoulders still shook. "I'm a polar bear."

"Oh!" she exclaimed. *No wonder he was so big!*

"Oh?"

"Oh," she reiterated.

"Oh, it is," he murmured.

"And Jessie? Is she also a shifter?"

Gunner grinned. "Yeah, she's a squirrel."

Erin giggled before slapping a hand over her mouth. "Sorry, please don't tell her I laughed."

"I doubt she'd mind. Speak of the devil."

Gunner pushed the answer button on his phone. "Jessie, you're on speaker phone."

"Hey!" called the chirpy squirrel. "Hey, Erin, how's it going?"

"Umm, fine, thanks, how's it going with you?"

The voice chuckled. "Peachy, is Gunner treating you okay?"

"Get to the point, Jessie," growled Gunner.

The squirrel clucked her tongue. "Okay, so just a bit of info for you, victim number four was called Hilda Billington. She was a beaver shifter, and she worked as a housekeeper for the Samuelson pack alpha and his family."

"Fuck, wolves," breathed Gunner.

"She'd worked for him for about ten years since she was eighteen, and she lived in a bungalow on his estate. She was a widow and didn't have a current boyfriend. I'm doing some checking about her past, but so far I can't find anything connecting her to a police report of any kind."

"Thanks, Jessie, keep looking."

"Okay, bye…"

Gunner cut her off, and Erin raised her eyebrows.

He caught the look and shrugged. "If you let her, she'll talk your ear off. Besides, we're here."

Erin looked up, and sure enough they had arrived outside a gaudy, and opulent estate. *The family home of the Samuelson wolf pack alpha, that appeared to have been modeled on the Parthenon.*

Gunner leaned out the window and told security who he was; seconds later, the gates swung open to allow them entry.

Before driving on, he turned to her and her breath caught in her throat. "Again, just let me do the talking."

Erin nodded her acquiescence and, satisfied, he drove up to the house.

*

Erin stood, hands on her hips, unsure where to start.

Gunner had exchanged a few words with their victim, Hilda's employers. The alpha's mate seemed to care for the loss of her housekeeper, but the alpha just seemed to find her whole death inconvenient. She could tell that the polar bear shifter barely managed to contain his temper around them, but he did. She was less thrilled at the fact that both wolves were looking at her like she was their next meal.

But, after a few inquiries, they headed to the crime scene. Gunner went off in search of the people Hilda worked closely with, like the maids and gardeners. Erin was left to her own devices in Hilda's home.

The more time Erin spent there, the worse she felt. Hilda's house was small but cozy. It was filled with knick-knacks, pictures of family and friends – it was everything a home should be. And knowing that someone had violated it, and what they had done... it was sickening.

She had to help find this sicko. She had to make sure they never did this to another woman. Erin didn't like doing it; it made her feel ghoulish, but she started touching Hilda's possessions in the hope that they might trigger something.

Hmmm, no such luck.

Erin made her way into the bedroom where the attack had taken place. She shuddered at the blood stain on the carpet. *Thank god she wasn't squeamish, or she'd be freaking out right now.*

Gingerly, Erin knelt on the floor. She pressed her fingers to the stain and breathed in and out.

"I wouldn't bother; it's already been scrubbed."

Erin squealed in surprise and scooted backward across the floor until she banged her head against the closet door. She pressed the heel of her hand into her heart and glared at the apparition standing by the window.

"You scared me," whispered Erin blandly as soon as she got a hold on her breathing.

Hilda smiled slightly. "I guess it's something I should get used to - scaring people."

"Most people won't be able to see you," admitted Erin sadly. "I'm sorry for what happened to you."

Hilda shimmered as she walked directly through the bed. "It's so strange; I should be angry or regretful, but I'm not. I don't feel anything, in fact, everything, my memories, my thoughts, feelings - they're all really fuzzy. I'm just... umm, what's the word?"

"Numb?" offered Erin.

The ghost shook her head. "No, I feel serene. Like, now that I'm dead, nothing matters. Like I said – strange. What happens to me now?"

"Sorry, I don't know. As far as I'm aware, ah, ghosts only hang around for a day or so after they die, or longer when they have something they want to impart to the living. Otherwise, they pass over – but that's the part I have no idea about."

Hilda cocked her head on one side. "How can you see me?"

"I just can. Is there anything you'd like me to pass on for you? Are there any messages you want me to give to anyone?"

Erin was dying to ask her about who killed her, but she had her priorities. Hilda was a well-loved woman, and if Erin could provide any kind of help to her loved ones, she wanted to.

Hilda mulled it over. "Could you tell my parents that I love them and that I'll be with Danny now?"

"Of course."

"Oh, and I want Alice Cooper's Poison to be played at my funeral. That's an absolute must."

Erin nodded and chewed on her cheek, pondering how to phrase her delicate question. "Hilda, do you know who killed you?"

The ghost knit her brows together. "I'm not sure. They came at me from behind. I never saw their face. But, it was a man, I was sure of that. And they were shorter than me; they had skinny arms, but they were very strong. Plus, I saw their watch. It was this fancy diver's watch with a red dial, and it was really familiar, I know I'd seen it before, but I couldn't be sure where. Does that help?"

"Yes, it does, thank you."

Hilda smiled at her. "I guess I should get going then."

Erin looked down as she pushed up off the ground, and in that second, Hilda disappeared. She stowed everything Hilda had said in her memory, in particular the promises she had made, and went off in search of Gunner.

*

Erin had traipsed around the grounds for more than half an hour before she gave up the search for her BBB. Instead, she made her way into the kitchen of the main house.

She was startled to find a teenage boy rummaging in the refrigerator. He looked up and sniffed before whirling around to fix her with amber eyes.

Crud. He was probably related to the alpha, and to him, she was trespassing.

"I'm sorry," Erin blurted. *No, stop apologizing for yourself you have every right to be there.* "I'm with the SEA, we're here about Hilda."

He nodded at her with wary eyes, one hand still paused inside the refrigerator.

She stood up straight and noticed that with heels, she was actually taller than the boy before her. He was unusual for a wolf shifter, shorter and more gangly. Males at his age tended to be already topping at least five-feet-ten inches, and they tended towards thick muscles.

Still, perhaps he could be helpful.

Erin took a couple of steps toward him. "Did you live here?"

His lips curled upward, and he directed his gaze back to the food. "Yeah, I'm Billy, the alpha's son," he said coldly.

"So, you knew Hilda well?"

He tensed but tried to shrug nonchalantly. "She worked for my parents. I saw her around the house."

Erin bit her lip. *Something was wrong.* She didn't have to be a shifter to know that something was off with him. But a hunch wasn't enough.

"I'd like to talk to Hilda's boyfriend…"

Billy slammed the refrigerator door closed and bared his fangs. "Hilda didn't have a boyfriend."

His eyes and his sharp teeth were terrifying, but what scared Erin the most was just what was on his wrist. *A diver's watch with a red dial.* A coincidence, perhaps. But every screaming instinct inside her told her it wasn't.

Belatedly, she recalled that she had left her purse containing her gun in Gunner's car. *Fat lot of good it was doing in there.*

Billy narrowed his eyes as he saw her staring at his watch. He couldn't possibly have known what she did about the watch, but his suspicion was evident.

She needed to get out of there and find Gunner, she would tell him what she knew, and then they could work out what to do next together. She mumbled an excuse and headed for the door, but the suspicious wolf was already upon her.

With a strangled yelp, she was dragged to the floor, and the young wolf shifter was upon her, his strong hands wrapped around her neck. She tried clawing and scratching at his arms; she tried kicking her legs, but it was all to no avail. He was too strong. This was it; she was going to die at the hands of an adolescent wolf on her first day of work. *Vaguely, she wondered whether Gunner would come to her funeral.*

But, no, wait, she was saved!

A huge roar shook the entire frame of the McMansion. The boy trying to squeeze the life out of her howled and leaped away from her. She coughed and spluttered as she tried to suck air into her deprived lungs.

Her vision swam as an angel appeared before her. He had pale blonde hair, startling pale blue eyes, and the most ruggedly handsome face she ever saw. *Why was the angel yelling at her?*

"Erin! For fucks sake!"

Oh, her angel was Gunner. *And boy did he look pissed.*

Carefully, he pulled her body up and propped her against a muscled arm. She coughed and buried her face in his shoulder. Yes, this was nice, this felt right. Oh, she could just fall asleep right here in the arms of this gorgeous man.

No, her conscience screamed, what about Hilda?

Erin snapped her eyes open to see the fury and concern marring Gunner's handsome features. "That boy," she croaked, "he killed Hilda."

Gunner stiffened and flicked his eyes in the direction that the wolf had disappeared. He was torn between staying with her and going after him. She made the choice easy when she rasped at him to go.

"Stay here," he ordered and stormed through the house, raising his gun.

Like she had a choice. *Ooh, look, Gunner remembered to bring his gun.*

Erin dozed with her head lolling against a kitchen cabinet. *Ugh, so tired.* Her eyes lifted as she heard the startling crunch of metal followed by screams and shouts. At that point, she gave up and fainted.

CHAPTER FOUR

Beep... beep... Paging Doctor Smyth to the obstetrics ward... beep... beep...

Erin blinked awake and then immediately regretted it. Her head hurt like a bitch. *What the heck?*

Sterile white walls, crisp, itchy linen, disgusting bleach smell – *oh, she was in a hospital.* She had to get out of there, pronto.

She sat up and tried to will her sluggish limbs to move. *Why was everything so hard?* She needed to get out of there; she didn't want to spend another second in a hospital. She swung her legs off the bed, and they immediately crumpled beneath her. Instead of hitting the ground, she found herself gripped by two, warm, comforting arms. *Oh, no...*

"Just take it easy," murmured Gunner.

"You take it easy," she grumbled.

She looked up to see surprise on his face; he wasn't expecting that – *admittedly lame* – sass. She couldn't tell whether it was amusement or annoyance twitching at his lips.

"For my sake, take it easy."

He lifted her back on the bed as if she weighed nothing more than a bag of potato chips. *And she knew she weighed substantially more than that.*

Erin patted her hands over her clothes. At least she'd been allowed to keep them. No embarrassing opportunities to flash her sizable rear in an unflattering, backless hospital gown.

Gingerly she rubbed her raw neck. *Darn wolf shifter.* Gunner's eyes were hooded, and he folded his huge arms over his chest. *Damn, sexy polar bear.*

"What happened?" she asked uncertainly, trying to distract the more libidinous portion of her brain. *Fat chance...*

"Where was your gun, Erin?"

She frowned as he avoided her question. "It was in my purse, which I left in the car..."

She leaped a foot in the air as he smashed a fist into the wall. "Fuck!"

A nurse burst through the door; her face was ablaze with fury, which dimmed the moment she saw him. "Agent Christiansen, please refrain from destroying our walls, I don't think they'll stand up to an assault by you."

"Sorry."

The nurse nodded and giggled before backing out of the room again. Erin scowled as she felt a wave of jealousy. *The woman was old enough to be his mother for hell's sake.*

His contrite attitude vanished the moment he looked at Erin again. He strode over to her and leaned down, his seething face inches from hers. "You could have been hurt." He pushed away from her and scrubbed his hands down his face. "Why do you even want to be a field agent?"

"To help people..." she said lamely. *Okay, so she didn't exactly follow procedure...*

"Is what you did today helpful? That wolf shifter, Billy Samuelson, said you accused him of murdering Hilda and when he tried to leave, you attacked him."

"What? I... well... I... that's not true at all! He murdered Hilda."

Gunner glared at her. "You know that for a fact?"

"Well, a ghost told me," she admitted lamely. "Or, at least, she told me about his watch…"

The polar bear shifter looked like he was about to explode; his eyes shimmered to the dark brown of his beast. "A watch? A fucking watch?"

Erin crossed her arms, thoroughly annoyed at where this conversation was going. "I know it's him. Hilda told me that her attacker had a diver's watch just like the one Billy wears. When I was talking to Billy, I thought that something was wrong, so I tried to leave, and that's when he attacked me. I didn't accuse him of anything, and I certainly didn't try to jump him. I'm a puny human, remember? One not good enough to be on your team. I certainly wouldn't have done something crazy like try to take on a wolf shifter. In spite of what you may think of me, I'm not actually suicidal."

His nostrils flared, and his lips were set in a grim line. *Had she gone too far?*

Moving on… "What happened after you left the kitchen?"

Gunner exhaled deeply. "I ran after the boy; he jumped in his father's Porsche and was about to get away, except he backed into his mother's car. Guess he didn't realize it was in reverse. He's in hospital here, too."

Erin gulped and fingered her neck. "Not near me though, right?"

Gunner looked affronted. "No, other side of the hospital, and he's being watched by Cutter and Avery."

Phew, no way did she want to repeat their earlier meeting.

"His parents are threatening to sue us. The director's going mental."

Erin felt tears welling in her eyes. *Embarrassing, unprofessional tears.* "I'm sorry, but I'm sure it's him. I bet if we searched his room we'd find…"

"*We* won't be doing anything. Once the doctor clears you, you'll be going home to get some rest."

"But…"

"No buts, Erin," he snapped. "What happened today was a mess. Forget the fact that we're about to get sued by one of the most powerful alphas in Los Lobos, you could have been seriously hurt, and all because you forgot your fucking gun. How could you have been so reckless?"

She opened her mouth to retort but thought better of it. "I'm sorry, what do you want me to do?"

Gunner stared at her, hard for a few beats. "If you're well enough, I just want you to go home. Wayne will drive you."

Yes, he wanted her home, out of the way, where she can't do any damage.

"Okay," she said quietly.

"Good."

He stalked to the door but stopped when he got there. He turned back and gave her a pained look. She held her breath, her silly, twittering heart, hoping that he'd give her something, any sweet word, but he said nothing. He shook his head and left.

Crud.

*

Erin stared at her apartment dejectedly. It wasn't a great place, but it was decent enough, and it came furnished.

The hospital had wanted her to stay overnight, but after a lot of cajoling, whining and outright complaining, the irritated doctor gave in and allowed her to sign a release form. If she died at home, it was completely her fault. *She was fine with that.* At her lowest ebb, she wondered about how many people actually would care if she died. Her sister, maybe, but would anyone else? *Would Gunner?*

She had to stop thinking about him. Clearly, she was just an inconvenience to him. *An embarrassing one at that.*

Wayne had diligently driven her home. He didn't talk much, thank heavens, but at least she hadn't noted the abject anger and disapproval evident in

Gunner's demeanor. When they arrived, he actually asked her if she needed anything. No, she just wanted to curl up and cry. *She didn't need anything to do that.*

She replayed the events of the day over and over, and, surely, Gunner was overreacting. Okay, she'd forgotten her gun, and that was a big no-no, but it wasn't her fault that the wolf shifter attacked her. She really hadn't tried to incite him. Gunner was acting like she'd committed a grievous offense in getting attacked – like she had a choice in the matter!

Erin walked over to the refrigerator and pulled out a piece of cheese to nibble on. Unbidden, she had a vision of the refrigerator being installed. The landlord was shouting at the deliverymen about how they were trying to rip him off.

Great, it was going to be one of those nights. Sometimes, she had the most random and pointless visions. Just little pockets of memories that served no other purpose than to drive her absolutely bananas.

She really didn't want this, not that night. She was tired, and she wanted a shower, so she resorted to the only way she knew how to dull the visions. She grabbed a beer and tripped off to the shower. *Yep, a soothing shower and a beer, worked every time.*

*

The banging wouldn't stop.

Reluctantly, Erin dragged herself to her feet and shuffled over to the door. She'd downed two beers and was thankfully starting to feel a little numb, but also, a little braver than usual.

Ugh, it was probably her pervy landlord come to get the rent. She'd met him twice, and both times he'd openly leered at her. She imagined he did the same to all his female tenants, and she'd bet her head that he came by late to catch her in her pajamas.

Well, he was in for a treat, because she was currently decked out in a pair of baby blue pajamas with polar bears all over them. A birthday present from her parents who had no idea about her likes and dislikes. *Although, she couldn't deny the fact that polar bears were suddenly more appealing.*

She flung the door open, ready to bawl out her landlord for coming by so late. Instead, she almost fainted at the sight before her. *Gunner.*

Erin opened her mouth to say something witty, something charming, hell, something at all, but no sound came out.

"Can I come in?" he asked quietly, since it was obvious she wasn't capable of more than a fish impression at that moment.

She nodded and instead of sidling past her, he walked straight toward her, forcing her to back up. He shut the door behind him and made a show of locking and bolting the door.

His eyes were immediately drawn to her neck, and a hard look flitted over his features. *That tiny change was chilling.* Thankfully, he relaxed a little as he looked her up and down, before raising an eyebrow at her pajamas. She felt the heat rushing to her cheeks. *Oh, kill me now.*

"You don't have a peephole," he said thoughtfully, running a hand up and down her door. *Lucky door she thought facetiously.*

"Umm, no."

"You should always ask who's at the door before answering," he rebuked her lightly.

"To be fair, flimsy doors like that wouldn't keep out most shifters." She said it jokingly but he just nodded in agreement.

"You should really live in a building where you have to buzz your guests in. It's not much, but at least it would stop just anyone wandering up and down your halls."

But it would have stopped you getting in. "Did you come all the way over here to discuss my terrible security? Or was there another reason?"

"You've been crying," he said accusingly.

She couldn't deny it. She'd cried over the dead woman, she'd cried over the fact that she might have made a mistake about the boy, and she'd cried pathetically over what a mess she had made on her first day of work. *Pity party – table for one!*

"I'm worried that you might be right, about the boy. I'm worried that I was wrong…"

"You weren't wrong," he declared curtly.

"What?"

He sucked in a deep breath. "When we searched his room, we found pictures of women he'd clearly been stalking, and three of those women included the ones who were attacked. We found his roll of duct tape; it had some splashes of the third victim's blood on from when he hit her. It was him. When we questioned him, he finally admitted it. The first three victims were girls who rejected him. But he broke down about Hilda; apparently he'd loved her for years, but fearing that she'd never love him back, he killed her."

Erin let out a sob, and she felt her legs give way. In a flash, she was encircled by strong, warm arms, and was soon deposited on the couch. He didn't move away like she expected, no, he hovered over her, concern evident on his handsome face.

"Do you want me to get you a glass of water?"

"No! No, thank you, just don't leave me… I need a few moments."

How could she say, I like having you so close to me? How could she articulate feelings that even she didn't understand?

Gunner seemed satisfied with her answer and settled into the couch next to her, shoulder to shoulder. *Or rather shoulder to bicep.* He really was big. The drunken part of her mind wondered whether he was in proportion, *you know*, in all areas, but Erin quickly scolded herself. *Now was not the time!* Would there be another time?

"Getting this guy so quickly was a real boon, Erin. It's a good job you were there."

She felt pleasure at his words blossom within her. *Actual praise!*

"But, the way you went about it today…" He exhaled deeply. "Things could have been a lot worse. We got lucky finding that blood on the duct tape. If we hadn't, he could have argued that everything was circumstantial. And worst of all, you could have been seriously hurt. No, you could have been killed."

"I'm sorry," she whimpered.

"Please, stop apologizing," he groaned.

"I'm…" She caught herself before she said it again.

"Look, I came over here to say well done but also to bawl you out on the whole gun thing. So considered yourself officially told off."

"Okay."

Erin pinched the skin on her hand, and he watched her curiously.

Gunner turned to look at her, searchingly. "Seriously, how are you feeling?"

She shrugged. "My neck's really sore."

He ran a finger over the burgeoning bruises, and she shivered under his touch. She clamped her legs together as she felt her sex moisten. It ought to be illegal the way he made her feel. She wondered if he elicited the same reaction in all women? A spark of anger ignited in her. She didn't want any other women to think of him that way. *Only her.*

His finger stopped as it reached her collarbone, and jeez, she almost begged him to keep going further until he reached her aching nipples. Her sex life had always been more of a pull your pants down, two minutes later it was all over, kind of deal. She couldn't recall any man ever taking the time to touch her breasts even, but here they were, burning to feel this man's touch. Yearning to feel, his big, rough hands on them. *Even if Erin didn't know what she wanted, her body sure did.*

Erin licked her lips, and he actually moved an inch closer to her. For a moment, she thought he was going to kiss her.

Instead, he mumbled the word, "Drink."

The spell was broken. "Huh?"

Gunner leaned back, and she almost mewled at the loss of heat from his large body. "The team always goes for a drink after we close a case, or when we're stuck on a case, or when we just want a drink. We don't really need an excuse to drink. You're welcome to join us."

She was tempted, sorely tempted, anything to prolong her time with this man, this shifter, who incited such feelings in her. But, she wasn't really up to dealing with other people. *Other judgmental people.* "I'm a little tired, and I already had a couple of beers."

His jaw ticked. "Next time."

"Yes," she agreed half-heartedly.

"I better go."

Gunner bounded toward her door and started pulling at the locks and chains like he couldn't get out of there quick enough. He paused before leaving, "You'll be at work tomorrow, right?"

"Of course."

"Good, I'll see you then. Make sure you lock the door behind me."

With that, he was gone. She gaped at the door before rushing to lock it; she didn't want to give him an excuse to chastise her again.

Was he her boss or her dad? Right now, it was hard to tell just what he was trying to be. Why did she feel so confused around him? Why did she feel like he had some kind of hold over her?

Whatever it was, she couldn't wait to see him again. *Yikes, he'd been gone a minute and already she was missing his company.*

Is this how everyone felt about their first crush? If it was, it was a wonder that anyone ever managed to get any work done!

Oh, she was screwed.

CHAPTER FIVE

Fuck, this was bad.

Gunner stared into his beer. His bear – *his usually, sullen asshole of a bear* – was practically dancing around like he hadn't a care in the world. Stupid beast was no help. He couldn't see the problem, but Gunner did.

It was all very well to find one of your teammates attractive; it was quite another to be desperate to rip her clothes off and sink inside her luscious body. He'd never felt such a deep-seated need for a woman. *And god help him, it wasn't just sexual.* If it were, he could understand it. It would just be an itch he could scratch. But, oh no, couldn't be that easy, could it? No, when he'd seen Erin, tear-stained and bruised, he'd wanted nothing more than to pull her onto his lap and cuddle with her. He wanted to be intimate with her. *Fuck, he was losing it.*

He'd felt the thrill of arousal from the second he saw her. It wasn't so unusual to feel an immediate pull to a woman, but she really wasn't his type. She was smaller, curvier, and another species - to name a few differences, but hey, attraction was attraction.

No, it wasn't until she'd looked at him across the conference table that he really knew he was in trouble. *She didn't look away.* His beast stared right at her, and she didn't flinch, or bare her neck in submission. It kind of pissed off his dominant side, but that was eclipsed by how much it turned him on. If she were a shifter, she would have looked away. *She would have been forced to.* But no, she met his gaze with those deep, soulful eyes. She trapped him with the vulnerability he saw flashing in them, and, fuck, he wanted to reach over that damn table and pull her into his arms.

Fuck, this was bad.

Why did she have to come to work wearing a figure hugging skirt and blouse? It showed off far too much of her curvy legs, and damnit, ended in those come-fuck-me heels. *Yes, he already wanted to, he didn't need those heels making her look any hotter than she already did.* From the brief touches he'd allowed himself, he was already besotted with her. He wanted to run his hands all over her. No, not just his hands, he wanted his mouth on her. He wanted to taste, lick, nuzzle, and savor every inch of her delectable looking skin.

Why the hell did she have to be human? She was so frail, so fragile. What if he hadn't been there today? That fucking wolf would have ripped her apart. His heart almost stopped when he heard her yell, and his beast was only just really starting to calm now. He knew it was a bad idea to have a human on the team, but he had no idea how bad. He couldn't trust her to be on her own. What if she got into a dangerous situation and he wasn't there to protect her? He couldn't trust Cutter or Wayne to look after her.

Gunner banged his fist onto the table as his beast roared in fury. No, they were males, he wouldn't allow them anywhere near her anyway. *Who knows what they might try!*

No, he needed to be with her, he needed to protect her. God knows she wasn't doing an adequate job herself. The security at her apartment was pathetic. Barbie protected her dream house better than Erin did herself. Something had to be done about that.

"Hey, BBB!"

Gunner smothered the growl that wanted to escape as he was surrounded by his teammates.

Jessie bustled into a seat beside him, ignoring the glower on his face. *The squirrel was far too brave for her own good.* "There you are!"

Wayne called over to the buxom waitress for a round of beers. She simpered and purposefully squeezed her breasts together. His animal chuffed in annoyance. Usually, he liked this bar. It was a supernatural friendly bar that a lot of the SEA agents frequented. There was always a strong sexual charge in the bar that, ordinarily, he found appealing. At that moment, it was just pissing him off. A shifter could meet other shifters, and also human groupies who were dying to be bedded by shifters. Not that he'd ever been with a human; they'd never appealed to him. Before today, that is. *Until a certain curvy brunette human with big doe eyes barged into his life.*

Avery made a big show of looking around the table and its occupants. "Where's Erin? Didn't you invite her?"

Gunner bristled. "She was tired; she's had a big day."

Jessie creased her brow in sympathy. "Was she injured badly?"

Too badly for his liking. "She'll have bruises for a few days, but she'll be okay."

"The perils of being human," mused Wayne.

"Maybe she'll remember her fucking gun in future," grumbled Cutter.

Gunner let out a warning growl. "Not a word."

Avery slapped the grumpy wolf on the back. "Yeah, go easy on her. Without Erin, we'd still be running around re-interviewing people. She cracked a case within an hour that would have taken us days or even weeks."

Cutter huffed in irritation. "We would have gotten there eventually."

Jessie looked at Gunner hopefully. "She is coming back tomorrow, right? We haven't scared her away?"

"Yeah, she'll be back." She better be, or he had half a mind to stalk over to her badly protected apartment and drag her out, kicking and screaming. Actually, throwing her over his shoulder didn't sound half bad. *No, not bad at all.*

Shit, he had to get his lust for the damn woman under control. He muttered about needing to take a leak.

His teammates ignored him, *thank the freaking gods*, at least he appeared to be acting normal, even if he felt like his insides were tearing apart over the darn woman. He reflected that all he had to do was be grouchy and terse, and he'd get away with it.

Although, when he went out drinking, invariably, it ended with him taking a willing female home. He needed to get around that somehow, without enduring the jabs about his virility that would inevitably come if he didn't. But there was no way in hell he could be with another woman, not when his every thought was directed at the human. He had a raging hard on, but the thought of sinking inside someone other than Erin seriously cooled his ardor. *Not that his irate bear would ever allow him to do anything like that.* Yes, that was it; he had to imagine other women. He had to go back through all the women he'd been with, and that would make his current, *ahem*, condition a little more manageable. *Or a little less able to pound nails into wood.*

"Gunner," called a silken voice.

The tigress shifter caught up with him just as he was about to escape into the bathroom. Fuck, well that was enough to make him wilt. It wasn't all bad he supposed.

"Isis," he growled.

She leaned against the wall, blocking the way. She was an attractive woman, and she knew it, mercilessly flirting with anyone and everyone in the Agency who could possibly advance her career. And, heaven save him, they'd spent more than a couple of nights together. As he recalled, they'd spent some very satisfactory hours together. Not satisfactory enough to make him lose all his senses, like she was hoping, and recruit her to his team, but satisfactory. The nights together stopped when it became clear he didn't want someone on his team that he'd slept with. He just didn't think that people could work together when personal feelings were involved. Although, he hadn't slept with Erin, and he was losing his mind over her anyway. So maybe he should rethink that policy. *Just in case he was lucky enough to get anywhere with her...*

Isis pouted full red lips at him and flicked her red hair over her shoulder.

"I met your new teammate today," she sneered. "I give her a week."

His bear snarled at him to defend Erin, but Gunner held his tongue and grunted noncommittally. If he said anything, it would put Isis' guard up and make the tigress think something was going on between him and Erin. Which it wasn't. No way. *Well, not yet anyway.*

"First day and she's already almost been killed by a wolf shifter. She's a fucking joke. Gerry's losing it."

Gunner raised an eyebrow. *Now that was something he could object to.* "The director knows what he's doing."

Isis pounced on that. "So you think having her on your team is a good thing?"

How to phrase this delicately? "I'd rather she wasn't a field agent, but I can't deny that her abilities will be helpful. I'd prefer her to be my consultant."

There – easy peasy. *Mostly because it was the truth.* He hadn't wanted her on the team before because he thought she'd slow him down. Now, he didn't want her on the team because he was terrified she might get hurt.

The tigress thought that over for a few moments and then nodded her head in agreement. Ruthless and fearsome though she may be, Isis was a good agent. Begrudgingly, and against his bear's wishes, he admitted that she was a much better agent than Erin could ever hope to be. *But then, she didn't have Erin's gifts.*

Isis grinned, and her eyes flashed to the yellow of her beast. "You know, Wes would love to have her on his team. He was jealous when he found out you were getting her."

Gunner smothered the snarl his bear wanted to release. Wes was Isis' team leader. They were the Gamma team, and they dealt with thefts and robberies.

"You could suggest a swap to the director?"

She fluttered her eyelashes and Gunner almost couldn't withhold his snort. No, even if he thought for a second the director would agree to it, he wasn't going to suggest that. He could probably cope with Isis on his team, but he didn't trust the idiot, Wes to keep his Erin safe. Not for one second. *No, the only place for her was on his team.*

"The director won't go for that," he replied gruffly. "Excuse me."

He pushed past her, ignoring her outraged growl and bolted for the bathroom. He hoped he was safe from her in there at least.

If his interaction with Isis reminded him of anything, it was that people who slept together shouldn't work together. The problem was that he wanted Erin, badly. His bear wanted her, and his body yearned to be with her. But, if they were together, his need to protect her would just sky rocket, and it was already pretty unmanageable. But, he didn't trust anyone else in the whole of the SEA to protect her, either.

He was caught between a rock and a hard place. *And no, that had nothing to do with his cock that was downright unbearable at that moment.* He wanted her, but he didn't want to turn into a possessive psychopath.

Gunner shook his head, ignoring the infuriated wails of his beast. He had to keep his dirty paws to himself. To protect her, he couldn't really be with her.

Huh. *Well, that sucked.*

He was seriously unhappy about that. Maybe it was for the best though. He had his doubts about what kind of mate a human would make for a polar bear. She was such a small thing, would she be able to cope with bearing his young?

Well, he wasn't about to find out. Because, in spite of a certain hairy, sulky beast's disapproval, he was going to keep his distance. It was for the best.

Yep, he kept telling himself that.

There was just one issue that had him gravely disturbed. What was he supposed to do if she started dating someone else?

Ugh, life wasn't fair.

CHAPTER SIX

"Erin, you're late," growled Gunner.

Erin leaped out of her chair in surprise, spilling coffee all over herself and her computer. Gunner groaned audibly, making numerous other agents look around.

She dabbed ineffectively at the liquid while mumbling an apology. Rolling his eyes, he knocked her hands out of the way and began mopping the coffee himself. He leaned over her in the tiny cubicle, pinning her to her chair and brushing his hard body against hers. He diligently got every last drop from her computer, and then started dabbing at her clothes; it was only when he skimmed her breast, and she let out a moan, that he stopped. *Was it her imagination, or was there a light dusting of pink over his cheeks?*

He cleared his throat and stood up, towering over her, completely oblivious to the interested looks of everyone else in the office. "Just to be clear, if you break your computer, you have to pay for it."

"I'm sorry, you startled me."

What did he expect? He practically crept up on her and shouted at her! He was just lucky the contents of her cup didn't go all over him.

"Yes, I seem to be making a habit out of that," he muttered. "You're late."

"I was…"

54

"Save it, the director wants to see us, you can explain it to him."

Shoot. Just what she needed - a meeting with the boss' boss while sporting a very unbecoming brown stain. Even worse, she'd been wearing a white shirt and the wetness was making it cling to her, showing off the curves of her breasts and the shape of her bra.

"Do I have time to take my shirt off?"

Gunner sucked in a breath and his eyes widened marginally.

Erin cringed over her clumsy mouth. "I mean, do I have time to change?"

"No, he wanted to see you at 9am. It's now half past; we better go. You've only seen the nice side of the director; you don't want to see his other side."

Without waiting for her, Gunner strode away, leaving her to scramble after him, avoiding the snickering of her teammates. She puffed and panted as she caught up to him. *Yeesh, he could have at least walked a little more slowly for her.* She only had small legs! Apparently the brief concern he'd showed her the night before had been a fluke; now, he was trying to live up to his moniker of BBB.

Erin found it irritating, but worse than that, it did nothing to quell her attraction to him. And that really annoyed her. Usually, she hated bossy and domineering people, finding them to be intimidating and rude. But, if anything, it just made him hotter.

Ugh, maybe moving to Los Lobos had been a bad idea. *Wouldn't she have been better in her sexless little bubble back in Playa Lunar?*

*

Gunner listened as Erin recounted her reason for being late to the director. Was the director mad? No, if anything he was impressed by Erin. *Great.*

Erin had made some promises to the ghost of their victim, Hilda, and she had spent the early morning visiting Hilda's family to pass some messages on. *Typical.* She couldn't have just slept in or gone to get her nails done like a normal woman. No, she had to do something selfless and kind that made him want her even more. *Erin had no consideration for his desire for her!*

Last night, after he'd promised himself he'd leave her alone, he'd left the bar to go for a run – as his polar bear. The damn beast had taken advantage and ran all the way over to Erin's apartment. They'd spent the night watching her window. It had been torturous being so close to her, but not actually being with her. But at the same time it was somewhat soothing, knowing that while he was there, she was safe.

He'd come up with a different solution to his problem. If the director deemed her unfit for field duty, she would have to stay in the office and work as a consultant. Then they could be together. *It would be the perfect solution.* Of course, he didn't expect Erin just to volunteer for desk duty, so he had to be the one to make the director see she wasn't fit and able. He found that part of the plan very distasteful, but necessary. He'd thought he had a win when Erin was late, but, sadly, no. She just had to find another way to prove how lovely she was. *It was maddening.*

In the interim, Gunner had resolved to be a testy jerk – *well, raving asshole* – toward her. If he could create some distance between them, it might make it easier on him not to just press her up against a wall and shower her with kisses. *He'd replayed that scenario in his head numerous times.* It also might help to dim the arousal he saw in her big brown eyes every time she looked at him. Yeah, he wasn't blind or cursed with no sense of smell - he knew she wanted him. It just made it harder to stay away.

He'd almost completely slipped up that morning. While cleaning her spilled drink, he almost lost complete control and fondled her. A well-timed moan from her was definitely a wakeup call. He just wished he didn't have such a good view of her breasts now; her sodden shirt wasn't leaving much to the imagination, which also meant none of the other males in the building had to use their imaginations either. *His bear was not a happy beast.*

After the director was done with her, mostly congratulating her on a job well done, and barely even chastising her for her faux pas with the gun, Gunner was leading her back downstairs.

Erin's gratified smile at the director's words lit up her whole face, making her glow. He felt a softening in his heart, and his defenses started to slip as she beamed at him, eyes twinkling. What he wouldn't do to be the one to make her look like that.

That feeling didn't last long. As they walked back down to their office, they passed Diaz, a jaguar shifter and leader of the Beta team. He cocked his head at Gunner, but his eyes were riveted to Erin's bosom. *Fucking cat was practically drooling.*

It was enough to send Gunner into a bad mood for the rest of the day.

*

Erin perched on a bar stool and pinched the skin on her hand. *Okay, out for a drink with her teammates – she could do this.* All she needed to do was be quiet, join in with the laughter, and not say anything that could be considered as loopy. Also, it would really help if she would refrain from seeing ghosts or having visions.

Gunner gave her an interested look as he watched her pulling on her skin, but he didn't say anything. Not that she would have minded if he did; it was just a little coping mechanism she had for when she was nervous. *Although, it probably wasn't a good idea to admit to a predator that she was nervous.*

Erin fidgeted in her too-tight t-shirt. She'd borrowed a shirt from Avery that, undoubtedly, looked fabulous on the lithe lioness, but actually made Erin look like an overstuffed sausage. *Or maybe that was just her opinion.* She wasn't used to wearing tight clothes. Nobody else said anything. In fact, she had caught a couple of the male agents eyeing her speculatively. Sadly, it didn't seem to have an effect on Gunner. He'd been interminably grouchy all day.

She'd spent the day first of all filling out wads of paperwork over what happened the previous day. Then Jessie absolutely insisted that Erin be given a tour of her work area. It consisted of a fairly large office, home to numerous computers and various pieces of electronic equipment that Erin daren't touch. It wasn't much of a tour, but Jessie was chatty, friendly and seemed to enjoy her company. They spent the afternoon basically gossiping about other agents in the building. Jessie seemed to know everything about everyone, in particular who was sleeping with whom, who was secretly dating, and so on.

Erin had to hide her chagrin at learning of Gunner's own entanglement with a feisty tiger shifter. The same shifter who had been less than welcoming on her first day. The same shifter who happened to be about six feet tall, toned, red-headed, and drop dead gorgeous. Yep, she was just the kind of woman who would suit Gunner. Erin hated her on principal.

Still, even if her schoolgirl fantasies about her sexy boss weren't likely to come true, at least she had a friend in Jessie. That was something she never had in Playa Lunar. There was even talk of the two of them going out to lunch and shopping. It gave her a warm feeling right in the bottom of her belly.

Other than enjoying her time with Jessie, however, she'd been informed by Avery that she was expected to undertake further firearms and hand-to-hand combat training. The thought of it left her with a dry throat and sweaty palms, but at least it could have been worse. The hand-to-hand training would be with Avery and the weapons with Wayne. Avery was forthright but friendly, and Wayne seemed to be softening toward her. *Cutter could barely stand her.* The idea of being trained in anything by him scared the hell out of her. Which was strange; Gunner was easily bigger and stronger than him, and yet even when he was yelling and punching walls, she didn't feel scared. Sure, he made her jump – *the guy moved like a darn cat* – but she always felt safe with him.

At that moment, she was avoiding looking at Cutter; the wolf shifter just sneered when he caught her eye.

Jessie drummed her hands on the table. She was so bouncy; she looked like she was about to shift and start zipping around looking for an acorn. Erin stifled a giggle as she imagined Jessie shifting into a sabre-toothed squirrel akin to the creature in the Ice Age movies.

"So, Erin, here's to your second day of work. You got through a whole day without someone trying to strangle you – kudos!"

Erin flushed as everyone but Gunner sniggered. "Yeah, well, the day's not over yet."

"That's the spirit!" laughed Avery. "So, Cutter, how are things going with Lucie, the nurse?"

Cutter let out a grunt of displeasure. "Nothing is going on with the nurse."

Wayne smirked. "That's not what she says."

The wolf shifter let out a protracted sigh as his friends continued to rib him.

Gunner leaned toward Erin. "How's your neck?" he asked quietly.

"It's…" She was going to say fine, but it would be a lie, and she didn't want to lie to him above all people. "It's really painful."

He let out a soft snarl. "This wouldn't have happened if…"

Oh, not again. "I know, I know, if I hadn't been dumb enough to leave my gun in your car. Again, I'm sorry. Trust me, I already feel like a complete idiot. You don't have to remind me."

Gunner's mouth gaped open in surprise. "I was going to say it wouldn't have happened if I hadn't left you on your own. I shouldn't have. You're on probation; I should have been there with you. I'm sorry I wasn't. What happened is on me. I realize that now, and I shouldn't have overreacted yesterday. I'm sorry if I scared you at the hospital."

"You didn't!" she exclaimed. "Scare me, I mean. You don't scare me." She hoped that didn't sound defiant; it wasn't meant to. She meant it to sound like she was comfortable with him.

He looked at her wryly. "I don't? Gee, I must be losing my edge."

Erin snickered at the expression of mock misery. "Oh, I think your edge is safe." *If the roar he let out yesterday was anything to go, it darn well was!*

"Just as long as people don't start comparing me to a teddy bear, I reckon I'll survive."

"Teddy bear?" she teased. "Perish the thought."

Gunner chuckled, and his eyes sparkled. *She just had one question, if she swooned, would he catch her?*

"Ugh!" uttered Jessie in annoyance. "Heads up, Tigger's on the prowl."

She nodded her pink streaked hair in the direction of Isis, who seemed to be making her way to their table. Erin gulped. Not a fan of confrontations, she wanted just to fade away into the background, lest the tigress say anything to her.

Isis approached the table and bid hello to everyone. Jessie and Avery groaned, while Wayne and Cutter nodded. Erin felt a thrill of satisfaction that Gunner hardly even acknowledged her presence. He stiffened when she approached but nothing more.

Surprisingly though, Isis was very cordial to her. "Hi, Erin. How's it going?"

"Ah, fine, thanks."

Isis nodded before affecting a sympathetic expression. "How's your neck? Wolf shifters are such bastards."

Cutter snarled in objection, but soon piped down when the squirrel shifter slapped the back of his head.

Erin pressed her fingers to her sore skin. "It's fine; it looks worse than it is," she lied. *It was one thing admitting weakness to Gunner, but it was quite another to do it to this female.*

The tigress gave her a toothy grin that seemed to be a staple of felines. "We were all really impressed by how quickly you cracked that case yesterday."

She shuffled in her seat. "It was just luck."

Isis clucked her tongue. "Nonsense, no one else here could have gotten that clue. My team leader would love to meet you. Hang on, I'll get him. Hey, Wes!" she roared.

Dang, if Erin thought she showed a lot of teeth when she smiled, it was nothing compared to when she roared. *So many sharp, white teeth.*

Hmmm, maybe Erin had misjudged her. Although, a spiteful voice still resented the fact that the tigress had been involved with Gunner, and for all she knew still was. Sneaking a peek at Gunner, Erin was shocked by the intensely angry look on his face, but she was mighty relieved it wasn't directed at her. *No, that was all for the tigress.*

A tall, although not as tall as Gunner, male wandered over. He had an easy, cocky smile that bordered on arrogant, but it wasn't that big of a surprise. He was extremely handsome – *disturbingly so* – and the women in the bar stopped what they were doing to watch him walk by, much to the dismay of the males they happened to be with them at the time. He was a lot slimmer than the polar bear, but Erin didn't doubt that he still packed some vicious strength in his sinewy muscles.

He purred out a 'Hi' to the table that had Wayne, Cutter and Jessie rolling their eyes. Avery went very quiet; Isis grinned, and Gunner looked like he wanted to murder the interloper.

"Hi," croaked Erin.

Wes' eyes roamed over the occupants of the table until they landed on Erin, and he gave her a predatory smile.

"It's nice to meet you, Erin. I've heard so much about you. I'm Wes; I lead the Gamma team."

"Nice to meet you, too."

Erin inhaled as a question popped into her head but then hesitated. With surprise, she noticed that Gunner's attention was now firmly on her, and he was watching her closely. Cheeks burning, she blurted, "What species are you?"

Wes chuckled. "I'm actually a liger."

She gasped. "Really?"

He nodded. "Yep, my mom's a tiger and my dad's a lion."

Erin looked at him with frank fascination, and she could have sworn that Gunner groaned. "But I thought that for shifters the babies usually either took after their mom or their dad – they were one or the other."

"Most of the time that's true, but sometimes when the different species are compatible the offspring gets characteristics of both."

"Wow, I had no idea." *There was so much she didn't know about shifters.*

"Yeah, don't worry, like I say, it's only where the species are compatible, you're not going to see a half-polar bear, half-tiger mutant walking around like if Gunner and Isis had a baby."

Gunner's jaw clicked, and his eyes melted to dark brown as the liger shifter slapped him on the back.

Wes smiled suggestively at Erin and waved his finger in a circle. "But, if we had a baby, it could easily be a tiger or a lion and have your abilities too. Double species are rare, but they happen."

Erin noticed that Gunner had balled up his fists, and she was dismayed when he asked Isis if he could speak to her. Oh, no, why does he want to talk to her alone? *Crap, what if they were going to have sex?* She knew that shifters were quite lascivious creatures, and even she couldn't fail to notice the sexual undercurrent in the bar – *heck, a number of patrons were almost having sex in their booths!* But would Gunner just ditch her like that to be with the beautiful tigress?

Isis and Gunner disappeared into the crowd, and Wes eagerly hopped into Gunner's vacated seat. He started asking her numerous questions about life in Playa Lunar, about her abilities… She answered with as much spirit as she could, while obsessing over what Gunner and Isis were doing together.

*

"What the fuck are you doing?" snarled Gunner as soon as he was sure they were out of earshot of his nosy teammates.

Isis fluttered her eyelashes theatrically. "What do you mean?"

His bear roared at him. "Don't act coy with me, what the fuck are you playing at?"

She rolled her eyes at his attitude. "Wes wanted to meet her, so I said I'd introduce him. It's perfectly harmless."

The tigress affected a look of innocence, but Gunner didn't buy it for one second. "No, Wes is hoping that he can talk her into requesting a transfer to his team. And you're helping him because you think that means you can get onto my team. Well, you can stop right now because it's not happening."

Damn right, it's not happening. He wasn't about to let that damn liger get his claws into Erin. Alright, so under different circumstances, Gunner might have considered him an okay guy, but he was trying to steal Erin and that made him the enemy.

Isis pursed her lips. "You can't control what Erin chooses to do. If she decides she's better suited to working with Wes, then that's up to her."

No, Erin wasn't allowed. "She won't do that."

"Cocky, aren't we?" sneered the tigress. "Wes can be very persuasive."

Gunner felt his ire rise, and he pushed his claws into the palm of his hands to stop his beast from lunging at the irritating tigress. "To be clear, Isis," he hissed, "even if Erin did leave my team, for whatever reason, I wouldn't give you her spot."

"Now you're just being spiteful."

If Isis took Erin away from him, he'd be more than just spiteful! "What you're doing won't work, so call off the liger."

"We'll see," she hissed and flounced away.

Gunner took a few moments to compose himself and calm his irate bear. He couldn't allow himself to lose control. Not over a woman. Not even if she was the most perfect woman in creation... *damnit.* He had it bad.

His bear nudged him. Just what was he doing standing at the other side of the bar when Wes was probably flirting up a storm with his human? *Shit. The bear was right.*

Gunner promptly shouldered his way back to their table, and was thoroughly alarmed to see that it was almost entirely empty. In particular, he was panic stricken to see that neither Wes nor Erin was there anymore. What if they had left together? What if they were going back to his apartment to have sex? The fucking liger could have his feline tongue down her throat at that very second. No, he had to stop them.

"Where's Erin?" he growled.

Wayne and Jessie, currently in the middle of an argument about the benefits of his gator wearing Kevlar, looked up in surprise. They both shrugged and got back to their conversation.

Useless. His bear snarled. *Find her!*

Gunner sniffed the air, trying to decipher Erin's delicious vanilla scent, but he had trouble picking her out of so many sweaty bodies. *Fuck.*

He would call her. He would tell her there was an emergency, and he needed her right away. Whatever she was about to do with Wes would have to stop. He stalked to the exit, almost knocking over Rory the SEA medical examiner as he did. He howled as a small, curvaceously familiar body careened into him while exiting the ladies' bathroom.

His hands clamped down on her shoulders, and an inordinate amount of relief washed through him. She looked up at him in shock, an apology dying on her lips when she saw who it was.

"I'm leaving; I'll drive you home," he declared forcefully, not waiting for her to catch her breath.

"Oh, okay," breathed Erin, not unhappily.

He nodded and grasped her arm, leading her out of the bar and to his car. He knew he was being unfair; refusing to be with her but trying to stop her from being with anyone else. Part of him knew how awful that was, but a larger part of him didn't care. *She was his.* She just couldn't be his yet. And while he waited, he'd make damn sure she didn't become anyone else's either.

*

"How are you feeling?" asked the doctor.

Tom 'the hammer' Murphy raised his tired eyes. He lifted his leaden hand to remove the oxygen mask. He struggled to get it off and the doctor, in spite of Tom's glare, helped him. Tom didn't like that he needed help; he resented feeling weak in front of anyone, in particular in front of a lesser shifter like this damn badger doctor.

"Fine," he growled.

"Your vitals look excellent, better than expected. You can rest here for the night and then your, ah, friend can take your home."

The doctor nervously nodded to the corner of the room where Tom's bodyguard, Alfie, a tough-as-hell elephant shifter, was sitting in a chair. To the casual observer, he seemed to be relaxed and engrossed in a paperback copy of, surprisingly, Pride and Prejudice, but Tom knew that the slightest nod of his head would have Alfie thundering across the room and ripping the badger apart.

"What if I want to go sooner?" asked Tom belligerently. He hated to be told what to do no matter the circumstances.

The doctor shrugged unconcernedly. "Then go. This isn't a hospital. If you fall down dead the moment you get out of here, it won't be our problem."

Tom pursed his lips, appeased slightly. "I'll leave when I'm ready."

"Okay, holler if you need anything. I'll be down the corridor watching LLPD Bloopers."

The doctor spun on his heel and ambled out the room. Tom tracked his movements. *Ugh, prey.*

He ran his hand down the front of his chest. He'd have a scar for the rest of his life, but after a couple of weeks it would knit itself into a thin silver line. He could already feel himself mending; he could feel his heart – his new heart - beating more strongly, thumping as it did forty years ago.

It was incredible, unbelievable and absolutely exhilarating. He felt like he could climb a mountain, jump out of a plane, and take several young women to his bed without breaking a sweat. *Just like the good old days.*

He had to admit, the doctor did good work. Perhaps he could persuade the doctor to come onto his payroll, couldn't hurt to have a talented – *yet disreputable* – medic on hand.

Yep, it had been worth every cent. Although the behavior of the asshole who put all this together still rankled. He deserved respect, he deserved better than a pipsqueak upstart talking to him like he was nothing! Red-hot rage boiled in his veins, his heart pounded in fury, and for the first time in months he felt... he felt fine. He was back to his old self! It was amazing.

That moment, his life began anew.

CHAPTER SEVEN

The next two weeks almost became routine. At work, Erin was put through torturous amounts of training by Avery and Wayne while Cutter looked on and sneered. The only case they had during that time was a murder, which solved itself when the murderer handed himself in and confessed. There were whispers of further missing shifters, but as it wasn't their case, they didn't get a lot of details.

Spare time was spent going through open cases. On the plus side, she got to spend time with Jessie, going out to lunch and shopping. *Jessie loved shopping.* On the down side, Gunner seemed to be going out of his way to avoid her at work.

The team went out numerous times to the bar for drinks, and every time Gunner would insist on driving her home. She daren't turn down his offer of a ride; *she dreaded disappointing him.* The ride home would always mirror the first time. Gunner asked her various innocuous questions about her likes and dislikes, and he seemed pleased when she asked him things, too. When they reached her apartment, he would insist on walking her to the door, he would lament her poor security, linger as if he was about to kiss her and then leave abruptly.

It was frustrating as hell!

Erin wondered at his behavior. She didn't exactly have a lot of experience where men were concerned, but she suspected he did have feelings for her that surpassed those of just a colleague. He bordered on frosty to her at work, but he seemed overly concerned after hours. Sure, he could have just been worried about her as a friend, but she didn't see him behaving that way to Avery or Jessie. But then, he trusted that the two of them could actually take care of themselves. *She knew he didn't think she was capable.*

She considered saying something to him, but if she really did have the complete wrong end of the stick, it would be absolutely mortifying. He'd probably laugh at her for being dumb enough to think that someone like him would even give an average looking human like her the time of day. She wasn't blind; she could see the way women eyed him at the bar. Hell, she could see the way other agents ogled him at work. It left her steaming and frustrated as hell because she couldn't rightly tell them to keep their slutty eye-fondling to themselves.

Erin prayed that the situation would come to a head – *and soon* – because there were only so many cold showers she could take.

*

Gunner rolled his shoulders as he loaded his gun. *Yep, a bit of target practice couldn't hurt.* It had been weeks since he'd done any.

The door behind him opened, and he heard a muffled gasp. He didn't need to hear that to know it was her, though; her vanilla scent invaded his senses, making his beast whimper in delight.

"Oh! What a surprise, I didn't know you'd be here," she exclaimed, unable to hide the sliver of happiness in her voice.

He turned a round and smiled at her. *But he knew she would be.* She'd started a routine of target practice whenever she could at about 7pm, choosing that time because the place was usually deserted by then. There was generally a mass exodus of the building at 5pm.

Gunner gathered from Wayne that Erin was hesitant and shy about her own prowess with a gun, but was desperate to improve. She just wasn't keen to practice in front of other people. Given how pleased she was to see him, she didn't seem to have an issue with him being there.

"I just thought I'd get a little practice in; it's been a while," he said nonchalantly.

Erin bobbed her dark head. "Me too, not that it's been a while for me, I need all the practice I can get."

She laughed nervously and looked at her feet.

Gunner shrugged. "You just have to give it time."

"Oh, I don't think I'm ever going to be any good at this." Her cheeks flushed as she realized that perhaps she ought not to have admitted that.

"Come on, everyone needs practice. You don't think I was born this amazing, do you?"

"Yes," she breathed before gazing at him through her eyelashes.

Heat pulsed through his body, and the desire, the want, and the need of the past two weeks reached boiling point.

"Erin, I…"

He was cut off by the laughs of two male shifters making their way into the room. His bear was furious at the interruption, and Gunner wasn't far behind. *They were the reason he was down there in the first place.*

Erin's habit of practicing had also become apparent to other people in the building, namely Diaz and Wes. *The jaguar and the liger.* According to Wayne, who pretty much knew all the comings and goings of people around the building, the two a-hole shifters had also taken it upon themselves to come to the shooting range, just when Erin happened to be there. *Gunner had to put a stop to that.*

He suspected that Wes was just trying to get her to join his team, figuring that a psychic would make his job a lot easier. Diaz, on the other hand, he was sure that the cat wanted to get into her pants. Gunner wasn't blind; the guy wasn't wholly repulsive, and if the jaguar managed to hide his smarmy personality, Gunner was sure that a woman might take pity on him and agree to go on a date with him. *He just didn't want Erin to be that woman.*

The two men stopped when they saw the huge polar bear shifter glaring at them. He was a little pleased to note that their shoulders dropped a smidge on seeing him there. No way could they cajole Erin into doing what they wanted when he was around.

They grudgingly nodded at Gunner and said hello to Erin, who waved in return.

Gunner was gratified when Erin ignored them and turned to him. "Could you give me a few pointers? I don't think I'm standing right, my shoulder really hurts after I'm finished."

As if in explanation, she twisted her shoulder around.

"Of course," he agreed, delighted to have any excuse to get her away from the other males. *Other, inferior males.*

He led her as far away from them as possible, and set her up with a gun and ear protectors. He indicated for her to start shooting. It was almost painful to watch. She crunched up her face, hunched up her body and completely tensed as she let off the first round. She hit the paper target; she just didn't hit the silhouette of the man.

Wordlessly, he repositioned her slightly. His hands roamed over her arms, gently tugging them. He swiveled her hips, and couldn't help but notice that she gulped when his fingers accidentally – *on purpose* – trailed over her plump ass.

Dang, how could he have failed to notice her ass before? He'd completely neglected it, preferring to obsess over her rounded breasts and pretty, pink mouth. *It was just the right size for his hands…*

Crap. She was looking at him expectantly. He ignored his mounting arousal and made a big show of twisting her body ever so slightly to the left. He gave her the thumbs up, and she tried to shoot again. She actually managed to hit the silhouette, right in the arm.

Gunner nodded encouragement and then tried to loosen up her arms. He stood behind her; his muscled chest grazed her back. He took each arm and slowly made her stretch. After that, he positioned her and motioned for her to try again.

The look of surprised glee on her face when she hit the center of the silhouette was charming. He chuckled as she did a happy little jig, and almost thought she was going to give him a hug. He would have let her too, in spite of being under the watchful eyes of Wes and Diaz.

After that, she couldn't get enough. They stayed for ages, practicing over and over. Even Wes and Diaz gave up and left before they did.

He wondered at all the people who had ever tried to teach her to shoot. *It had been so easy.* Perhaps they just weren't as patient as him. Still, it made him proud at how she blossomed under his tutelage.

Finally, he had to admit it was getting late. He pulled off his ear defenders and indicated she should do the same.

"We've been here a while; we ought to go."

"Yeah," she agreed unenthusiastically.

"Drink?" he offered.

"No, I don't really feel like it. I'm not much of a drinker."

"I'll drive you home."

"You don't have to do that, I don't mind taking the bus," she said, bashfully.

His hackles rose at that as his bear grumbled. *No way was he letting her ride the bus at night.* "I don't have to; I want to," he replied simply.

Judging by the smile she failed to conceal, that had been the right thing to say.

*

The ride home was like the other nights. He asked her a few basic questions, nothing very intimate, while she darted quick little glances in his direction, pretending she wasn't completely infatuated with him.

It had been an unexpected pleasure to find Gunner at the shooting range. It also meant she was spared from having to deal with Wes and Diaz. They were nice enough guys, but she could hardly practice when they were asking her questions every five seconds. Plus, she didn't particularly enjoy their laughs of derision when she missed the target.

Gunner didn't laugh though. *No, he helped her.* He showed her what she needed to do, and for once, she actually felt like she was making some progress. Just when she thought her warm, fuzzy feelings for the bear couldn't get any stronger, he had to do something like that.

All too soon they arrived at her apartment. Would it be weird if she asked him to circle the block a few times just to prolong their alone time? Probably. *No, definitely.*

As usual, he walked her to her door and waited for her to unlock it and go in. She hesitated when she entered and turned back to see him filling the door frame. She had to say something or do something. Otherwise, this was what it was going to be like for the rest of their lives. Her panting, dreaming and obsessing over him, while he acted chivalrous and apparently completely blind to her lust for him.

Yes, she had to say something that would make him see the depth of her feelings for him. "Would you like some coffee?"

Ugh, well it was better than nothing, she supposed.

Gunner cocked his head on one side. "Sure."

Yes! He said yes!

He ambled into the apartment and locked and bolted the door. It reminded her of the first time he'd ever visited her.

She turned and made her way to the kitchen before stopping and groaning.

"What's wrong?" he asked, inches behind, making her jump.

Seriously, he made no noise when he moved! *The darn bear needed a bell.*

"I don't have any coffee," she admitted quietly.

He sucked in a breath. "I don't want coffee," he murmured before she felt his scorching lips on her neck.

Erin let out a small whimper before sagging against him. He twisted her in his arms, lifting her off the ground and pulling her tautly against his body. *Oh, it was really happening!*

His lips crashed against hers, devouring, tasting, and unleashing passion she hadn't even begun to guess at. Finally pulling away, he leaned his forehead against hers, breathing heavily.

"Oh my..." she breathed as she saw his sharpened teeth.

Gunner winced slightly. "Sorry, my beast..."

She didn't know what came over her, but she pushed her lips against his open mouth and licked her tongue over his teeth. *Oh, it was such a turn on!* The idea that this man, shuddering against her, could be such a deadly beast, was ferociously arousing.

Erin drew away and delighted in his growl of arousal.

"Fuck, Erin, do you have any idea what you do to me?"

What she did to him? *Was he kidding?* If he weren't holding her up she'd be a puddle on the floor right about now.

Gunner started rubbing his hands over her body, kneading the globes of her ass. *Mmmm, that felt so nice.*

His expression turned dark. "We don't have to do anything you don't want."

"I want to," she whispered against his mouth, scarcely believing that this wanton creature was her.

He laughed roughly. "Thank fuck for that, because I was lying. I'm taking you to bed right now, and short of an earth quake and the roof falling in, nothing is stopping me."

"Oh, that sounds nice," she blurted before groaning at her uncontrollable mouth.

If anything, it only served to incite him more. "Babe, the things I am going to do to you… Bedroom?"

Erin waved her hand in the direction, and he fairly flew there. In a whirlwind of hands and arms, he divested her of her clothes, and she was squirming on the bed, as Gunner, now shirtless, shoeless and sockless, was licking and kissing her skin.

He tugged on her earlobe, before flourishing kisses over her neck and nibbling on her collarbone, and, oh, she almost died when his mouth found her breasts. She threaded her fingers through his hair and strained towards him, eager for him to take more. He smoothed his tongue over her heated skin, lightly biting her nipple before moving onto its twin.

She almost cried when he released her and drew back to kneel between her legs. His eyes did a slow sweep of her body and, *knock her over with a feather*, he certainly seemed to like what he saw.

"Do you have any lube?"

Erin flushed all over. "What? No."

His brow crinkled. "Have you never used it?"

What sort of question was that? "Well, I, umm, last time I was, uh, intimate with someone he used a lubed condom. That was enough. And he was only inside me for less than a minute."

Erin slapped her hands over her face. *Why did she just say that?* She was lying in bed, naked, with the hottest guy she ever met just waiting to make love to her, and she was making a complete ass out of herself.

"Stop laughing," came her muffled voice under her hands. She couldn't see him, but she knew he was shaking in silent laughter.

She felt his body heat seeping into hers as he leaned over her. Gently, he pried her hands away from her, *undoubtedly*, tomato red face.

He laced her fingers with his as he placed soft kisses over her cheeks. "I'm sorry, babe. You don't have to feel embarrassed about that; you can tell me anything. I'm guessing you don't have much experience, am I right?"

She bit her lip and nodded. *This conversation was so humiliating.* Yet, when she admitted to her lack of sexual prowess, he almost seemed to sigh in relief.

"And I'm pretty confident that I'm a lot bigger than any of the guys you've been with before…"

"Someone's conceited!" she blurted.

Gunner chuckled throatily. "With good reason," he purred. "And I just want to make sure I don't hurt you. But, I have a better idea."

Erin frowned as he slid off the end of the bed, but squealed as he grasped her legs and pulled her body down to him. He placed her legs on his shoulders and positioned his mouth at her sex.

Holy hell! He was going to… Her thoughts were interrupted as Gunner did indeed swipe his tongue over her slit. Her body arched at the unexpected and alien sensation. Her fingers gripped the bed sheets, and she threw her head back as he began his sensual attack.

Her toes curled as her body trembled under the delicious onslaught. Neither of her sexual partners had oral sex as part of their sexual repertoire. One claimed it was just something you saw in porn flicks, and the other said he didn't want to put his mouth down there. But, dang, it was the most unbelievable thing she had ever felt.

Gunner slid his fingers over her thighs, rubbing his fingers over her flesh as his tongue mercilessly plundered her channel. Remorselessly, he licked at her, lapped at her, sucked and nibbled her clit, alternating between fast and slow, and once or twice stopping to just blow on her – that almost had her shooting off the bed.

It wasn't long before Erin felt her body tensing, and then shaking, preparing itself. Gunner sensed the change in her, as she readied for her climax, and he sped up his movements, eager to push her over the edge. Within seconds, she gasped, and her body held still as she hit her peak. *Then she was flying.* She screamed and writhed as pleasure cascaded through every inch of her. Even then he didn't stop, he continued his marvelous assault as her body thrashed in ecstasy.

Erin collapsed onto the bed; she felt like a sobbing, quivering mess. Gunner stood up, towering over her. *She must have looked a sight.* But, if the lust etched into his face was anything to go by, he certainly wasn't put off.

Never taking his darkened eyes off her, gracefully, he slipped out of his jeans. She didn't even bother to hide her gasp as she saw his thick, hard manhood straining toward her. No wonder he was so cocky! *In proportion nothing, he was freaking huge.*

Gunner grinned at her reaction as he dipped his fingers inside her sex. She held her breath for a second as she expected him to start massaging her inner flesh, but he didn't. No, he covered his fingers in her honey and then began smoothing it over his member. He did this repeatedly as she watched, entranced. She was amazed to see him grow even bigger.

"We'll go slow," he rasped huskily.

Erin nodded. At that point, she didn't care. She wanted him inside her, and she'd have agreed to absolutely anything he said. She licked her lips in anticipation, and he groaned.

"Get in the middle of the bed," he ordered.

Erin scooted up as if to get away from him. But escape was the last thing on her mind. He knelt one leg on the bed and slowly crawled over her. His eyes were the dark brown of his beast, and Erin shivered at the thought of being taken by this man. She'd never been with a shifter before, and the thought of being with a man half controlled by a wild animal was thrilling.

Gunner covered her body with his, careful not to crush her. Her legs instinctively parted for him, and he nestled between her thighs, sighing as he did.

"If you need me to stop, just say the word," he breathed.

Erin rolled her eyes impatiently. "I will, please just…"

She was about to tell him to hurry, but she caught herself. Gunner got her meaning though, and the smug look on his face was almost unbearable. She couldn't stand to see that and surprised him by kissing him. She raked her fingers through his hair as she nibbled on his bottom lip. Judging by the shudder that coursed through his huge frame, he liked that.

Distracted by his sinful tongue, she didn't even realize Gunner had reached down between them, and was aligning their sexes until she felt the blunt tip press against her entrance. Instinct told her to tense, but she willed herself to relax. She wanted this, more than she wanted air at that moment, and nothing, not even her shy, scaredy-cat nature was going to stand in the way.

Erin hooked her legs round him and tried to pull him toward her. She sensed his satisfaction and was pleased when he started moving inside her. He was big; there was no denying it, but it wasn't painful, not in the least. Her flesh parted for every inch that pushed inside her. And with every inch came a stronger feeling of rightness.

When he was finally fully seated in her body, she broke his ardent kiss and threw her head back to let out a sultry moan. *Yes, this was how it should be.* Taking him inside just felt so right, so perfect, like it was meant to be.

She lifted her eyes to his face and was dazzled by the look he gave her. *Hungry yet also reverent?* It was too much for her. She clutched her inner muscles, tightening around him even more, and he let out a lusty groan.

"Oh, Erin," he breathed.

Slowly, he withdrew part way and then thrust back inside her. She moaned again, and a deep rumble vibrated through his chest. She rubbed her hands over his muscles, enjoying the feel of his silken skin under her fingers. He plunged in and out of her, snarling softly as her body undulated beneath him.

Gunner rocked inside her, and she moaned every time he filled her. His beautiful body, his patience, and rough sensuality obliterated all of her past trysts. *Not that there had been many.* She wanted this moment to last forever, to be endlessly excited, but she knew she couldn't. Her body was already trembling with the promise of a climax even more satisfying than the last. And, oh, she wanted him to come, she wanted to reciprocate the amazing release he had given her.

Instinctively, she lifted her hips to meet his thrusts; her legs dug into his waist urging him to go faster. With a roar, he did. He sped up his movements until he was crashing against her body.

"Are you okay?" he gasped as he drove in and out of her.

He was concerned about her, but he needn't have been. No way did she want him to stop. "Don't stop…" she whimpered.

Gunner flashed her a predatory grin as he swiveled his hips. He grazed her clit, once, twice and she screamed as an orgasm thundered through her.

She bucked against him, clawing at his shoulders, rippling and tightening around his cock, buried so deeply inside her. It was the most intense sensation, and she was caught between wanting it to end and needing to ride out the waves.

It was too much for Gunner; with one final plunge inside her body, he stilled and bellowed her name as he reached his own completion. They clung to one another as they shook and trembled through the aftershocks.

Finally calming, he twisted onto his side, keeping his softening manhood firmly sheathed inside her. He hooked her leg over his hip and ran his hand up and down her smooth skin as his sex pulsed and softened.

Erin marveled that even at half-mast he filled her. It was strange yet comforting to feel him still within her. It somehow felt more intimate than when they were actually having sex. *Probably the post coital bliss she'd only ever read about.* Her other partners would already have been zipping up their pants by now. She'd half-expected Gunner to just up and run too. She wouldn't have minded if he did. *Heck, a wooly mammoth could run through her living room at that moment, and she'd just smile and wave at it.* Good sex, no, *great sex*, was certainly enough to make you forget your troubles, momentarily at least.

She considered telling him that it was okay if he wanted to go; he didn't have to stay if he didn't want to. He certainly didn't owe her anything. But, oh, the hands cupping and massaging her ass felt so good; the feel of his hard chest against her breasts felt so pleasant. *Maybe just a few more minutes.*

"You okay, babe?" he rumbled.

"Yes," she breathed.

"I didn't hurt you?"

"No."

"Did you enjoy yourself?"

Erin slapped his arm as forcefully as she could, which wasn't very at that moment in time. *No, at that moment, she felt almost boneless.*

"You're just fishing for compliments."

"True," he chuckled. "You were amazing."

Gunner placed a kiss on the top of her head, and dang it if her sex didn't just start fluttering. Forget the ecstasy she'd just been given, she was ready for more. *So greedy!*

Apparently she wasn't the only one. Erin let out a garbled 'ooh' as he swelled inside her.

"Round two, babe?" he asked smugly.

What she wouldn't give to do something about that damn smug tone. *Maybe after…*

"Yes, please," she murmured.

Well, she was only human.

CHAPTER EIGHT

Gunner jerked awake as Erin started mumbling and twitching. Disorientated for a couple of seconds, he soon recalled the events that had led him to this unfamiliar bed and smiled.

He hadn't intended to spend the night with her. He'd only intended to drive her home as usual, but that look of hopefulness when she'd offered him coffee made him pause. He'd never dated a human, but he'd been told that the invitation to have coffee was actually code for something else. But, given that it was Cutter who told him that he couldn't be certain as to the truth, so he'd been careful as to his next move. The shifters he'd been with had never bothered with a code. When he'd taken them home they'd eagerly blurted out, 'let's fuck,' and he was never in any doubt as to what they wanted. But then most of them did just want a meaningless coupling; it was rare for them to look to him to become anything more.

Of course, when Erin had confessed she didn't have coffee, he knew what she had meant. *And lord, he hadn't been able to stop himself.* His bear had pushed him, and he'd given in, uncaring as to the consequences, uncaring as to his previous resolves. Not that he could possibly regret what had happened. The feel of her body entwined with his had been breathtaking. *He'd never known such… fulfillment.* Something he was keen to repeat as soon as damn possible.

Erin had fallen asleep in his arms, but during the course of the night, she had somehow managed to work her way over to the other side of the bed.

And if her frantic little movements were anything to go by, she was having a bad dream.

He reached over and gently pulled her closer to him. His bear whimpered at the painful moans she emitted as her sleeping face scrunched up. *He guessed she dreamed about the horrific things she saw in her visions.* It troubled him to know that he could never do anything about that. If punching something could make her gifts any easier to handle, he would, but sadly, life wasn't that easy. He settled for running his thumb down her forehead and making soothing, hushing noises. He'd seen his mother do that for his nephew once, and was gratified when Erin seemed to calm. He pressed a kiss to her temple and slipped out of bed.

Gunner gave himself a quick tour of her apartment and was altogether unhappy with what he found. *The place was shabby.* The wallpaper was peeling in several places, the furniture looked like it had been rescued from underneath an overpass – *presumably after being thrown over the overpass* - and the kitchen appliances looked like they had never worked properly even when they were new – back in the 1970s. *What was Erin thinking living there?*

He shook his head and peeked into her refrigerator. It was disturbingly bare, containing little more than orange juice, milk teetering on the edge of being out of date, and some leftover Chinese food. *Jeez.* He moved onto the rest of her kitchen, becoming increasingly dissatisfied with the contents.

Gunner closed his eyes and banged his head against a shelf. Taking care of his little mate was even harder than he thought. He was all for eating junk food. *Hey, he could down two dozen donuts in one go without pausing to take a breath.* But, seriously, that had to be combined with proper meals like a nice slab of juicy meat, some mashed potatoes, green beans, crusty bread slathered in butter... *Mmmm,* his bear rumbled happily at the thought. The scrappy bits of food in Erin's kitchen could barely even be called food. Microwave meals, noodle pots, and cheap ass corn chips were not filling or nutritious.

He needed to make sure she started eating better. It wasn't the only thing he needed to change. He really needed to improve the locks on her apartment. He'd wanted to before now, but had been hesitant about it, fearing that it might have been crossing a line. Instead, he'd dropped hint after hint in the hope that she might be spurred into doing something herself. *No such luck.* She was perilously oblivious to safety matters. *Something he intended to change.*

Then there was this nonsense about her getting around on the bus. He was trying to drive her everywhere that he could, but he was aware that he couldn't be with her all the time. If he couldn't persuade her to get her own car, then he'd find a way to make her use his. He'd borrow one of the Agency SUVs. As a team leader, he was entitled.

Gunner wondered how she would react to these proposed changes. It wasn't like he was trying to change her - *he wouldn't dream of it* - but he wanted to improve her life. *Isn't that what mates were supposed to do?*

He was cut off from his thoughts when he heard a confused whine from the bedroom. He quickly made his way back there to find his disheveled little human half-awake and frowning at his empty side of the bed.

She caught sight of him in the doorway. "Are you leaving?"

"Nah, babe."

He sidled over to the bed and slid under the covers. He moved her around, so they were spooning, and wrapped his burly arms around her small frame.

"Good," she mumbled and then promptly fell asleep.

Yes, it was good.

*

"Hey, what are you doing?"

Erin jumped at the softly spoken words. She felt like a thief in the night, slinking out of bed and leaving her lover. *Yes, her lover.* There, she thought it. Although, there was no way in hell she would say it out loud. It would most likely send Gunner running for the hills if he knew she thought of him that way.

"I'm sorry; I didn't mean to wake you. I forgot that I'm supposed to be seeing my family for lunch today. It's kind of a party to celebrate my sister's engagement. Tons of my family will be there." It wasn't how she wanted to spend her Saturday, but she didn't exactly have a choice.

She'd stayed in bed as long as she could before she absolutely had to get up. She'd spent an hour watching Gunner sleep; memorizing every inch of his perfect body, and completely mesmerized by the rise and fall of his massive chest. Being with him had been, what? *Incredible? Outstanding?* But, just lying in bed with him, that was more comforting than anything she had ever hoped for. He hadn't run off under the pretext of needing to get up early the next day; unlike the others, he'd stayed with her for the whole night. Not that she'd ever really wanted her exes to spend the night. No, there was only one man in the world she wanted in her bed and, *dagnabbit,* by some miracle, there he was.

Gunner's forehead creased as he sought out his watch. "Lunch? It's 9am."

She knew that. She wouldn't have been anywhere but in that bed if it weren't necessary.

"I know, but I have to get a bus to the coach station, and then a coach that'll get me there for about 11.00. I don't want to be late. I don't really get along with my family, and I don't want to make things worse."

He scowled at her. "Have you even had breakfast yet?"

Erin prickled at his response. *What did that matter to him?* "No, I'll probably get a breakfast burrito on the way."

His eyes narrowed at her. "Where do they live?"

"Feather Point."

He rolled his eyes at her. "That's like an hour away by car."

"For people who have cars, sure."

He whipped the covers off his naked frame and Erin blinked at him. *How, oh how, had she tricked this god-like man into her bed?* As she recalled, he seemed to want to be there. *It was mind boggling.*

"I'll drive you," he said simply.

"You'll what?" she spluttered.

He shrugged and strode into the bathroom; she scuttled after him as he stepped into the shower. After a few minutes, it was clear that she was just watching him showering. Although she was enjoying herself as he soaped up his massive muscles, common sense kicked in, and she dragged herself out of there before the urge to jump in and scrub his back became too much.

Minutes later, as she paced her apartment wringing her hands, he strode out of the bathroom, with a big grin on his face and smelling like her shampoo. He collected his clothes and pulled them on. Fleetingly, she thought it was a shame to cover up such yummy flesh.

Erin bit her lip. "You don't have to do this. I don't want to feel like I'm making you do this."

He frowned as he came to stand in front of her. "I don't do anything I don't want to do."

"You didn't want to accept me onto your team."

She immediately regretted her words, but rather than the anger she feared, he merely chuckled softly and wrapped a strand of her hair around his fingers.

"Fair point, but if I really didn't want to be on the same team as you, I could have quit. I'm glad the director hired you. And as for this morning, you're not asking, I'm offering."

"Thank you." She warmed at his words. He was 'glad' to have met her. *Alright, it wasn't exactly romantic, but it was better than what he could have said.*

"Will you introduce me to your parents?"

Erin couldn't help it. Her eyes bulged at that. *He wanted to meet her parents!* Did he want to be permanently involved? Or was he just curious as to the people who had brought such a basket case into the world?

Gunner's eyes narrowed. "You don't regret last night, do you?"

"What? No, of course not, it was… it was wonderful." Something she wanted to repeat over and over again, and then a few more times after that to make sure she wasn't imagining it.

He sighed - in relief she thought. "Good, so let's go see your parents."

"Oh, umm, yes, let's."

Why did she feel like she was being railroaded? But then why was she so happy about that? Part of her seemed to think that if he met her family, it would be harder for him just to walk away and tell her it was a one-night stand.

He took her hand and started pulling her to the door; she had just enough time to grab her purse. "We'll get a proper breakfast on the way," he declared.

His tone implied that arguing the matter was absolutely futile, so she simply murmured in agreement.

*

Gunner stared at Erin, and she had trouble meeting his gaze. He assumed because of embarrassment, but he couldn't be sure. *Perhaps because of memories of the previous night.* Whatever it was, his bear didn't like it one bit. He feared that she was trying to pull away.

Reluctantly, he dragged his eyes away from her and started attacking his breakfast with gusto. She'd been amazed at just how much food he'd ordered, and he'd been amazed at how little she'd ordered.

He had to keep reminding himself that she was human. She wasn't like any of the shifter women he'd been with. *In more ways than one.* She wasn't free or open with nudity or her sexuality, and, by her own admission, she was seriously lacking in sexual experience. *Although, a few more nights like last night would soon have her caught up.*

No, lack of experience didn't matter - if anything he was grateful for it. Male shifters were territorial over their females, and he doubted his a-hole bear could have coped if she'd been half as wanton as he had been. *No, he wasn't looking a gift horse in the mouth.*

She was certainly a passionate creature, and he couldn't deny that being with her had been the best night of his life. But how could he explain to her that he thought she was his mate, and he expected her to bear his cubs? If she were a polar bear, this wouldn't be an issue. She'd have felt the pull to him, and by now they'd probably be bonded and maybe even expecting their first cub. But no, fate had sent him a human, and he couldn't deny that anymore. She was perfect for him and his beast.

But, how to make her his without scaring her away? His first thoughts on waking that morning had been that she was leaving him. No, she wasn't allowed. Well, he'd been in her apartment, so there was no way she would have gotten him out of there without a fight!

Nope, his bear had calmed when she'd offered a perfectly rational explanation. And even better, he'd managed to wangle an opportunity to meet her parents. He understood that was a big thing with humans – *meeting the parents.* It wasn't the same for bears. In clans, it was more important for matings to be blessed by the leader of the clan. But since Gunner technically wasn't in a clan at that moment, he could do as he damned well liked. But he would try and follow human rules as best he could.

A deep rumble escaped him as she licked a drop of maple syrup off her bottom lip. *What he wouldn't give to do that.* Her eyes widened at him, and he leered in return, making her cheeks turn an adorable shade of crimson.

"Thank you, again, for driving me."

Why did she have to keep saying that? Why did she always act like she was some kind of burden to him?

"I told you; I want to be here. Stop thanking me," he snapped.

His bear immediately snarled at him for his tone, but she didn't seem to mind. Wisely, he changed the subject.

"So you have problems with your family?" he asked bluntly.

Erin immediately tensed, and he felt bad.

"You don't have to tell me if you don't want to," he said quickly.

She shook her head as she toyed with the pancakes on her plate. "No, it's fine. It's not really a secret. I had trouble dealing with my abilities when I was a kid, and my parents didn't know how to handle me. My whole family is human – in fact my whole neighborhood was human. Shifters and witches were just something you saw on TV, and they never really affected us."

She winced as she said it, but Gunner didn't react. The majority of the people in the world were human; he had no doubt there were numerous places where what she said was true.

"My dad was away a lot, and my mom couldn't cope with me and three younger kids, so the Council of Supernaturals found a home for me to live in."

"A home?" he repeated in disbelief. *Was he hearing this right?*

Erin concentrated on the soggy mess of pancakes and maple syrup. "It was kind of like a hospital for supernatural beings who had trouble coping."

Gunner leaned across the table and hooked a finger under her chin, forcing her to look up at him. "Erin, that sounds like a mental institute."

The painful look of vulnerability returned to her eyes and he wanted to hit something. *All the people who had ever hurt her sounded like a good start.*

"It was, but it wasn't as bad as it sounds. They did help me. If I hadn't gone there, I doubt I'd be where I am today. I've met others with my gift, you know, but instead of facing it head on, they try to drown it out with alcohol and drugs. They weren't as lucky as me."

Gunner looked at her doubtfully, but he removed his finger from her chin and instead chose to place his hand over hers. She smiled at the touch, and his bear let out a happy growl.

"Anyway, after I left the hospital, I went and lived with a foster family, with other kids who were kind of like me. Then I turned eighteen, and the

Council gave me a scholarship for college. My family visited me regularly when I was a kid, but we kind of lost touch after I finished college. But, about six months ago, my sister reached out to me, and since then we've been trying to patch things up. She's actually getting married to a shifter, so my parents are a bit more open minded about supernatural matters. You're gripping my hand too tightly."

Gunner flinched and eased up. "Sorry."

Damn, he wanted to hit something so badly. What kind of parents did that to their child? *They even had her thinking that it was a good thing!* His bear was unbelievably furious at the way they had treated his Erin.

A smile blossomed over her face. "It's okay."

Damn, she was beautiful she when smiled. But then, she was always beautiful, even when she scowled. *No, especially when she scowled, and a hint of fire entered her eyes.*

"What about you? How come you don't live in a… umm… I want to say clan?"

Gunner chuckled. "Spot on, bears live in clans."

"Phew!" She used her spare hand to wipe it across her forehead in mock relief.

Her other hand was still trapped by his, and he was currently rubbing a thumb over the back of it.

"Not much to tell; I was born into a clan in Alaska. I joined the army when I was eighteen, and after I got out, I joined the SEA. I've been in Los Lobos for two years now."

She thought about that for a few moments. "Do you miss home?"

"Yeah, but right now, I prefer it here. I visit when I can, and I figure I'll retire there one day." *Retire there with his mate…*

He frowned at her plate; more than half her pancakes and bacon were still there, and she hadn't even touched her hash browns. He'd finished all his food; every last bite of the six dishes he'd ordered.

He pointed at her plate. "Didn't you like it? Would you like to order something different?"

"No, it was lovely, it was just a bit much for me."

"You haven't eaten very much," he grumbled.

Erin raised an eyebrow. "Food seems to be a big thing with you."

"I want you to be healthy and to have lots of energy." His lips curled up, and he winked.

Her cheeks turned an enchanting shade of pink; undoubtedly she had cottoned on to what she needed the energy for. "I'm human; I can't eat that much. Besides, what might equate to energy for a shifter would just mean fat on me. And I have quite enough of that, thank you."

"I'd say you were just right," he murmured.

The inescapable scent of her arousal wafted toward him, and his bear almost went wild. *Hmm, must remember to compliment her more.* That wouldn't be too hard; although she was small, she had just the right amount of dips and curves to suit him. He could spend all day long worshiping her sinful body, and he'd planned to do just that before she dropped this family gathering bomb. Still, meeting the parents was a step in the right direction.

Erin let out a small moan; the sweetness sent all available blood rushing to his already hardening cock. He had thought the previous night might have alleviated his suffering in that department, but no. Now that he'd had a taste of her, his greedy animal wanted more. And the fact that she just made the same sound as when he first sank inside her body really wasn't helping.

"I guess we should get going," she said grudgingly.

"Just say the word, and we can turn around and spend the day locked in my apartment."

Erin giggled. *Crap, that was even worse than the moan.*

"That is tempting, but my sister's been so sweet to me, I don't want to let her down."

"How old's your sister?"

"Vanessa's nineteen; she was just a baby when I went into the home. But as soon as she was old enough, she used to write to me all the time. We were kind of like pen pals. I have two brothers, too, but we're not close."

Her eyes lit up, and she looked at him expectantly before hesitating. He'd come to understand this meant that she wanted to ask a question, but she wasn't sure if it was appropriate.

"Ask away," he said smugly.

She pouted. "Am I that easy to read?"

"I like to think that I'm just getting to know you."

Erin blushed, and he shook his head. It was a wonder her cheeks weren't constantly flushed considering how embarrassed she got over everything. He certainly wasn't complaining; it was one of the many things he loved about her.

Whoa, love? Fuck, he really was screwed.

The waitress came to collect their dirty plates and leave the bill. He used it as an excuse to remove his hand from hers. His bear didn't like that one bit, and even Erin wilted a little with disappointment. But, the sudden realization at how deep his feelings were was like a punch to the gut, and he needed to take a slight step back. He thought she was his mate, but mate didn't immediately equate to love.

With her freed hand, she traced patterns on the tabletop. "I was just wondering whether you had any brothers or sisters."

Ah, safe territory. "An older brother, he's the leader of my clan. He took over when my dad stepped down."

"Is that one of the reasons you left?"

His hand hovered over the bill. "How did you know that?"

"Just a guess. I kind of thought that if you were there, you'd feel like you had to challenge for leadership."

Gunner marveled at her perceptiveness. "Some guess."

"Maybe it's just that I'm getting to know you."

Their eyes locked, and his heart sped up until it was beating away like a jackhammer. He was tempted just to pull her across the table and take her right then and there, but the other diners might have a few objections. However, given the heat in her big, round eyes, he doubted she'd say no.

"Let me get that." She reached for the bill, and he snatched it away as his animal snarled in consternation.

The sizzling electricity between them cooled, and in that instant her confusion was met by his ferocity. *No way in hell was he allowing her to pay.*

"It's only fair," she reasoned. "You're driving, so let me treat you to breakfast, it's the least I can do."

"No, I should pay." He was a man; he was supposed to take care of his female. He found it insulting to suggest he wasn't capable of doing so.

"Because you're the guy?" she rightly assumed. *Wow, she did know him.*

His bear roared in agreement. "Yes, male shifters take care of the females."

"Humans prefer to go Dutch."

He looked at her completely bewildered. "Dutch? What do the Netherlands have to do with this?"

Erin giggled. "It means to split the bill, usually fifty-fifty."

Gunner scowled. "I don't like that idea." *Humans had some funny ideas.*

"How about we compromise and I pay 25% of the bill," she joked.

"I'm paying the bill; please don't fight me on this." His voice was as quiet and controlled as he could manage, but even she couldn't fail to detect the undercurrent.

"Okay."

Gunner took a couple of deep breaths, and when she didn't try to argue he nodded, and strode off to pay. He watched her as he handed over the money, lest she try and make a break for it from the crazy shifter. He really needed to rein in his controlling tendencies. Female shifters could laugh off his rough chauvinism, but Erin might actually be offended.

He almost collapsed in relief when she came over to him and smiled, unperturbed by his mini-outburst. That was a good sign; she wasn't completely put off by his need to show his dominance. Yep, he was an asshole, and he knew it; he just prayed that Erin could learn to live with it. *Speaking of dominance...*

"Out of curiosity, what type of shifter is your sister marrying?"

"Oh, fox."

Gunner sighed in relief. A fox was nothing compared to a polar bear. Good, he'd be the most dominant shifter at this shindig, and fully prepared to take on all comers if anyone even dared to say anything to Erin.

She looked at him wonderingly, but before she could ask him anything, he took her hand and laced his fingers with hers. "Let's go."

*

Erin sighed as she approached her parents' house. She hadn't been there in, jeez, more than five years, but it looked the same as always – depressingly so.

She dared a glance up at her handsome companion. He'd been a bit put out about the bill back at the diner, but he'd soon recovered his good mood and had regaled her with his misadventures as a cub up in Alaska. Mental note, never go ice fishing with him. *He was one crazy son of a bear.*

She'd thought he was joking back at the diner, and had been a little taken aback at his hardness on the subject over who got to pay. He acted like she was insulting him or something. *Yeesh, she was just trying to be nice, anyone would think she was casting none-too-pleasant aspersions on his parentage.* Second mental note – if they go anywhere together, just let him pay, it isn't worth the aggravation of an argument. *Shifters had some funny ideas.*

They were having such a good day; it almost seemed like a shame to spoil it by going into her parents' house. No one knew they were there; there was still time to turn around and take Gunner up on his offer to lock themselves away in his apartment. *Hopefully, for a repeat of last night…*

"Erin!"

Crud. Her younger, prettier sister was standing on the porch step, beaming like there was no tomorrow. No chance of running away now.

Oh no! That was something else she hadn't considered. What if Gunner preferred Vanessa to her? What if he suddenly woke up and realized how foolish he'd been in getting involved with such an average looking – *and clearly bonkers* – woman like her, when there were so many sweeter, lovelier creatures like Vanessa in the world? *Oh, this was a bad plan.* Vanessa was taken at least, but who knew how many single females lurked through those doors waiting to pounce.

Erin looked up to see the concern evident on his face. "Don't worry, it'll be fine," he whispered reassuringly.

At least he wasn't a mind reader. Better he thought she was worried about seeing her family, rather than just indulging her irrational jealousy over every other female that breathed air.

When they got to the door, Vanessa gawked open-mouthed at Gunner. Yep, that was probably the expression Erin had when she first saw him too. He was certainly big, imposing, rugged, handsome, swoonworthy… *damnit.*

Her sister was caught between trepidation and lust as she pulled Erin in for a half-hearted hug. *All her attention was firmly directed at the polar bear shifter.*

"Umm, Vanessa, this is… ah, Gunner. Gunner, this is my sister, Vanessa."

She almost introduced him as her boss, while an evil little voice suggested 'lover' just to see her sister's reaction. *What was she supposed to call him anyway?* He *was* her boss, and up until last night she would have categorized their relationship as friendly with a good dollop of yearning on her side. At least she'd thought it had only been on her side. Now, she didn't know what to call him. It wasn't exactly like they were dating.

"Nice to meet you," rumbled Gunner as he shook her proffered hand firmly, it sent ripples throughout her whole body.

"You too," she simpered in return. *Clearly lust had won over trepidation.*

After a few seconds of ogling, Vanessa snapped out of it. "Come on in, we're having a barbecue in the back."

Gunner smiled; Vanessa cooed, and Erin just wanted to throw up. They followed Vanessa through the house, and Gunner lightly placed a hand on Erin's back. Heaven help her, instinctively she arched her back into his touch, desperate to feel his hands on her in any way, shape or form. *Heck, she'd settle for a bear hug with his polar bear at that moment.*

Erin's mouth went dry at seeing so many people there; she recognized a few people as her parents' family and friends, but most were strangers to her. She guessed the others were Vanessa's fiancé, Roger's guests.

Darn. All the women were wearing floaty, flowery summer dresses, and she was wearing a pair of jeans and a striped t-shirt. She looked like she was playing Where's Waldo! *Like she needed another reason to feel inadequate or out of place.*

Vanessa clapped her hands together. "Everyone, this is my sister, Erin, and her boyfriend, Gunner."

Boyfriend?! Aww, crap. Would Gunner make a bolt for it? Should she?

People murmured uninterested hellos at her while trying not to stare openly at the beefy shifter standing behind her. A number of the party guests lifted their chins and sniffed before recoiling slightly. Erin guessed they'd figured out just what species he was.

And Gunner? His hand slid up from her back to her shoulder; his fingers splayed over her skin, and he took a step closer to her, so he was standing directly behind her. His warm body pressed against her, sending delighted shivers through her. *And she really didn't want to think about that bulge digging into her back.*

He also took an exaggerated sniff before booming out a hello. Numerous guests, the sniffers and therefore shifters, cringed a little. He shook a little in laughter at that. *Shifters were weird.*

CHAPTER NINE

Much to his chagrin, Gunner found himself gathered around the smoky barbecue with Roger, the sister's fiancé, Erin's dad, Erin's brothers, and the fiancé's dad.

What is it with men and barbecues? He could never really see the appeal, preferring to eat his meat fresh. *Fresh as in still squirming in his paws.* It baffled him that any enjoyment could be derived from crowding around a smoking fire, discussing the merits of coal over propane, and arguing with other men about why the food wouldn't cook.

Erin was nowhere to be seen. She'd pressed a beer into his hand and had spirited away, sylph-like. He sniffed, trying to seek out her delectable scent, but that only resulted in a nose full of smoke.

His bear was not happy. He wondered if she was hiding in the house.

Roger – the fiancé and fox shifter – coughed to get his attention. "So, uh, how do you know Erin?"

Gunner dragged his attention away from the house and fixed his gaze on the slender fox, who had the sense to tremble at him. His bear chuffed in gratification. "We work together."

Erin's father and brothers said very little to him; they just eyed him distastefully. Gunner presumed they were unsure how to feel about him dating Erin. That was fine with him; he wasn't altogether pleased with their treatment of Erin. If they were to say a cross word to him, he couldn't be certain his bear wouldn't lash out and, oh, accidentally kill them. Nah, he probably wouldn't. *Probably.*

Roger's father, the leader of their skulk, pursed his lips. "Where do you work?'

The older fox was displeased at the bear for not showing more respect and inclining his neck in submission. *Hah! Him submitting to a fox?* That'll be the day.

"At the SEA," muttered Gunner absently.

These men were boring him. He was somewhat aware of the fact that he should have been trying to make a good impression on them, but his focus was swayed by his absent little human. Besides, he doubted Erin's opinion would be affected by any of these buffoons.

It occurred to him that if this had been a clan, and he was an outsider trying to mate with one of the females, by now the males would have interrogated him over his life, his intentions toward their female, and whether or not he was a fertile male capable of producing offspring. *Yeah, there was zero privacy in a clan.* But these men didn't seem to think they had any claim on Erin's life at all, which, he supposed they didn't. If he thought of her family as a clan, she hadn't been a part of it since she was a child.

Erin had been on her own for nearly her whole life and damn if that didn't make his heart twitch, his bear furious and the need to give her a bear hug overwhelming. He was on his own out of choice – not wanting to find out what he might do if he lived in such close quarters to his brother – but Erin had been forced out, just for being a little different.

Fuck, he needed to go to her.

He pushed his half-drunk beer into Roger's hand and muttered something about using the bathroom. He strode away, ignoring the murmured 'asshole' comments. *Why would he give a shit what they thought of him?* There was only one person in this whole bunch who mattered to him, and he wanted to see her that very second.

*

Erin escaped her mother and her sister and decided to hide in the bathroom. She cared for her sister – she really did – but she could only listen to so much talk about wedding centerpieces for so long before she wanted to start pulling out her hair just for something to do. *She defied anyone to get excited about centerpieces!*

Ugh, being home always stressed her out. She was always so afraid of doing or saying the wrong thing that she worked herself up until she had a stomach ache.

She wondered how Gunner was faring. She felt guilty at abandoning him, but the 'boyfriend' comment had surprised her. Was he her boyfriend now? Did Gunner see himself that way? She knew the smart thing would be to ask him, but a crushing fear of rejection sent cold shivers through her. He could easily say no. He could easily laugh at her. *No, she didn't like the sound of that at all.*

Erin splashed cold water on her heated cheeks. There was a gentle knock at the door.

"Just a minute."

"It's me."

Oh, it wasn't fair how her stomach started doing flips over those two words. "Me who?" she teased – there really could be no doubt as to who that deep, husky voice belonged to.

"Me – I'm gonna knock this door down if you don't open up."

Erin pressed her lips together to stop from smiling and unlocked the door. He slipped into the room and locked it again.

"Hey," she murmured.

"Hey."

"Having fun?"

"Well, now that I've caught up with you…"

He reached out and snagged one of her hands, gently pulling her toward him. *Resistance is futile.* He bent down and captured her lips in a surprisingly tender kiss. She moaned into his mouth.

Gunner sighed as he drew back; he snaked his arms around her back, and in turn she rested her hands on his stomach. *It was like leaning against a stone wall.*

"Don't take this the wrong way, babe, but how soon can we leave?"

She looked up at him with wide, innocent eyes. "What? You mean small talk with humans and foxes, while digesting meat that's charred on the outside and frozen on the inside, isn't your thing? Well, color me surprised."

Erin batted her eyelashes at him, and he chuckled, sending vibrations through her frame. Ooh, she liked how petite he made her feel. Not something a lot of men could boast.

"What can I say? When I eat uncooked meat, I prefer it if it's still moving."

"Gross." *Sushi was her limit for uncooked food.*

"Not gross, it's natural," he insisted as his hands rubbed up and down. "You should come up to Alaska when I visit my parents; we could go fishing. Or at least my bear could go fishing, and you could watch."

Erin blinked at him in stark surprise. "You want me to meet your parents?"

"I met yours; it's only fair I return the favor. The difference is my parents will actually like you."

He leaned down and nipped her earlobe, before letting out an exaggerated 'ahem.'

"What?"

Gunner rolled his eyes mockingly. "That was your cue to tell me that your parents do like me."

She let out a small snort. "Oh, I missed that."

"Well? Aren't you going to say it?"

Erin bit her lip. She was under no allusions about her parents. They weren't happy at her for bringing a bear shifter with her. They still weren't altogether comfortable with supernatural beings, but they tolerated having fox shifters around because Vanessa was the apple of their eyes. *A lumbering bear shifter who looked like he could bring the whole house down with one well-timed sneeze was another matter.* But then she'd learned long ago that she was never going to be fully accepted by her family. She was happy enough to make the best of it, but she wasn't going to forgo a chance at her own happiness for their sakes.

"I would but I don't really like lying." She said it half in jest but half seriously.

Gunner huffed in mock annoyance, but he couldn't hide his grin. She seriously doubted that anyone's opinion mattered to the huge bear shifter. He really didn't lack for confidence. *Oh, what must that be like...*

She curled her fingers into his t-shirt. "If it makes you feel any better, I'm not sure my parents like me either."

"Their loss," he growled darkly. "My parents would love you for a... ah..."

"For a what?"

"A, uh, vacation. They'd love to have you visit for a vacation. They've always been curious about humans."

Jeez, he made it sound like she was some kind of newly discovered mammal. Now presenting, the previously undiscovered wonder that is Erin. *Yeah, right.* "Surely they've met humans before?"

Gunner shrugged unconcernedly. "Sure, but they've never lived with a human, I think they'd be fascinated by how little you actually eat." That darn frown returned to his face, and she just wanted to wipe it off, or kiss it off, or send his mouth further south for a repeat of last night...

"Oh? Would they try and fatten me up too? I'm not convinced you're not doing it so you can eat me."

His eyes sparkled. "Oh, I'd like to…"

"No! Stop right there, I know where this is going." *Was he a freaking mindreader?!*

"You do? Because you seemed mighty surprised by it last night." His lust-filled leer was positively panty wetting.

Erin buried her head in his chest, trying to hide her blush. "Don't pick on me."

He tangled his fingers in her hair and gently pulled her head back, so she was looking at him. "Wouldn't dream of it."

"No?"

He leaned down. "No, my dreams are much filthier," he whispered suggestively.

There was a loud banging on the door, and Erin jumped. She didn't know what surprised her more, the interruption, or that her hands had actually been trying to work Gunner's belt open. *They had a mind of their own.*

"Is everything alright in there?" called her mother.

"F… fine," replied Erin. "I'm just, err, on the toilet." *That's it - think of the worst thing to say.*

"Okay, you've been in there a while…"

"I'm fine, Mom," snapped Erin, ignoring the silent laughter emanating from the huge bear shifter.

She waited until she heard her mother's retreating footsteps before slapping his arm. "It's not funny," she told him primly.

"Of course not," he sniggered.

"As much as I'm enjoying hiding out in here, we should really go back out there."

"I don't know; the bathroom kind of has a charm to it. I bet we could spend hours in here if we tried. There're plenty of fun looking surfaces in here to try out."

His hand slipped down to her ass, and she smothered her moan by making light of the situation. If she did moan, one thing would lead to another, and before he could say abracadabra she'd be out of her clothes.

"Oh, why stop at hours? I'm pretty sure we could build a life in here if we really tried. It could be our little pied-á-terre."

"Don't tempt me, babe."

Erin was taken aback at the forcefulness behind those words, but before she could ponder them further, he was already leading her back out to the party. This time, though, he kept his hand firmly laced with hers. Apparently, he wasn't going to let her abandon him again. He needn't have worried, as she surveyed the sea of unfriendly faces, there was nowhere else she'd rather be.

*

Erin was surprised at how nice Gunner's apartment actually was. She'd seriously been expecting some kind of man cave deal, with the floors covered in unwashed clothes and pizza boxes. But, no, this was nice, clean and modern. Actually, it was a heck of lot nicer than her own apartment. Out of the two of them, she was the more slovenly one. *Oh, that bummed her out.*

Yep, somehow she'd found herself in Gunner's apartment. She just wasn't sure how. She knew the logistics, of course. After escaping the family barbecue, he was driving and lamenting how little she'd eaten, and then he'd suggested she come over to his apartment to watch a movie and get some takeaway… *That's where she got stuck.* She was sure that her scaredy-cat nature had reared her fluffy head and made some protestation, but somehow it hadn't got any further than that. He'd carelessly waved away her concerns and whisked her back here. Yep, he was a force of nature. *Hurricane Gunner.*

She sat on the edge of his plush couch and yelped as she sank into its depths. He smirked as he looked through his collection of DVDs.

"You have a lot of films," she offered conversationally.

"Yeah, what can I say? I like to relax by watching a film and drinking a beer. I can't stand TV, all the commercial breaks drive me insane, there're only so many times I can watch an infomercial about Viagra before I'm clawing at the walls."

Erin smiled. "What else do you like doing?"

Gunner laughed slightly. "Not much," he admitted. "Pretty much, I work, I train, I go to the bar, and then I come home and watch a movie. I'm not a lot of fun."

"Swap the films for books and get rid of the training, and it sounds like my life," she said ruefully. "I guess I'm only half as fun as you."

"Maybe we should make our own fun," he leeringly suggested.

Erin shook her head. He really could turn everything sexual. *Not that she was complaining…*

"You like movies?" he asked.

"Sure." She just didn't see movies often. There was something infinitely depressing about going to see a movie on her own. The last movie she watched, or rather re-watched, was Look Who's Talking on TV. *Talking babies, gotta love 'em.*

Hmmm, babies… Erin gasped and slapped a hand over her mouth.

"What?" He looked up in concern and immediately his body tensed.

"When we had sex we didn't use protection!" Why was it only occurring to her now? *She could already be baking a polar bear cub in her oven!*

He chuckled and relaxed. "It's fine; you're not fertile right now."

What the heigh-ho did that mean? "I'm… I'm not? How can you tell?"

Gunner shrugged his massive shoulders. "I can scent it."

She wrinkled her nose in distaste. "You mean, you can, like, scent when a woman's on her period?"

"Sure, and ovulating."

Eeuw. She didn't have to say the word out loud, but he could obviously tell what she was thinking.

"Shifters are part animal; we're driven to mate and produce young. We need to be able to tell when females are fertile."

That was kind of creepy. "So when you first met me, did you automatically check to see if I was fertile?"

He looked at her oddly. "No."

Oh, no. She couldn't help the questions that came out next. She didn't want to ask them, but they came out anyway. "So, as a shifter, having kids is important to you? It's something you'll want one day?"

Gunner stared at her for a few beats, and she wanted to shrink into his oversized couch. "Look, this is getting a little heavy, why don't we just chose a movie and store this conversation away for the future?"

Erin almost collapsed in relief. Babies were not something she wanted to think about. She'd only known Gunner for a couple of weeks. "Okay."

"What are you in the mood for?" He flicked through the numerous titles, awkwardness forgotten. "I have action movies, action comedies, and some more action movies."

She smiled impishly and folded her legs under her. "Well, gee, on that basis I guess I'll have to go for an action movie."

"Oh, babe, teasing me is not a good idea."

"Hmmm, I'm willing to risk it," she cooed.

He grinned at her. "So, we have Die Hard, True Lies, The Bourne Identity, The Expendables..." She scrunched her nose at the suggestions, and he kept looking. "Hey, hang on a second, I think I have some still in their plastic wrap my sister-in-law bought me for Christmas." He reached to the back of the shelf and pulled out two titles. "Okay, yeah, I have Ghostbusters and Jurassic Park. What do you think?"

Erin tapped her lips pretending to think, before, deadly serious, she said, "Who ya gonna call?"

He shook his head and chuckled. "Ghostbusters it is." He set the DVD going. "I'm going to order that pizza, what would you like on it?"

"I'm not really that hungry."

His expression darkened for a few seconds before he cocked an eyebrow at her. "You've barely eaten anything all day. You'll need your strength for tonight."

"Oh, do I have plans tonight? I'm so tired I might just fall asleep watching the movie."

The disappointed look on his face was absolutely priceless, and Erin just couldn't hold onto her mirth. She let out a chirp of laughter before burying her face in a cushion.

Gunner let out a playful roar, and on diving across the room he flipped Erin onto her back and proceeded to tickle her, eliciting hysterical shrieks.

"I warned you about teasing me," he purred as he easily controlled her flailing limbs.

"I'm sorry! I'm sorry!" she choked out between squeals.

He suddenly stopped, and gave her a stern glare. "Do you promise never to tease me again?"

Erin pouted at him. "Oh, I don't think I could I manage that. How about I promise not to tease you for the next twenty minutes?"

Gunner appeared to think about it for a few moments before growling 'no deal' and resuming his tickling torture.

She endured as much as she could before she had to admit defeat. She was only human, after all! "Alright, I submit! I submit! I promise never to tease you again."

His hands slowed down until he was just rubbing her stomach and hips. As her mischievous side calmed, her lustful side sat up and stretched, more than ready for a little action. She smoothed her hands up his arms, wondering how to phrase what she wanted him to do to her.

She'd never actually asked for sex before. The closest she'd ever come was admitting she wanted to be with Gunner the previous night. In her experience, men asked her repeatedly to have sex with them until she gave in and, somewhat, grudgingly let them.

It wasn't the same with Gunner. It didn't feel like just sex between them, it felt like a joining of hearts, minds, and bodies. Just coming out and saying 'please do me' seemed a bit crass. It needed to be more tender, more romantic, more... *where the heck was he going?*

Gunner released her and sat back up on the couch. She mewled at the loss of his hard body over hers.

"Something wrong, babe?" he asked innocently.

Her brow creased in bewilderment. *Didn't he want to have sex with her?* Hadn't he been the one disappointed when she intimated that she was too tired? "I thought..."

"First we eat our pizza and then we'll get to the fun portion of our evening."

Erin gaped at him. Was he kidding? Was he really policing her eating by threatening to not have sex with her? *Oh no, if he was she was doomed!*

Gunner chortled at her stricken face and pulled her up on the couch until she was tucked under his arm. "I wasn't kidding, babe, you're going to need all the energy you can get. But, if you eat your pizza like a good girl, I promise to put you to bed. Now, what topping do you want?"

CHAPTER TEN

Gunner groaned, and his sleepy polar bear yowled as he slipped out of bed and grabbed his phone, keen to stop the incessant ringing before it woke Erin.

He pushed answer and whispered hello into the phone.

"Gunner," intoned the director's cold voice.

The bear shifter cast one last longing look at Erin's sleeping, curvy form and reluctantly dragged his feet out into the living room.

"Problem?" barked Gunner.

"I need you at a crime scene. I'll text you the location."

Gunner hesitated. "I uh… I'm not alone…"

The director clucked his tongue. "Whoever she is, she'll wait. Get here now."

"The rest of the team?"

"Just you, for now."

The director hung up, and his bear huffed in irritation. Not at the snake shifter - his boss could be as terse as he wanted, and Gunner could give a shit. No, he wanted to crawl back into bed with Erin, he wanted to feel her smooth skin pressed against his, he wanted to hear her soft breaths lulling him to sleep.

He scowled as he received the text. No way did he want to drive across town in the middle of the night to stare at a corpse. *Still, he had to be responsible.* Not that the thought of waking Erin up for a quickie didn't cross his mind, his bear was all for that, but he quelled the urge because he wanted Erin to get her rest.

Gunner pulled on a fresh pair of jeans and a shirt. He gave himself a sniff and slapped on some truly dire aftershave. It was awful, but it served its purpose of covering up any lingering scent of Erin on his skin. He might cause a few crime scene technicians to pass out from the fumes, but at least Erin's modesty would be saved.

His beast chuffed at him. He wanted to revel in her scent, and he wanted his skin drowning in her sweet vanilla smell. He wanted every other damn male to know she was his and belonged to him. But no, Gunner couldn't risk it. *Not yet.* He needed to talk to Erin before he started spreading it around that he and Erin were intimate. Turning up at a crime scene covered in her smell was akin to flashing a neon light that said 'I had sex with Erin Jameson.' At least Cutter wouldn't be there. *That damn Lupine bastard was better than a freaking bloodhound.*

He squatted next to the bed and brushed a strand of hair out of her face before running a thumb down her pink cheek. She always looked flushed; always flustered and embarrassed or perhaps warmed from their lovemaking. *He wouldn't mind just watching her sleep...*

His bear growled as his phone beeped again. Undoubtedly the director was asking what was taking so long. It must be bad if the cold-blooded snake shifter was riled.

Gunner sighed and kissed her temple, whispering that he would be back soon. With one last look, he left her resting peacefully.

*

"Hey, Gunner, oh, yeuch, can you smell that?"

The rabbit shifter medical examiner, Rory twitched his nose as, reluctantly, Gunner lifted the crime scene tape for him.

Gunner shrugged and rolled his eyes. He didn't have time for the creepy little shifter any day of the week, but in the middle of the night, when his body and his bear were screaming at him to haul ass back to his luscious, little human, he was understandably short. "Can't smell anything."

Rory shook his head in disbelief as he struggled to keep up with the polar bear's strides. "You're joking, right? I hang around dead bodies all day, and I've never smelt anything that bad. Whatever cheap perfume your latest *woman* has been using, I suggest you pour it down the toilet – stat."

The polar bear curled his lips at the scorn poured onto the word woman. *The stupid rabbit was just jealous; he could never get a woman like Erin.*

"No wonder you're still single," hissed Gunner.

Rory frowned. "Because I can scent how bad you smell?"

"No because you hang around dead bodies all day."

Ordinarily, Gunner might be polite, but he was not in the mood. *Asshole rabbit.*

"At least I'm not trying to pretend I don't smell like fermented sewer water," muttered Rory before making a beeline toward the director.

Gunner sneered and followed. The director nodded at him but didn't react to the smell. Thankfully, he was too preoccupied to notice. Although whatever he was thinking about couldn't have been good.

"What do we have?" demanded Gunner irritably.

The director looked at him wearily, worry lines marring his usually clear face. "Dead hippopotamus shifter."

Not to seem heartless... "What else? You wouldn't have come out here if there weren't something more to this."

The snake shifter took a deep breath. "He's missing his heart."

Gunner exhaled and for a change, his beast was quiet. "Fuck, not good. Do you think…?"

"I hope not. Take a look at him."

The director turned away to talk to some local police officers, and Gunner stepped closer. Rory twitched his nose in annoyance but didn't say anything. It was a body of a naked young man, aged about thirty, and sure enough, he was missing his heart.

Gunner cocked his head at Rory. "How long's he been dead?"

"Can't you smell it?" asked Rory maliciously.

The rabbit shifter's eyes widened as the polar bear let out a low growl; Rory cleared his throat. "About two weeks, I would guess."

Wordlessly, he left the rabbit to it and found the director.

Gunner folded his arms over his chest. "What happened?"

"We're standing on the property of the Cinderella Waste Disposal Company. It's a company that handles some private contracts, but also contracts that include hospitals and even the SEA. They dispose of waste; or rather, they incinerate it in an environmentally friendly fashion."

"Spare me the company spiel," muttered Gunner.

"Anyway, one of their machines has been out of use for the last few weeks, so they've been backed up and all those containers," the director pointed to what looked that shipping containers, "are what are waiting to go in. They've been working overtime to try and get through all this. Earlier this evening, they had a rookie operating the crane that lifts them. He dropped one of the containers, it opened and out came our victim."

Gunner looked over to a pile of trash that numerous crime scene techs were wading through. "That the rest of the container?"

"Yep. The guys who work here pulled the body out of the trash and covered him with a blanket, out of respect."

"Sure. Has anything else been found in the rest of the trash?"

"A wallet, a shoe that would fit the victim, and a shirt. Hopefully, we'll find the rest of his stuff."

Gunner swung his gaze back to the body. A couple of years back, when he first took over the Alpha team, they had a case where a witch was kidnapping shifters, dissecting and using their organs to create potions. He was caught and currently resided in a high-security mental institute upstate. But he'd killed a lot of people before he was caught, and there was always the fear that someone else might try it too.

Hundreds of years ago, when shifters and witches truly hated each other, it was common practice to create potions out of the bodies of shifters. *Just like it was common practice for shifters to snack on a witch if they got hungry.* Times had changed, at least for most people they had, but there would always be a few people who would cling to their hate.

"What does Cinderella have to say to all this?"

The director quirked an eyebrow. "Not much, mostly because the guy I talked to is in shock. I imagine, they'll rally their lawyers pretty quickly though; I doubt we'll get much more than basic information from them."

"I guess it's possible that someone at the company decided to kill the guy and then get rid of his body this way."

"Or possible that anyone, who knew about their pickup schedule from the many companies they service, knew to put the body in with their regular trash."

His polar bear stirred unhappily. "Do you think we have another rogue witch on our hands?"

The snake shifter eyed him coldly and calculatingly. "My gut says no. I would expect that if someone went to the trouble of killing this guy for his organs, they wouldn't have stopped at the heart."

"Unless they were interrupted…"

"In which case I wouldn't have expected his body to have been disposed of so well. This machine breaking down is a fluke; the crane operator dropping it and it spilling everything are both flukes. If those things hadn't happened, then the body would already be incinerated."

"Hmmm, why didn't you want the rest of the team here?"

"I wanted to speak to you alone, to make sure we're on the right track. The last time bodies turned up missing organs it was a nightmare. The press went wild, accusing witches – it turned into a literal witch hunt! The number of witches hurt by angry shifters was phenomenal. And while Los Lobos was panicking like fuckwits, that bastard killed seven people. I don't want that happening again. No panic; as far as we are concerned, this is a straightforward murder for the time being. Got it?"

Gunner exhaled loudly. "Got it."

He didn't exactly agree with that, but he wasn't about to argue over it. Hah, maybe he was going soft in his old age. The thought tickled him for a second, until he was warmed by thoughts of Erin. Or maybe having met his mate had calmed him.

No, in his opinion, this guy was targeted for his heart. The cut marks in his chest just seemed too clinical for it to be a crime of passion. He'd had a case where an emu shifter actually had performed a little amateur surgery – she cut her ex-lover's heart out of his chest. *She said it was fitting that he literally was heartless after she was done with him…* This was nothing like that. Although, whoever had done it hadn't bothered to sew him back up, so clearly once they had the heart out, they considered the job done.

"We'll brief the team tomorrow," declared the director, "for now, we'll both interview witnesses, stressing the importance of keeping quiet about this whole matter.

"Let's do it."

All thoughts of crawling back into his warm, occupied bed were sunk. He put on his most professional face and decided to tackle the men who found the body.

CHAPTER ELEVEN

Erin looked up as Gunner stomped out of his office. His face was a picture of barely restrained rage. She hadn't seen him so angry since she'd been in hospital, and he punched the wall. *She wondered if he had to pay for that wall…*

The rest of the bullpen went quiet as Gunner stormed over to her and the rest of the team.

He eyed them all in turn before alighting on Erin. Cutter, Avery and Wayne had the grace to incline their head slightly in submission. Erin, in a hitherto unknown fit of defiance, jutted her chin and stared right back at him. *Moody bear.*

Erin was peeved. He had no right to be angry at her. He wasn't the one who woke up in the middle of the night, in a strange bed to find himself all alone! How would he have reacted if she'd just skipped out on him?

His eyes traveled down to the stuffed cat sitting next to her computer. He snorted derisively. Erin picked the cat up and began stroking its matted fur. She pouted at him. *Don't mess with my cat!*

He huffed. "Conference room, ten minutes," he barked, and turned away without waiting for an acknowledgement.

Seconds later his office door shut with a resounding slam, and everyone in the office sighed in relief. *BBB, indeed.*

"Wow, that was actually kind of mild for him," commented Avery, over the divider between their cubicles.

"Oh?" replied Erin, uninterestedly.

"Yeah, nothing got broken, no walls were hit, yep, this has to be one of his nicest bad moods yet."

"Good to know," she murmured.

She stowed the cat safely in her bottom drawer and stood up. "I'm going to the bathroom; I'll see you in the conference room."

Avery nodded as Erin walked away.

In the bathroom, she splashed cool water on her cheeks. She could kind of understand Gunner leaving her during the night. She assumed it was about work. At least she was praying that was what it was about. A horrible, tiny, little, niggling, oh-so-anxious part of her couldn't help but worry that he had left her to run off and see another woman. She didn't like herself for thinking it, but she couldn't help the unbidden thought taunting her. The truth is she had no idea where he went. Maybe if he'd left a note or texted her... *But nope, nothing.*

It sure as hell wasn't nice to wake up in the middle of the night screaming from a nightmare and find herself all alone. *And that was the crux of what upset her.* Having nightmares wasn't something new for her, but waking up and being disappointed that he wasn't there to comfort her was. She resented the fact that he hadn't been there when she needed him. Unreasonable? Maybe a little, but it sure as sugar had hurt to wake and find him gone.

Oh, well, better get going. Don't want to give him another reason to be mad. An insolent part of her considered hanging around in the bathroom, and purposefully being late. *Ha, that would rile him.*

Erin looked at herself in the mirror and giggled – *yes, actually giggled* – while the rest of the world seemed intent on staying out of Gunner's way when he was mad, she seemed to want to make him even madder. It was strange; she'd never been so... so... naughty or disobedient. *Usually her mottos were, don't make waves, blend in, pretend you're invisible...* But no, here she was trying to enrage a seven-foot polar bear shifter on purpose. She found it odd at how comfortable she was with him, and how she really didn't fear him hurting her at all. Well, not physically anyway. *Emotionally was a whole other ballgame.*

Well, she'd waited long enough. She really ought to get going.

She made her way out of the bathroom and ran smack-dab into a solid wall of chest. *Mmmm, a yummy solid wall of chest. Gunner.*

He steadied her and placed his hands on her shoulders. *Oh, she just wanted to climb him like a tree.*

"What have you been doing in there?" he demanded irritably.

And just like that, all sexy thoughts were vanquished.

"Why do you hang around outside women's bathrooms?" she asked with equal ire. This wasn't the first time she'd careened into him outside a toilet.

His mouth gaped open, surprised at the vehemence in her retort.

Erin squirmed under his gaze. "Shouldn't we get going?"

"They'll wait," he said gruffly. "Why did you leave this morning?"

She narrowed her eyes and squared her shoulders, not easy with the way he was gripping them. "I woke up alone, I didn't know where you were," she replied, trying to keep the hurt out of her voice, not altogether successfully. "But I knew I needed clothes, so I went back to my apartment."

"How did you get back there?"

Erin shrugged. "The bus."

"The bus!" he exclaimed incredulously, eyes bulging. "What time was this? You shouldn't be riding the bus at night alone. You shouldn't be going anywhere alone. You shouldn't have left my apartment."

"I could say the same to you," she muttered petulantly.

Gunner grimaced. "I had to work."

"Well, I didn't know that!"

Were fumes coming out of her ears? She suspected there might be fumes coming out of her ears.

Gunner visibly relaxed and stroked his thumbs over the edge of her shirt. "Okay, fine, you're right. But know this, I wouldn't have left if it weren't important, and I didn't think I was going to be so long."

Erin sighed as her anger melted. *She was such a pushover.* "It's okay, I was just worried when I woke up and you weren't there."

Gunner swiveled his head and scanned the empty corridor before giving her a quick kiss on the lips. "We better go."

They walked together, side by side, toward the conference room, both a little happier than they had been earlier that morning.

"It probably wasn't a bad thing for you to have showered at home and got fresh clothes," he said in an amused voice. "At least my scent won't be on them."

She stopped and cocked her head at him quizzically. "Oh?"

He shrugged his Herculean shoulders, making the fabric of his t-shirt stretch impossibly tight. "We don't want people to get the wrong idea."

"The wrong idea…" she repeated slowly.

A small pit of worry was forming in her stomach. Oh, she didn't like where this was going. *What the heck was the wrong idea?*

He furrowed his brow. "Yeah."

All her crossness and crabbiness from the morning came flooding back. "Okay, yeah, we don't want anyone to think there's something going on with us."

But instead of the anger-laced words she was expecting, he seemed almost fearful. "That's not what I meant."

"I think we should go in," she said prissily as she pushed the door open and ignored his almost inaudible groan.

Erin seated herself between Jessie and Avery and avoided looking at him altogether.

"About time," snapped the director.

Gunner huffed but didn't bother to apologize.

Succinctly, and in a low, hard voice, Gunner proceeded to tell them about the body they'd found. Gingerly, everyone looked at the crime scene photos. Erin could feel Gunner's eyes boring into her as she bent her head over the gruesome pictures, but she studiously avoided him. *Childish? Maybe, but he had it coming!*

"We identified our victim as James Silver," said the director. "He was part of the Roystan pod of hippopotami, and he was also reported missing almost two weeks ago."

Gunner looked up sharply. "He was one of the suspicious disappearances Zeta team was looking into?"

"Yes, he disappeared in the same way as the others. Potentially, we have to consider the possibility that they all died the same way too."

Wayne tapped the photos. "Why do we think his heart was missing?"

The director pursed his thin lips. "We don't know yet, it may yet just be a simple murder."

"Cutting out someone's heart is hardly simple!" scoffed Cutter.

"Let's not make any assumptions," rumbled the director. "We don't want anyone panicking about this. For now, it's just a murder. He was reported missing by his mother who found a note at his home stating he was leaving town, and some of his belongings were gone. But not many and his car is still parked at his home. She didn't believe it and reported it."

He passed the missing person file to Gunner, who flicked through it.

"We managed to retrieve his clothes, phone and wallet from the trash," said

Gunner. "So, whoever dumped him in that container must have hoped they'd be incinerated at the same time. Jessie, see what you can get from the phone."

He skimmed the phone across the table, and Jessie immediately picked it up and started studying it. He hesitated slightly. "Erin," he said softly, "do you think you could get something from his wallet? A, uh, vision or something?"

Erin ignored her heated cheeks and the interested glances of her teammates. "I'll try, can I touch it?"

"Sure, the crime scene techs are finished with it."

Gunner rose to his feet and loped around the table in easy strides. He passed her the wallet, rubbing his fingers against hers as he did. She withheld a moan and firmly clamped her legs together as she met his stormy gaze. It was woefully unfair just how much he turned her on with a slight touch and a look. At that moment, her inner nymphomaniac was practically winking at him.

Thankfully, she was soon distracted. As soon as she clasped the wallet with both hands a vision flashed before her eyes. Their victim, James Silver, was sitting at a high table in a club. He pulled out some bills and threw a couple on a waitress' tray as she handed him a drink. He then pushed one into the waistband of her blue hot-pants and leered. She gave him a suffering smile and walked away. He swigged at the drink and looked around at other women. He smirked as a tall, skinny blonde sauntered over to his table. She rubbed his arm, and he whispered in her ear, making her throw her head back, letting out a cacophony of high-pitched, fake laughter.

Erin blinked and was surprised to find Gunner kneeling beside her. One of his large hands hovered over her shoulder, unsure whether to touch her.

"Are you alright?" asked Avery tentatively.

Erin gazed around at the worried faces of her teammates. "Of course."

"You just went so pale, and your eyes went blank…" murmured Gunner.

She laughed lightly. "I wouldn't know; I've never seen myself have a vision before."

"You saw something?" demanded the director, ignoring the disapproving look Gunner hurled at him.

"Yes," she told him uncertainly, "I'm not sure how helpful it is. I guess it was from the last time he used his wallet. He was at a club, and there were neon flamingos on the walls and people dancing in cages."

Jessie raised an eyebrow. "Strippers?"

Erin, in spite of herself, blushed. "No, they had their clothes on, or at least they had their bikinis on. He paid for a drink, leered at the waitress, and then a blonde woman came up to him. I don't think he knew her." She smiled self-consciously. "It's not much help."

"It might be the last place he visited, and she might have been the last person to see him," said Gunner softly. "Did you get a good look at the blonde? Would you recognize her again?"

She nodded fervently. "Definitely."

Gunner stood up to his full height, towering over her. She tried to restrain herself from quivering.

"Cutter, go to the crime scene, see if you can pick up anything, and see how they're getting on with the search. Plus, it couldn't hurt to scare the hell out of the good people at Cinderella – just in case they're holding something back. Jessie look into his background, see what you can find, but go through his phone and get Wayne a list of his friends." He nodded at Wayne. "I want you to talk to them, and see what they can tell you about him. Avery and I will make the death notification to the family, and we'll check out his apartment."

Erin looked up at him almost coyly. "And me?"

"I need you to look through mugshots for the blonde woman."

"Keep me informed," ordered the director.

Everyone filed out the room, eager to get moving.

Gunner lingered at the door and gave her a meaningful look. "We'll talk tonight; don't leave this building without me."

With that, he was gone, too quickly for her to even argue. *Sneaky bear.*

Oh, well, here we go, desk duty – yay.

*

Erin yawned and licked at the mountain of whipped cream perilously piled onto her hot chocolate. Feeling bored of looking through photo after photo of young blonde women, she decided to take a short break, and had taken refuge in the coffee shop across the street.

Mmmm, perhaps coffee might have been a better choice. She hadn't exactly had a lot of sleep in the past two nights – *she had something much better to do* – but now she was starting to feel a little weary. And the bags developing under her eyes certainly weren't helping her self-esteem.

Gunner didn't look weary at all. *Damn, lucky shifter.* No, he'd spent half the night pleasuring her, and the rest of it traipsing round a crime scene, and he still looked as fresh as a daisy in his tight, muscle-hugging t-shirt and jeans that looked like they'd been sprayed on…

No, stop it, she was still annoyed with him. She knew there was a policy against teammates dating, and she had briefly thought about that before she threw herself at him, but she hadn't really thought about how he'd feel about it. He said he didn't want anyone to get the wrong idea. *But what idea was that?* That they were dating? Was that wrong? Bad, troubling thoughts sought attention, and it was becoming difficult to ignore them.

He didn't want anyone to know about them being together because he was planning on dumping her.

He didn't want anyone to get the impression they were dating because it had just been a one-night stand for him - or rather, two-night stand.

He was embarrassed by her and didn't want people knowing that he had slept with the decidedly un-skinny, human nutjob.

Apparently, she was good enough to have sex with, but not good enough for anyone to know about!

She felt her blood boil but then tried to calm herself. She was thinking the worst of him, and that wasn't fair. He deserved the benefit of the doubt. *Hmmm, but how could she know that?* She'd only known him for a little over a couple of weeks. For all she knew, he was a full-on horndog who regularly seduced and dumped women. And yet... she felt like she'd known him forever. *That she was meant to know him.* Everything felt so right and so natural when they were together. It certainly explained why she was so quick to rip off her clothes for him. *Or maybe that was just the prudish part of her trying to justify the newly discovered sex maniac.*

Maybe he was just concerned about their jobs, she rationalized. Maybe he really enjoyed working with her and was worried they wouldn't be able to if the director knew there was something between them. *Yes, yes, she liked that idea.* It was so much more palatable than the alternatives.

"Erin!"

Ah, crap.

Erin bit back the sigh that wanted to escape as Isis gracefully sat down in the seat opposite. She crossed her long legs and flashed a dazzling smile.

"I'll have my usual, Tony," she called out to a gangly teenager behind the counter.

To the frustration of everyone waiting to be served, the smitten Tony immediately whipped up a skinny latte for Isis. She winked at him when he placed it on the table for her, nudging Erin's purse out the way. He looked like all his dreams had come true. *Pretty mediocre dreams thought Erin grumpily.*

"So, how's it going?" asked Isis seemingly amiably.

"Fine," mumbled Erin.

"What's that? Hot chocolate?"

"Yes," she hissed, a little self-conscious. *She had no reason to be!*

"Good for you," said the tigress condescendingly and patted her pancake-flat stomach. "I have to watch my weight."

Erin looked at her doubtfully. She bet Isis was naturally toned, and she was fortunate to have a shifter's metabolism. Erin struggled to maintain her current, curvy shape, and even that was a little big for her taste.

Isis leaned forward, resting her elbows on her knees. Her eyes were filled with fake concern. "How's it really going? I know there were a few... objections to you joining the team."

She prickled, even though she knew it was true. "No, it's fine."

The tigress eyed her keenly. "How's Gunner treating you?"

Oh, very well. The things he had done to her... Erin desperately tried to ward off the rising heat threatening to reach her cheeks.

"Fine, we get along fine. I enjoy working with him; he's... he's a good guy."

She'd almost said *amazing, wonderful, the man of her dreams* – but she caught herself. Nothing good could come from Isis knowing about her feelings for her boss.

Isis nodded absently and clapped her hands together. "I'm going to get some sweetener."

Erin raised an eyebrow. *Why didn't she just get her lapdog Tony to fetch it?* He looks like he'd do just about anything for the thrill of getting a wink from the beautiful shifter.

Isis smirked at her, and Erin felt a small shiver of alarm. *What was she up to?*

The tigress rose to her feet, *to her more than a little intimidating six-foot-one in heels height*, and started to walk away. She brushed past Erin, grazing her arm and Erin froze as a vision flittered in front of her eyes.

Erin gasped and gave a lurch forward, spilling hot chocolate all over, and inside, her purse.

Isis made an unsurprised 'oh' sound. "I'll get napkins."

Within seconds, Isis returned and pressed a wad of napkins into her hand. Erin diligently mopped up the mess and began emptying her purse to clean everything inside.

Unconcernedly, Isis stirred sweetener into her coffee. "Something wrong?"

"No," muttered Erin, her head bent to her task.

No, nothing was wrong. *Nothing at all!* She'd just had a succession of visions of Gunner and Isis having sex – why the freaking hell would anything be wrong?!

Isis must have been thinking about it when she brushed against her arm. She guessed Isis did it on purpose. A lot of psychics saw the memories closest to the surface, and Isis was probably hoping Erin would see that, *that, montage,* of sex. *Well, Isis had lucked-out – those images were now seared into her psyche for all eternity.*

Erin tried to ignore the images of a very nude Gunner and Isis looking like they were enjoying themselves just a bit too much in her opinion. There was altogether too much screaming, moaning and groaning for all that to be okay!

"So," started Isis, sounding far too chipper, "is Gunner dating anyone at the moment?"

Erin stopped and looked up into Isis' smug, catty face.

"No, not as far as I'm aware," she replied in an even voice.

Which was actually kind of true. She wasn't sure that Gunner did actually consider them to be dating. As far as she knew, he could still consider himself to be footloose and fancy-free. Yeesh, that depressed her more than she felt comfortable admitting.

"You probably already know that Gunner and I dated a while back."

"Oh? I hadn't heard that you *dated.*"

She stressed the word. She knew they'd hooked up – *and sadly she now had that mental image for life* – but she didn't think it actually amounted to dating. In Jessie's words, 'they did the pelvic mambo until stripy bitch-face realized she wasn't going to get a promotion out of it.' *That squirrel sure had a way with words.*

"Yeah, well, we did. And since I'm not seeing anyone at the moment, I was wondering if he wanted to hook up again."

Isis said it nonchalantly, but the way her eyes sharply watched Erin for a reaction were a dead giveaway. The cat was trying to get a rise out of Erin. *Perhaps she was angling for a cat-fight.* Well, she would be sorely disappointed.

"Oh? Are you lonely?" asked Erin sweetly.

Isis' jaw tightened ever so slightly. "Not at all," she growled before her voice turned to a husky drawl. "It's just that Gunner is one hell of a fine, big specimen if you get my drift."

Of course Erin got her drift – the two eavesdropping middle-aged women from three tables over got her drift!

Erin cocked her head to one side, ignoring her rising hackles. Everything about her wanted to scream at the female shifter to stay the hell away from her polar bear! But no, she wouldn't do that, and not just because she wasn't sure if he actually was her man. No, getting angry and throwing things - *punching walls* – was the shifter way to react. She was human, and she was going to react the human way – by calling her bluff.

Erin plastered a huge, sickly smile on her face, pretending she'd had a marvelous idea. "Shall I talk to Gunner for you? Shall I let him know that you're interested?"

Isis' eyes started turning yellow, a sign that she was annoyed, and that her cat was trying to muscle in on the conversation. "No, there's no need for that."

"Nonsense, I'd be happy to let Gunner know."

"Really, there's no need for that," snapped Isis, cheeks turning puce.

Erin shrugged exaggeratedly and felt inordinately happy. Hey, it was a small win, and the tigress deserved it – *she was trying to steal Gunner!*

Time to go before she managed to do anything embarrassing and spoil her – *admittedly small* – triumph.

Erin got up and threw the used napkins in the trash. She then went back to the table and swept her hot chocolate sodden possessions into her purse.

"I better go. I guess I'll see you back at the office."

Isis grinned, displaying an alarming amount of straight white teeth. Her displeasure had all but evaporated, and she suddenly seemed very pleased with herself. "Yes, Erin, I'm sure you will."

Erin's heart sank as she hotfooted it back to the office. *That wasn't good.* Isis was far too happy and clearly up to something; Erin dreaded to think what that might be.

She just better stay the heck away from Gunner. This inner jealous bitch was a little new to Erin, so she wasn't entirely sure what she was capable of. But if Isis tried to get her claws into her polar bear, Erin was sure she'd find a way to teach her a lesson.

Yep, I am human, hear me, ah, scream really loudly!

CHAPTER TWELVE

Gunner gazed around the victim, James Silver's bedroom. It was modern and sparse, decorated in white, black and chrome. *Erin's bedroom was cornflower blue.* The color suited her; it was pretty against her flushed skin.

There were dozens of pictures of family and what Gunner assumed were friends and maybe ex-girlfriends. *Erin didn't have any photos in her apartment.* That thought made his bear unhappy. She deserved to be surrounded by people who loved her. Well, now she had him, and he could surround her. Would it be too much if he bought her a picture of himself for her apartment?

Silver's wardrobe was neat beyond compare. He'd never met a guy who had so many pairs of shoes. *Erin had a grand total of six pairs of shoes.* She didn't seem to be interested in clothes. But then she looked lovely in plain, simple clothes.

Fuck! He had to focus. Everything he did just brought him back to her, and as much as he enjoyed that, he really needed to concentrate on what he was doing.

Gunner, Avery, and about half a dozen crime scene technicians were poking around the apartment. There were no unusual scents to be found, but it wasn't impossible to mask scent, and those of the SEA techs were muddying up whatever was already there.

A number of items of clothing and a suitcase appeared to have been taken, as well as his deodorant, a toothbrush and so on. It was unlikely that Silver packed the suitcase himself, given what happened to him. The theory was that whoever abducted and/or killed him packed a suitcase to make like he'd left town, and then typed out a note on his laptop to say he was leaving town. They'd already bagged the laptop.

Whoever it was didn't exactly do a good job. They hadn't taken anything personal like family photos. Either they didn't care enough to try, or they had no clue as to what a person would take with them if they were leaving town forever. Honestly, it looked more like he'd gone on holiday.

Silver's parents and sisters were devastated when they learned the truth. Death notifications were brutal and the worst part of the job. Either the family broke down or they didn't care. Gunner hated both reactions.

He'd considered bringing Erin with him to talk to the family, but he decided against it. His bear was still a bit antsy where she was concerned. When he arrived home in the wee hours of the morning to find her gone, the beast was frantic. A million fearful thoughts raced through his mind, centering around her leaving him or being abducted. Unable to calm the bear, Gunner had allowed the shift, and the bear ran all the way to her apartment to make sure she was there safe, and alone. She was. *Thank heavens!*

But those moments of uncertainty still worried him, and her safety was foremost in his mind. Luckily, he'd found a way to keep her nice and safe in the SEA building for the day. She hadn't liked it, but it was the only way he had been able to appease his animal. The only other option was to keep her glued to his side, which wasn't exactly feasible. *Appealing - yes. Feasible – no.* If the two of them were going to have a long-term relationship, then they needed to find a middle ground that allowed his bear the control he needed but also meant she wouldn't be restricted to office duties.

Of course, that depended on her and whether she still wanted him. Fuck, she had looked mad earlier. Mad about him leaving her alone in the night, and then mad about him wanting to keep their relationship private. He needed to explain it better. There just hadn't been time. Fuck, she looked cute when she was angry – all pink cheeks, flashing eyes and heaving chest. If he weren't so sure it would have a detrimental effect on his sex life, he would actually consider purposefully trying to annoy her.

He needed to set things straight with her; that was for sure, and soon. But first of all he needed to decide how to handle the situation. They couldn't date because they worked together - it was against office policy. His bear huffed and chuffed at him. So what? Screw that! He wanted Erin, and who knows, maybe they could make it work. He'd worry about her no matter what, so having her closer would actually make that easier to bear. Maybe if he threw himself on the mercy of the director, or even better, maybe if he got Erin to throw herself on the mercy of the director …

Avery swept into the room, and he looked at her guiltily. She frowned. "What are you doing?"

Daydreaming. Fuck, he needed to get it together. "Nothing, there's nothing here."

The lioness sighed and stretched. "I agree. I listened to his answer machine; there were a ton of messages on there from friends and colleagues wanting to know what was going on." She gave Gunner a sad smile. "Popular guy."

"Maybe Jessie will find something in his background check."

"Yeah, maybe. Wayne called; so far he talked to four people, and they all say the same thing – nice guy, can't think a reason anyone would want to hurt him."

His family said the same thing. He had no problems with work, no financial issues, and no nasty breakups. His mother reluctantly admitted that he was a 'ladies' man,' but he never treated women badly and was on speaking terms with his exes.

"What should we do?" asked Avery.

"Bag everything up and ship it back to the office; maybe Erin can get a vision from this."

*

"Hey."

Erin let out a small yelp and jumped out of her seat.

Gunner chuckled. "At least you weren't holding coffee this time."

"Hey," she breathed and sank back into her chair.

"You're still here," he said wonderingly.

Erin shrugged and smiled impishly. "Yeah, some control-freak bear ordered me not to leave the building."

Gunner arched an eyebrow. "Really?"

She nodded solemnly and bit her lip. "Yep, he was all mean and serious when he said it too."

He let out a long breath. "Wow, he sounds like a… like a… real swell guy to me. A keeper, some might say."

The amused expression on her face died, and she started pinching the skin on her hand. Fuck! What did he say wrong? *Hell, human women were strange creatures.*

Erin cleared her throat. "How did it go with the family?"

Gunner sighed. "It was pretty brutal. We couldn't really get much out of them; they broke down when they realized he wasn't coming home."

"Poor people," she murmured sympathetically.

"Yeah, as far as we can tell he went out for a drink one night and then just disappeared."

And as far as his family were concerned he was the most perfect son and brother on earth. The harder, more cynical part of Gunner was considering nominating him for sainthood.

"You find anything?" he asked.

"No, not yet," she admitted sadly. "I can see the woman I'm looking for as clear as day, so I'm sure that I'll find her eventually."

If she has a record, Gunner silently added. More than likely, Erin was just on a wild goose chase.

Although, if it kept her safe…

Erin inhaled sharply and looked at him brightly, before hesitating.

"Ask away," he chuckled. *She had the cutest little quirks.*

"I've tried touching all the belongings we found with the body, but nothing else came up, maybe I could, ummm, actually touch his body…"

"Really?"

Gunner didn't bother to hide his displeasure. His bear sure didn't like the sound of it either, and made no bones about letting the man know.

"It's worth a shot," she said, prickling defensively.

"Let's uh, let's think about it again in the morning." His bear chuffed in relief; a morgue was no place for his female, and hanging around the creepy medical examiner was not something he wanted to subject her to. "I had crime scene techs bag up some of his possessions from his apartment for you, maybe you could try touching them."

"Mmmm, maybe."

Her whole body looked tight, and her countenance was laced with frustration. He wanted to ease her somehow. He didn't want her to push herself into trying to get a vision, and make herself sick.

Gunner flicked his eyes around the empty office, making sure they were alone, and ignored the flicker of irritation on her face. He pulled her up to her feet and placed his hands on her shoulders, rubbing her tight muscles. She groaned happily. Aha, his little human liked getting back rubs; perhaps a full body massage was on the cards. *He could just imagine his oiled hands skimming over her delectable curves…*

His fingers became more forceful, and she moaned *that* moan. *His moan.* Surely, it belonged to him. It was that sweet little moan she always made when he filled her, when he took his pleasure in her perfect, soft body.

He stooped down. "Where's that toy cat?" he whispered huskily.

"Hmmmm," she cooed, "why? What do you wanna do to it?"

He threw back his head, laughing as he twisted her round, so her back was to him, and his hands moved up and down her frame.

"Nothing, babe, just wondering."

"Avery told me you don't like us to have things on our desks, so he's in hiding from you."

"He?" growled Gunner, as his bear took offense.

His hands stilled as Erin started hooting with laughter and gasping for breath.

"It's not that funny," he grouched.

"Don't tell me you're jealous of Waldo?" she spluttered in between giggles as he resumed the massage.

"I don't like the idea of any male cat holding your affection."

"Well, this one's four inches long, and not much of a talker. He's really no competition."

Gunner wished he could say the same for the other male cats in the building. On the way back from their victim's house, Avery disclosed that she'd heard a number of males in the building had made bets on who would get into Erin's panties first. The current frontrunners were Diaz and Wes. *Fucking cats.* His odds were apparently lower than Cutter, the director and the female ostrich who worked in tactical. *How little they knew...*

"I've had him since I was four; I got him in a kid's meal. It's no big deal, really. It was before I got my visions; my mom was pregnant with my oldest brother and my dad didn't have to travel for his job yet. My dad used to hide the cat all over the house and then I'd find him. That's why I called him Waldo. It was the last time that we... that I... it was just a time that we were really happy."

His bear ached for her. He leaned down and kissed a freckle on the back of her neck. "I want to make you happy."

Erin slipped round in his arms to face him. She bit her lip. "You already do."

She looked at him with big, guileless eyes, and he trembled inside. He and his animal were a big tangle of want, need, love, and fear. He'd never met a woman who could potentially hurt him as badly as Erin could, and it was a little daunting. Just the thought of her leaving him, of being with another man, of not loving him was devastating. *However, he did make her happy...*

His pleasure at her words was cut short. Gunner looked up and scowled. "Fuck, Isis," he snarled.

"What?!" exclaimed Erin in alarm.

"I can scent her; she's coming closer."

Erin sighed in relief. "Thank god for that, I thought you were calling me Isis."

Gunner frowned at her. "Why would you think that?"

She didn't answer, just shrugged a shoulder and smiled.

Hmmm.

"Look, I'm done for the day; I'll drive you home."

"Well, I was thinking about looking through some more pictures..."

"Please? I haven't seen you all day."

His bear sneered at him. Yes, he sounded whiny and needy, and he never would behave this way with any other female, but Gunner couldn't give a crap. It would be seriously damaging to his alpha male pride, but he wasn't above getting down on his knees and begging her to spend more time with him. *Although, while he was down there, he could think of something much more fun to do...*

"Okay," she said with a suffering sigh, although she barely contained the look of delight on her face. "I just need to go to the bathroom, five minutes; I'll meet you by the elevator."

She grabbed her bag, and he swatted her ass as she walked past him. Erin let out a shocked little 'oh,' but he did notice she put an extra little wriggle into her walk.

Gunner made his way to the elevator, trying to avoid Isis altogether. *No such luck.*

He groaned inwardly, as Isis' overpoweringly flowery perfume assaulted his senses. His bear growled and turned his back. The animal had always been against getting involved with the tigress, and now his feelings were clear. *I told you so, and you're on your own with this one.* Pussy bear.

"Hey, Gunner," she called sweetly. "Fancy meeting you here."

He gave her a baffled look. "Where we work?"

Isis definitely had an overinflated sense of how sexy she was. Her attempts at flirting were irritating.

She cocked her head at the elevator. "Going down?" she cooed.

Ugh. He jutted his jaw. "I'm waiting for someone."

Her lips twitched before curling upwards. "Erin?"

Gunner stared at her coolly, and it was obvious she knew his answer.

"How's Erin working out? I know how opposed you were to having her here."

His bear harrumphed at that, even thought it was true. *But that was before he met her.* "Good," he rumbled.

Isis' eyes widened in exaggerated disbelief. She looked like she'd never heard anything more astonishing in her life. *It was right up there with learning that a Smurf had been declared supreme ruler of the world.*

"Really? No more problems?"

Gunner folded his arms and clung to the remnants of his fraying temper. He had given up his previous resolve to get Erin benched. He didn't want to hurt her in any way. And he seriously didn't want anyone else trying to do the same.

"Whatever you're doing, stop," he said in a low, menacing voice.

"Moi?" She placed her hand on her chest and graced him with such fake wide-eyed innocence that he was tempted to howl with laughter. His bear just wanted to howl.

"Erin's a valuable member of my team. She's doing good – better than good – she's doing great."

Isis licked her lips. "Are you so sure about that?"

"Cut the crap, Isis," he barked and was pleased that she flinched at his harsh tone. "If you have something to say – say it."

He hated women who played games and was thankful Erin wasn't like that. She might be a little hard to read, but she usually said what she thought. Usually she blurted it out, and then turned a bashful shade of beetroot red. *Adorable.*

"Would you be surprised to learn that Erin left her gun in the coffee shop today?"

Gunner felt a chill run through him, and even his bear stopped snarling to pay attention. "What?"

Isis pulled a gun out of her purse and handed it to him. He looked at her searchingly, and she nodded.

"Yep, clumsy, little Erin spilled her hot chocolate all over her purse, got all the contents out, and then managed to leave her gun on the floor of the coffee shop. Luckily, I was there to diffuse the situation when the manager found it. But I think it would be a career ender, don't you?"

Fuck. This was bad. Losing your gun and leaving it in a public place was really, really bad. She'd be suspended for that, and most likely fired or reassigned to the worst SEA outpost they had. *Most likely northern Alaska where the only thing to do was concentrate on not losing your toes to frostbite.*

His bear pushed forward, unsheathing his claws, and roared at Gunner to do something. *Something vicious to the tigress seemed like a good option.* "What do you plan on doing?" he bit out.

"That depends; if you can get her to ask for a transfer and then request that I join your team - nothing."

Unbelievable. She pursed her lips in displeasure and growled lightly as he let out a hollow chuckle.

"You're blackmailing me?"

"Just think of it as motivation," she rationalized patronizingly. "I can see you like her; I'll bet she's the little sister you never had."

Gunner almost choked at that. *The feelings he had for her, and the things he had done to her, could hardly be described as familial.*

"So, if you like her, get her to do this. This whole thing is not worth ending her career over. I mean, it's not a very promising one, but I'm pretty sure that she doesn't want to get fired over this."

He watched her through narrowed eyes as the elevator arrived, and she hopped in; his limbs quivered as his bear fought to be let free.

She pressed the button for the lobby. "Let me know what you decide."

Isis blew him a kiss and gave him a finger wave as the doors closed.

"Gunner?"

Crap. He pushed her gun into the waistband of his jeans, pulling his shirt down to cover it, and slapped on his most innocent smile.

"Ready to go, babe?"

Erin frowned. "Was that Isis?"

"Yes, c'mon," he said impatiently.

"What's happening? Are we going to the bar?"

"No, we need to do something that I've wanted to do since the moment I first saw your apartment."

"Oh?" she breathed. "That sounds exciting."

*

"What?" barked Tom 'the hammer' Murphy into the receiver.

"Feeling better?" asked a familiarly arrogant voice.

Tom sneered. "What do you want? You got your money."

"And you got your brand-spanking new, illegally obtained heart, so you might want to check your attitude. You got a fair deal."

"Fair?!" spluttered Tom.

"More than fair, unless you prefer breathing hooked up to a machine. Because, if you like, that can be arranged."

Tom gritted his teeth at the cold, callous tone being leveled at him. "What do you want?" he hissed.

"The body of the shifter who generously donated his heart to you has been found. The SEA is investigating."

He felt a swell of contempt. "So? Why the fuck should I care?"

"So, I'll go ahead and assume that you don't want the SEA scratching at your door anyway, but do you really want them to confiscate that nice, new heart? After all, it is evidence of a crime. So, keep your mouth shut and lay low. Most people already think you're dead, so, for your health, keep it that way. Got it? Good."

Tom stared in disbelief at the phone as the fucker hung up on him. Again. He hung up on him again? Who the fuck did this guy think he was? The asshole had no respect. Jumped-up, little pipsqueak. Tom was putting shits like him in their place before he was even born!

No, this was too much.

Tom rubbed his chest thoughtfully. He had his new heart, and he was healthier than ever. He had what he wanted and now, this guy needed to be taught a lesson.

CHAPTER THIRTEEN

Erin sighed as the warm water cascaded down her aching limbs. No way would she admit it out loud, but she was feeling just a teensy bit sore and tired after spending the last few nights with Gunner. She couldn't remember the last time she had gotten so much exercise! *But if other exercise were half so enjoyable, she'd be trying out for the Olympics by now!*

It wasn't quite what she imagined Gunner had in mind, but last night he had changed all the locks on her door and windows. She was tighter than Fort Knox now.

Her landlord objected and started making sounds about the security deposit, but the creepy skunk shifter – *yes, a skunk shifter, she'd never have guessed* - was soon quelled by a look from Gunner. *He could scare bark off a tree.*

It was actually kind of baffling. She could see that, in theory, he was kind of scary, but, to her, he was just one big teddy bear. Hmmm, she wondered what his actual polar bear was like. She had yet to meet the creature. *She wondered if he would let her pet him.*

After the locks were changed, they had fun on the couch while eating Chinese takeaway – she really must learn how to cook, all this fast food was not doing her waistband any favors. And then, they soon moved to the bedroom. He'd spent the whole night with her – again.

It was wonderful, but it kind of niggled at her that she didn't know where it was going. He'd made it clear that he didn't want people to know at work, and okay, yeah, after the first worry of rejection, she whole-heartedly agreed with that. *She didn't want to be known as the office slut!* Well, actually, the nympho in her was a little titillated by the idea, but no, she didn't want that. *Surely that role was already taken by Isis, she thought viciously.*

Erin squawked, instinctively covering herself as the shower curtain was thrown back with gusto.

Gunner, in all his acres of nude glory, grinned at her in a predatory manner – all teeth and lusty eyes. She almost swooned at his deliciously naked body. It really wasn't fair that he was so naturally gorgeous.

He raked his eyes up and down her form. "No need to cover up, I've seen it all before."

"But not in the harsh light of day," she mumbled holding a sponge over her sex.

Gunner clucked his tongue. "Oh, babe, you've no idea how beautiful you are, do you?"

Erin gave a half-embarrassed shake of her head. That was not a question she got asked often, or ever, even.

"Good."

She blinked at him as he stepped into her small shower, crowding her. "What?"

"Good, I don't want you to know how beautiful you are. Once you realize, who knows how long it is before you're skipping off into the sunset with some asshole wolf shifter or worse, a damn cat shifter. Horny bastards."

Erin thought of the surly Cutter and the slimy Diaz and shuddered. "Not likely."

"Hmmm, well just in case, I better not pay you too many compliments."

"I don't think there's any danger of that," she murmured, ignoring the heat seeping from his solid body into hers. Moisture was starting to pool between her legs and, yep, the nympho in her had officially woken up and decided she wanted a repeat of the previous night. Erin scolded her for being greedy. *Surely she'd had enough last night!*

"Hey, babe," he crooned as he pushed his body closer to her, crushing her against the cool tiled wall; she shivered but soon warmed under his hot skin. "All joking aside, I never met a woman I found more attractive."

"Puh-lease," she muttered.

He hooked a finger under her chin and lifted her head to look at him. "You think I'm kidding?" he asked in a surprisingly harsh tone.

His eyes were dark, brown pools. Oh, his animal must have been close to the surface. *Yikes, that sent electric arousal coursing right through her.*

Erin sighed, she didn't want to tell him how she really felt, but she wasn't one for lying. Evading the truth, however, was another matter. "I think men would say anything to get what they want," she admitted.

Gunner let out an impatient grunt. "Fuck, Erin, don't throw me into the same category as any of the assholes you dated before me. They weren't even fit to kiss your feet."

"You don't even know them." Although she was secretly pleased, and not above agreeing with that sentiment.

He ran his hands down her sides, teasing her skin with his deceptively soft touch. "I know no one is good enough for my psychic princess."

"Princess, hmmm?"

"Yep." He nodded seriously before his mouth twisted into a smirk. "Besides, I don't have to flatter you to get into your tight little panties; I'm pretty sure I'd just have to wink, and you'd jump right into my arms."

"Ugh! You are unbelievable!"

He puffed out his chest. "Yeah, I'm pretty sure you screamed that last night. By now I'm guessing everyone else in the building knows."

Double ugh!

Erin playfully slapped at him, and he pulled her up his body, pinning her against the wall with his hips, his manhood throbbing between them. She wrapped her legs around him, and he laced his fingers with hers, pushing her hands back against the wall.

"I don't think this shower was built for two," she said wiggling her hips.

"I'm sure we can manage," he groaned.

"Not when one of the two is enormous," she added as his tongue swept up her neck, eliciting a tremor from her sensitive body.

"You flatter me, princess."

"That's not exactly what I meant... although it's true."

She dug her heels into his taut buttocks, trying to pull him even closer to her. He obliged by grinding himself against her. Damn, her arousal was blossoming at an alarming rate; she might just come from this.

"Didn't I tire you out last night?" he asked amusedly.

"Not likely," she breathed, pushing herself against him, rubbing the tight buds of her nipples against his chest.

His manhood swelled even harder against her. A deep growl vibrated through his chest. He let go of one of her hands, and just as quickly caught it with his other. His free hand reached between them, brushing against her clit before he aligned their sexes.

"Well then, I must try harder," he whispered as he drove inside her.

He took her to the hilt in one, and she let out a strangled moan verging on a gasp. Yes, this is what she needed. To be filled impossibly full by this man, this bear.

Gunner stilled for a few moments, a happy expression on his face. "Oh, Erin, you are amazing."

He stooped to kiss her quickly before he started his pleasurable assault on her body. He snaked his hips up and down, thrusting and crashing into her body, mercilessly rubbing against her tender nub. It was almost too much for her; the pleasure he effortlessly wrung from her body was almost overwhelming.

Erin twisted and turned, trying to free her hands from his steely grip, but he held her tightly. One hand captured her wrists; the other grasped the soft flesh of her thigh, and his hips trapped her against the wall.

As her orgasm neared, pleasure hurtling through her body, she needed to touch him, to caress him, to show him how she felt, to try and give him back some of the wonderful feelings he incited in her.

Instinct took over, and she smoothed her tongue over his neck, sucking and tasting him. He let out a soft snarl and sped up his movements. *Oh, he likes that.* Emboldened, she started nipping and biting at his flesh and soon he was calling her name with every plunge inside her body.

Feeling herself near, Erin bit his neck with as much force as she could. Gunner threw back his head and roared as he exploded inside her. She latched onto his neck, feeling the throb of his pulse, as she reached her own climax. Her body rippled around him as ecstasy soared through her.

Gunner freed her hands, and she gratefully wrapped her arms around his body, clinging to him for all she was worth. He did the same, almost crushing her to him.

"Holy hell…" he breathed.

She seconded that.

*

"Jessie texted; she found a club that she thinks fits the description you gave of your vision."

Jeez, does that squirrel never sleep? She was a small ball of efficiency and made Erin feel increasingly lazy. Jessie was probably diligently working while she allowed herself to be ravished by a bear.

Gunner shut off his phone. "Cutter's on his way there; we should join him."

Erin pulled on a light blue shirt and almost mewled in pleasure when he stared at her with frank appreciation.

"Hmmm."

Gunner raised an eyebrow. "Not a fan of the wolf shifter?"

"More like he's not a fan of me," she muttered.

The wolf had a major chip on his shoulder about her, and she had no idea why. It wasn't her fault she was born human and, therefore, was physically weaker than the rest of the team. Just like it wasn't his fault that he was born a wolf and, therefore, more of a dickhead than the rest of the team. *Oh, she liked this emerging inner bitch.*

"He's a grouchy asshole. Give him time, he'll soon warm up."

Erin pursed her lips doubtfully. *Although she definitely agreed about the asshole part.*

Gunner pulled a shirt over his head, and she almost sighed; it was such a shame to cover up all those exquisite pectorals. He'd had the foresight to keep a change of clothes in his car. The prude in her had wanted to be outraged that he just assumed he would get lucky and would be invited for a sleepover. However, the nympho had practically jumped up and down in excitement, and these days, her voice was much louder.

"He's actually quite a fun guy when he lets loose," continued the man mountain, running his big hands through his hair.

Ugh, thinking about the snarky wolf shifter – way to douse a good mood.

"Whenever that happens," she muttered petulantly.

Cutter still looked at her like he wanted to eat her, and not in the good way that Gunner did. Not that she would want that from Cutter. No, she couldn't imagine being with anyone other than her polar bear.

"I don't know, he almost wet himself laughing after Avery and Isis got into a cat fight over the last bag of salted nuts at the bar a couple of months ago. They turned into their cats and everything."

Erin looked away from him quickly, biting her lip and remembering what Isis had told her. Lord, just the mention of the cat tied her up in knots. *Would she really be able to hold onto him when Isis was vying for his affection?* A puny human with an excess of curves compared to a lithe, beautiful tiger shifter who had just the right amount of curves? *There was no contest!*

On the plus side, Erin had managed to refrain from doing something completely off-kilter in front of Gunner yet. Yep, she'd managed to avoid waking up screaming bloody murder after a nightmare and completely avoided having to interact with some pissed off ghosts in front of him. It was the ghosts that sent her last boyfriend running for the hills. Nobody wanted their girlfriend having an argument with an imaginary person in the middle of a Stop 'N' Go while shopping for toilet paper. It wasn't Erin's fault that the woman had been crushed by some falling tins of kidney beans, but because Erin was the only person who could see her, she got the brunt of the woman's anger.

Gunner placed a finger under her chin, and directed her face back to his. "What's with the big, sad eyes?"

"Nothing," she replied unenthusiastically.

"Erin," he growled impatiently. "Don't lie to me."

She let out a sigh. *How could she say this without sounding needy?*

"I know about you and Isis and I'm worried that you're going to leave me to be with her."

She buried her face in her hands. *Yep, she may have missed subtle and calm by just a smidge.*

To make matters worse, Gunner chuckled. No, not just chuckled, she would go so far as to say laughed uproariously.

"You think this is funny?" she griped.

Why did he find her uncontrollable mouth so hilarious? It was humiliating.

"Yeah, babe, you're too cute."

Cute?! Her nympho fumed.

"There's nothing between me and Isis. We slept together a few times, but there's nothing there."

"So you admit you slept with her?" she asked quietly.

Gunner hunched his shoulders in a 'so what' motion. "Of course, why wouldn't I?"

Oh, no here it comes, that question her big, fat mouth was desperate to ask. "Was it good?" *Ugh, why did she want to know that?*

He looked torn between mirth and frustration. "You really want to know whether I enjoyed having sex with another woman?"

"Seeing as you're so blasé about it, why not?"

In her old Gunner-free world, sex was just something done in the dark, and you never talked about it afterwards. But then, she was loosening up quite a lot. She'd just had sex with her bear lover during the day! And in a shower! *She was feeling mighty loose at that moment!*

Gunner raised an eyebrow. "It was functional."

Erin, in spite of her burgeoning jealousy, barked out a laugh at the absurdity of what he just said. "Functional, huh? Wow, I dread to think about what you say about me."

"It's not the same," he growled forcefully. "What happened with Isis really wasn't the same as us. Isis and I just wanted sex, so we had sex. It wasn't romantic. It just scratched an itch. It was, like I said, functional."

"And what is it between us?" She bit her lip and gazed at him uncertainly.

"Oh, Erin." He pulled her into his arms and buried his face in her hair.

"That's not an answer," she squawked, her voice muffled in his shoulder.

"I know; I don't want to scare you off."

His hands skimmed down her back until he reached her buttocks and started kneading them. *Yeesh, he knew how to manipulate her body.* Just a little petting had her sex weeping for joy.

"You wouldn't," she murmured, tamping down her excitement. *She was trying to be serious, damnit!*

"You say that now," he said with a heavy sigh. "For now, can't we just say we're dating?"

Gently, she managed to peel herself away from his possessive arms.

"For now?"

He nodded solemnly.

"And the future?"

"Just know that I want more."

In surprise, she realized she did too. For once though, she managed to keep a tight rein on her wandering mouth and instead said, "okay, and I thought about what you said yesterday, and I agree, I don't think we should tell anyone at work."

"Yet," he added.

"Yet," she agreed, thrilled at that one word.

Gunner smiled, and her insides quivered. He gave her a quick peck on the lips and started striding to the door. "We better go. I'm guessing Jessie was the one who blabbed about me and Isis?"

Erin shrugged as they hurried to the car. She wasn't exactly keen to get her friend in trouble.

Gunner mirrored her shrug. "It's not a big deal. It was months ago, and it was hardly a secret when it happened. Why would you think I'd dump you for her?"

Her cheeks started to pinken with the effort of keeping up with him as they walked. *At least it hid her embarrassment.* "She told me she was interested in, umm, hooking up with you again."

He stopped and paused, one massive hand on the car door handle. "When was this?" he asked quietly.

Erin felt a frisson of fear at the soft tone of his voice and the darkness pooling in his eyes. She wasn't afraid for herself; she was afraid for a certain stripy shifter. She didn't like Isis – *mostly out of jealously, and she wasn't ashamed to admit it* – but she didn't want her to become a polar bear chew toy.

"It's not a big deal…"

"When was this, Erin?"

His eyes bore into her, and she considered that under that gaze even the most hardened criminal would be tempted to spill their guts and admit to crimes they'd never even committed.

"Yesterday, we bumped into each other at the coffee shop across the road."

His jaw tightened, but otherwise he didn't react. He swung the passenger door open for her. "We better get going."

*

"Well?"

Erin nodded as she surveyed the neon flamingos and the giant birdcages. "Yep, this is it."

Before Gunner could stop her, she marched over to the table where she had seen their victim, James Silver sitting. She pulled herself up onto his stool and drummed her fingers on the table. She closed her eyes and breathed deeply.

Gunner hovered around her while Cutter scowled, and the club owner watched her warily. They waited in their respective poses until the club owner couldn't take it anymore.

"What is she doing?" he hissed.

"Fuck knows," muttered Cutter.

Gunner snarled at him quietly, but with enough force to shut him up.

Erin shuddered as she flashed back to her vision. The familiar scene of Silver pushing a bill into the waitress' hot-pants unfolded before her eyes. The blonde woman approached him. They spoke to each other; she couldn't make out the mumbled words, it was like watching them through water.

The blonde laughed, throwing her head back with wild abandon. *As if anything in the history of the world was ever that funny.*

She stepped closer to him, resting a hand on his shoulder, and he slid an arm around her waist. She whispered something in his ear, and a grin split his face. She slipped away from him and swung her hips as she walked. He almost fell over his feet to chase after her.

She led him through the club, dodging the swaying bodies. They exited the back way, into an alley. The door slammed shut behind them. She turned to look at him and... and... Silver screamed in agony as two men grabbed him and pushed a needle into his neck. The blonde woman hurried away, not looking back, as Silver struggled helplessly. Soon enough, his struggles waned, and he collapsed into their arms. They dragged him over to a waiting car...

Erin shuddered violently and gasped for breath. She calmed as warm hands gripped her shoulders.

"Shhh, Erin, it's okay. I'm here."

Gunner curled his arms around her and pulled her back against his body. She slumped in his arms as she panted, and he pressed kisses into her hair.

"Everything okay?" called out Cutter uncertainly.

"Yes," snapped Gunner, "go back inside and grill the owner."

"Inside?" asked Erin, bewildered.

"We're in the alley," he murmured soothingly.

"Oh."

Erin blinked as she looked around and sure enough, they were out in the alley, standing in the very spot Silver was abducted from. She hadn't even realized she'd wandered out there.

"When you started moving, I wasn't sure what to do. I called out your name but… but it was like you didn't hear me. It was like you were gone." His arms tightened around her, and his voice was thick. "It was… I don't know. It freaked me out."

She was surprised at his tone, but it hit her – *what happened scared him.* Her big, fearless bear had been scared when she suddenly zoned out. She felt sympathy for him but also a big selfish dollop of joy. It was silly, but his fear for her showed her that he cared. Although it definitely wasn't something she wanted to put him through again anytime soon, but she knew it would happen again. *It had happened before…*

Erin rubbed a hand over his arm. "I'm fine. I'm sorry you were worried. It just sometimes happens."

He let out a deep, almost painful breath. He didn't move, didn't say anything, he just continued to hold her. She suspected it was more for his benefit than for hers, but she was more than happy to oblige.

After a few minutes, she related what she had seen.

Gunner grunted. "Was he alive when they took him?"

"Yes, he was definitely breathing."

"Huh. We better get back inside. I'm guessing Cutter is about ready to wring the toad's neck."

"Toad?"

"The club owner."

"No wonder his eyes are so bulbous. I heard that toads can lick their own eyes. I wonder if he can lick his own eyes."

Gunner shook with laughter against her. "Let's go inside and you can ask him."

CHAPTER FOURTEEN

Gunner groaned at the flurry of activity in the SEA office. Various researchers, analysts, and civilian employees were running around as dozens of phones rang shrilly.

He snagged hold of a chipmunk shifter, who gulped at finding himself being manhandled by the gruff seven-foot polar bear.

"Hey, Milton…" rumbled Gunner.

"Marvin," squeaked the chipmunk shifter. "But you can call me Milton!" he added on seeing Gunner's 'don't fuck with me' expression.

"What's happening, Marvin?" Gunner gestured a big paw around at the office. "What is all this?"

Marvin looked around, probably hoping to find someone else to give the bear shifter the news. *Gunner wouldn't so much shoot the messenger as pulverize him.*

"The uh, news, about your victim missing his heart, has been leaked. The tip lines have been going crazy."

"Fuck!" snarled Gunner, very loudly, although few people bothered to turn around. *They were used to him.* "When did this happen? How did this happen? Who did this?"

Gunner gripped Marvin's collar with increasing tightness and brought his furious red face directly in front of the chipmunk. The polar bear looked like he wanted to rip something apart – anything – *and since he already had hold of something...*

Marvin tried not to whimper, but he needn't have worried. Within seconds, Gunner's anger dissipated as Erin placed a hand on his forearm.

"Uh, Gunner, I think we've imposed upon Marvin enough for today," she murmured soothingly.

He carefully let Marvin go, and to the surprise of the chipmunk shifter, he actually straightened out his collar.

"I'm sorry Marvin," he muttered.

"No, no, no problem," stammered Marvin, beating a hasty retreat, "it was probably my fault."

Gunner grunted in agreement, but Erin gave him a scowl.

He spread out his hands. "What?"

"It says a lot about a person's personality and their behavior when they virtually attack someone, and then that someone blames himself for it."

"I didn't hurt him," griped Gunner defensively.

Erin rolled her eyes. "No! You just scared the hell out of him."

What was this about? He'd acted this way since... well, forever, and no one had ever called him on it. *Maybe no one had ever dared to.* His bear, he noticed, was unusually silent, torn between agreeing with her and actually standing up for his behavior. *Now who was the pussy?*

"Maybe you should try being a little nicer," suggested Erin.

She sounded like an admonishing school teacher. Actually, that was kind of sexy. He could imagine her in thigh-highs and glasses trying to teach him, her unruly student. *Of course, he'd be the one doing the spanking...*

"Yeah, bossman," said Cutter, roughly cutting through his fantasy, "you catch more flies with honey. That's always been my motto."

Since when?! His beast roared in consternation. *Cutter was an even bigger asshole than he was!*

"If we're being picky, you could catch more flies with manure," grouched Gunner. "C'mon."

He took hold of Erin's upper arm, leading her through the throng to Jessie's office, and ignoring the urge to punch Cutter right in his smug, wolfy face.

"Anything?" demanded Gunner brusquely as soon as they saw the bubbly squirrel shifter.

Erin threw him another glance of disapproval, and his bear nudged at him. *Fine!*

"Hello, Jessie, how are you? Do you have anything for us?" he amended.

The squirrel beamed at him in delighted surprise while Cutter tried to stifle chuckles of derision - unsuccessfully. He didn't care though, *well, maybe a little*, but it was worth it to see the shy approval in Erin's smile.

"Well, since you asked so nicely," grinned Jessie. "I'm still going through his financials, nothing seems out of the ordinary, but there are a couple of large charges that I'm still figuring out. As for his background, he's as clean as a whistle. Wayne's still interviewing his friends, and Avery's trying to find a way that the body made it to Cinderella's facility. She's trying to talk to all the people who have contracts with Cinderella, but there are a lot of them."

"I see," he growled.

Gunner let out a long, ragged breath. Ordinarily this would be the point where he would be frustrated at their lack of progress and would throw things across the room. He could see that Jessie was actually standing in front of her desk, trying to shield all the items on there, and Cutter had taken a few steps away from him. *Well, they needn't have worried.* In deference to his little human, who he was all for impressing, he was going to try a calmer approach.

"Anything useful from the tips?" he asked, almost casually.

Jessie scrunched up her nose in surprise and let her guard down a little. "Ah, umm, yes, maybe. We had one that said the heart had been bought for an illegal transplant, and it gave us a cell phone number of a person to contact about it."

"That's pretty specific for the tip line," mused Cutter.

Erin looked between the three of them. "Oh?"

"Yeah," explained Jessie, "usually we just get tons of calls about alien abductions and people trying to blame neighbors they don't like for it. It's rare that we get anything helpful."

Gunner rubbed his jaw thoughtfully. "Did you get anything from the number?"

Jessie shook her head. "It was from a burner phone, which I'm guessing has been dumped by now. But, I did get the location of where the call was made from; it's a diner down by the docks."

She passed him a post-it with the details. Gunner showed it to Cutter, and he nodded. It wasn't exactly the most reputable part of town, so it was probably worth a look.

"Cutter and I will check it out. Erin, tell Jessie about your vision and see if you can get any security footage from around the club that night. Otherwise, I want you to check out Silver's belongings, and see if you can get anything from them. Jessie, check in with the director and let him know what's happening."

"Me?" squeaked Jessie, in dismay.

"Yes, you. Keep in touch."

As they left, Gunner felt Erin tugging on his arm. He told Cutter to wait for him in the car, and, grumbling, the wolf shifter stomped away. *Moody bastard.*

Gunner looked at her in concern. "Everything okay, babe?"

He'd been a little edgier than usual ever since the incident at the club. Seeing her like that, in a trance, had been chilling. *His bear hadn't liked it one bit.*

"I just wanted to tell you to be careful."

He smiled, warmed by her sentiment. "I'll be fine, you be careful, too."

Erin gave him a rueful smile. "I'll try not to get too many paper cuts, or drop a stapler on my foot."

"That's my girl."

He would have kissed her goodbye, but at the moment Diaz came sauntering down the corridor. *Fucking jaguar always seemed just to pop up whenever Erin was around.* Diaz grinned at Erin in no doubt what he thought was a panty-wetting smile. His bear snarled lowly. *That cat better keep his damn paws off.* Diaz nodded at him and gave him a sour look. *Huh.* Whatever Gunner did to deserve that, he sure hoped it had hurt the jaguar.

He settled for squeezing Erin's shoulder. "I'll see you later."

*

The diner was a pretty sleazy affair called The Brown Bear because it was run by a brown bear. It appeared to be popular because it served alcohol.

Cutter and Gunner sat outside watching the diner from a distance.

"Do you reckon they have security cameras?" asked Gunner.

The wolf shifter snorted. "Doubtful, I can't imagine anyone would want video evidence of what goes on in there."

Gunner grunted in agreement and scanned the surrounding buildings. They were mostly run-down apartment buildings, and it was unlikely that they had security either. They were hesitant about going into the diner. Although the two of them could hardly be called the most civilized of shifters, they would be made as cops immediately. They didn't want to risk whoever made the tip actually getting tipped off that they were looking for him.

Instead, he replayed the recording out loud. Jessie had sent the audio file to his phone. It was a gruff, voice, and it was clear that the speaker was trying to put on an accent to hide his voice. Unfortunately, no one in the world spoke with an accent like that, so it just made him more conspicuous. It also indicated to them that the speaker thought they might know his voice if they heard it.

"I've heard the voice before," said Cutter.

"Me too," added Gunner. "I've heard it, but it's not someone I interviewed or arrested."

They played the recording a few more times while watching the entrance to the diner, before getting lucky.

Gunner jerked his jaw up in the direction of the diner door. "Look."

Cutter snarled as he saw the man in question. It was Alfie Morehouse, number one stooge to Tom 'the hammer' Murphy – one of the nastiest creatures to ever step foot in Los Lobos. *He gave all shifters a bad name.*

"That's the voice – it's Alfie," muttered Cutter shaking his head in disbelief.

Gunner seconded that. "We should have recognized it."

They watched as the hulking frame of Alfie lumbered into the diner. The man could never be described as graceful, but as an elephant shifter, he was freaking tough. Added to the fact that he had no morals to speak of and a penchant for inflicting pain, if you saw him charging at you, you got the hell out of the way – fast.

"Haven't seen him in a while," said Gunner, thoughtfully.

Cutter gave him a significant look. "Not since Murphy disappeared."

About a year ago someone hired a hitman to come after Tom. Not just any hitman, a vampire hitman. Whoever hired him must have paid a fortune, because he didn't work cheap. It was strongly suggested that after years of suffering, Tom's own daughter had snapped and done the hiring. The details of what happened were kind of fuzzy, all the reports said was that the hitman managed to stab Tom in the heart with a silver knife and then Tom ripped the hitman's head off. Tom hadn't been seen since, and, given that silver is deadly to shifters, it was widely believed that Tom was dead.

Of course, if Tom had managed to cling to life, his heart would be beyond the repair of his natural healing abilities, and he would need a new one. *And Tom just happened to be a hippo shifter.*

They watched, eagerly, as Alfie ambled out of the diner, carrying three big brown bags, presumably filled with greasy food. He hopped into an SUV and started moving.

Gunner started the engine. "Let's go find out what Alfie is up to."

He followed at a discreet distance, trying not to spook the elephant shifter, who seemed to be driving a little erratically. Gunner shook his head; all he was doing was drawing more attention to himself. *Not the brightest bulb...*

Cutter folded his arms and tapped his foot impatiently. The wolf shifter didn't like to be driven anywhere; he liked to drive. But then, so did Gunner. They both were in possession of an asshole alpha gene and while they generally coped, the need for control, the need to be in charge was always there. It just meant that they became grouchy and angry over the smallest things. Gunner felt satisfied and appeased his beast by leading his team; he wasn't too sure how Cutter ever managed to placate his howling wolf. *He doubted he would catch Cutter doing yoga...*

The wolf fidgeted and huffed. "I don't know why we're even bothering to investigate. Why don't we just go back to the office and wait for our psychic to see a vision? Or even better, wait for her to have a tea party when the ghost of our victim shows up."

Gunner ignored the furious wails of his bear. *It was just Cutter being Cutter.* He put Wayne through hell when he joined the team, and Avery just about had to claw his eyes out to prove she was capable. If anyone other than Cutter had made such sneering remarks about Erin, he wouldn't have let it go, but he and Cutter went back as far as the academy. They'd both transferred out to Los Lobos together. Hard to believe, but they were actually the best of friends. They were just the kind of friends who didn't pry into one another's lives.

"Why don't you give Erin some slack?"

Cutter's lips curled upwards. "You asking that because you think she deserves it or because you're sleeping with her? And don't bother denying that."

His bear let out a warning snarl. "How did you know?"

He snickered. "You're not exactly James Bond. I see the way you look at her; you look like a thirteen-year-old girl who just got tickets to see her favorite boy band. The sappy, dreamy look on your face makes me want to puke. Then there's your scent, you two can slap on as much aftershave and perfume as you want, but the two of you reek of each other. And don't even get me started about when you were kissing her hair in the alley earlier. Then there was…"

"Does anyone else know?" Gunner interrupted forcefully.

"Not from me, how long's it been going on?"

"Just a few days."

Cutter blew out a breath through his teeth. "You planning on this going somewhere? Because I don't think she's the type of woman who would be okay with a couple of quick fucks and then curtains. She looks like a clinger. The only way to get rid of her would be to get her to latch onto someone else."

Gunner roared furiously, almost jerking the car as his bear tried to push forwards. *No one else would touch his mate!*

Cutter snorted. "Jeez, you're screwed. The director's going to toast your marshmallows for this. Seducing his new pet? He's going to be pissed."

He gripped the steering wheel tightly, making sure his hands didn't accidentally stray and wrap themselves around Cutter's neck. "He'll get over it."

The wolf made a tut-tut noise. "He won't let you work together."

"We'll deal with that."

"Do you think the director will choose you over her? You'll be lucky if you don't find yourself down in the archives for breaking up his dream team."

"I don't care," hissed Gunner at Cutter's increasingly heated tone.

"You don't care that you might get booted off the team?" asked Cutter incredulously.

"No," he replied simply, and he was surprised at himself. He hadn't really thought about it before, but if he did have to leave the team for her, then it was a sacrifice he was willing to make. He loved her, and he'd do anything to keep her.

Crap. He loved her. He'd fallen hard and fast, and that was that. He just wished that he'd realized how strong his feeling were for her when he was with her, instead of trapped in an increasingly stuffy car with an increasingly irate wolf shifter.

"What about us?"

The wolf had been sullen, petulant even, and Gunner almost laughed. From obnoxious man to whiny child in two seconds – *nobody could say the wolf shifter was boring.*

"I'm replaceable."

"Replaceable? Fuck you. Did you even give any consideration to the rest of the team? Or were you just thinking with your dick?"

Gunner bared his fangs. "Are you kidding me with this? You're pissed at me because you think I'm letting my dick do my thinking?" *That was the pot calling the kettle horny...*

"I spent two weeks thinking of the consequences, but when it came down to it, I just wanted her. She's my mate, and I'm not letting anyone stand in the way of her being mine."

Cutter sucked in a horrified breath. "Rather you than me."

He rolled his eyes. Yes, he imagined the thought of only being with one woman for the rest of his life would be horrifying to the wolf.

"Well, what are we supposed to do in the interim? Teammates can't date."

"No, but they can get married."

Dumb rule as far as he was concerned. The idea was that married couples were more settled and less likely to cause upset among their teammates. It didn't work that way. Only a couple of shifter co-workers had gotten married, and they had both fought tooth and nail right up until they divorced, and both requested transfers to different ends of the country.

"You're seriously thinking of marrying her?" exclaimed Cutter in disbelief.

Gunner was torn between being affronted that Cutter really couldn't see why anyone would want to marry his perfect Erin, and pleased that the wolf was immune to her charms that had him panting for breath. *He was a contrary fool.*

"I told you, she's my mate," he bit out, holding back his raging animal. *Why was the wolf questioning that fact?*

Cutter narrowed his eyes. "Have you told her any of this?"

"Not yet. Right now, she thinks we're dating." *Ugh, dating.* Not the kind of thing he usually went in for, but he couldn't deny that just spending time with Erin wonderful.

"Don't tell her, she'd probably run for the hills."

Gunner raised his eyebrows. "One second I can't get rid of her and the next I can't hold onto her. Is she clingy or running for the hills?"

"I'll bet she's just a typical human female. Only wanting things she can't have, and when she gets them she runs away scared."

Given Cutter's track record with women, taking advice from him was never going to end well. "How you ever manage to get laid is a complete mystery to me," he muttered.

"Must be my looks," preened the wolf.

"Well, it's not your personality; that's for damn sure."

Cutter snorted. "The situation's not all bad, at least I'm going to win the bet."

"Bet?"

"Yeah, the one about who's going to sleep with Erin first. Or who was, it's a moot point now."

Gunner growled ferociously, but Cutter ignored him. "Unless our Erin is a dark horse, you got there first, and since I put a large bet on you this morning, it means I'm going to win. Your odds went way up when I placed the bet, by the way. Diaz was not pleased."

As opposed as he was to the bet, he couldn't help but feel a prickle of pleasure at that. *No wonder Diaz had looked like he wanted to turn him into a bearskin rug that morning.*

"Look, he's stopping."

Alfie pulled up in front of a trailer in an empty construction site, and Gunner stopped a way back to watch as Alfie took all the bags of food into the trailer.

"What do we bet that Murphy's in that trailer?"

Gunner gave him a grim smile. "Let's go find out."

*

Gunner folded his arms over his chest and tried not to laugh as Tom 'the hammer' Murphy tried to wriggle his considerable bulk out of a narrow window.

Cutter had banged on the door while Gunner went round the back, just in case something like this might happen. *He wouldn't have missed it for the world.*

"You okay there, Tom?" drawled Gunner lazily.

The hippo shifter looked up at him and sneered. It was Tom Murphy alright; from his bulbous nose to the scar bisecting his face, no one could fail to recognize his ugly mug.

"Just going for a walk," he lied as he reluctantly backed up through the window.

Gunner scratched his chin. "I'd advise using the front door in future."

He could hear Cutter's annoyed voice coming from inside the trailer, asking what the fuck was going on.

"I'm coming in," said Gunner. "Don't worry, I'll use the front door."

He jogged around and was soon inside the cramped trailer. It was probably okay under normal circumstances, but now that four large, male shifters were inside, it seemed to be groaning under the weight.

Tom was sitting on a shabby couch, idly flicking through channels on a portable TV like he hadn't a care in the world. *Like he hadn't been declared dead and just tried to escape out of a window.*

Alfie was leaning up against the trailer wall, eyeing them distastefully. "Something we can help you with, agents?"

"Just following up on the tip you made about a murder victim," said Gunner nonchalantly.

"Tip? What tip? I don't know anything about a tip," replied the elephant shifter in a rush.

Tom stopped pretending to watch TV and looked up at the ceiling, muttering to himself. *Yep, Alfie might be scary and a good guy to have on your side in a fight, but he didn't do subtlety.*

Gunner nodded at Cutter, who played the recording. "That's you, Alfie."

"Prove it," he spat.

"It's your voice, fuckwit," said Cutter slowly and condescendingly. "That's all the proof we need."

Alfie let out a loud trumpeting noise as his own animal fought for control. *Shit, that was all they needed, a freaking elephant bursting forth in that tiny trailer.*

"Don't even think about it!" snapped Tom. "You'll destroy the trailer." He turned his vicious gaze to Gunner. "Have you come to harass my associate for doing his civic duty? By the sounds of it, you have a lunatic on your hands, and Alfie here was just trying to help you out. Instead of wasting your time, why don't you go and look for some real criminals."

"There're plenty here," growled Cutter, never taking his eyes off Alfie.

The two of them were trying to outstare one another, trying to prove their dominance. *They could be there all day.*

Gunner spoke directly to Tom, it was pointless addressing Alfie - he was just a puppet for the hippo. "We need to know how Alfie came by his information."

Tom hunched his shoulders. "We hear things."

The bear paused for a few moments. "You look remarkably well for someone who was stabbed in the heart with a silver knife."

The hippo let out a rumble. "Is that what you heard?"

"Strange coincidence, you getting stabbed in the heart, a hippo shifter turning up dead missing his heart, and then you making a full recovery."

Tom smirked. "We truly live in an age of wonders."

"I wonder what we would find if we took a DNA sample of that heart in your chest."

"Good luck with that." Tom waved his hand around. "I may not be living in the same splendor as I was a year ago, but all this is temporary, and I still have five lawyers on retainer. You'll never get a search warrant to go rooting around in my chest."

"You think you're untouchable?"

"I think I can survive anything," replied Tom, smugly.

If Tom had survived something like getting stabbed in the heart, then yes, he might start to believe that he truly was invincible. The thought almost had Gunner shuddering; the bastard didn't need a confidence boost. *He already acted like a dictator to anyone who unfortunately crossed his path.*

Tom switched the TV off and leaned forward, resting his elbows on his knees. "But just say I did get stabbed, and I did need a new heart. What would I do in that situation? Would I go on a hospital waiting list? Do you have any idea how often shifter transplants are performed? But, oh boy, it would be mighty helpful if there were someone out there who was willing to find a donor and then do the transplant for me. Don't you think? And I'll bet there are lots of other shifters who feel the same way."

Gunner stared at him placidly. "I'll bet you're right."

"I usually am," laughed the hippo shifter. "Now, if you don't mind, I'm a busy man. Come back when you get a warrant."

"Let's go, Cutter."

He turned and strode away with a reluctant and grumbling wolf following him.

Cutter waited until they were on their way back to the office to let rip. "What the fuck? We could have taken them!"

His bear let out a warning yowl to the wolf. "We weren't there to 'take them.' We were there to get information about our victim and we did. He was a victim of circumstance. He happened to be the right species, the right sex, and the right blood type, so he was picked to donate a heart to that asshole Murphy. We now know it wasn't personal."

Cutter threw himself back into the seat mumbling and flexing his claws. "I still say we should have beaten them up. They're culpable for this murder, too."

"If it came down to it, they'd argue that they had no idea where the heart came from. They could claim that they thought this was all legal. Those two are a fight for another day. Right now, we have to focus on finding the guy currently relieving people of their vital organs."

"You think the same thing happened to our other missing shifters?"

Gunner sighed. Unfortunately, yes he did. Which meant they were looking for a serial killer - a crafty, money-grabbing serial killer, but a serial killer nonetheless.

"Short answer, yes. We need to get back to the office. We need to start looking into this as if all the missing shifters are victims are dead, and work out how the killer is picking them."

Before he picks the next one.

CHAPTER FIFTEEN

The director tented his fingers. "So our theory is organ trafficking?"

They were in the director's office updating him on what they'd found.

Erin and Jessie were sitting demurely in the seats facing his desk while the other four larger shifters prowled around the room, trying not to bump into each other.

"This is more like a made-to-order service," said Gunner. "Our theory is that people who need organs contact our killer, he finds someone who's a match, abducts them, takes their organ, then kills and ships them off to the waste disposal plant."

The director mulled that over. "Any luck in finding out how Silver's body ended up at the plant?"

Avery shook her golden head. Erin was dazzled for a second; she looked like she had a halo.

"No, the body couldn't have been taken to the plant and then put in one of the containers; it must have been thrown in with other trash. But, given that they were so backed up, it could have come from anywhere all over the city. I'm looking into it, but I don't have much hope."

The director swung his gaze over to Erin, and her teammates were peeved to notice that he softened a little for her. She immediately flushed. Hey, she had no idea why the director liked her so much! *She'd done nothing to deserve it!*

"Have you made any progress finding the woman from your vision?"

"No," she admitted sadly, "and we couldn't find any useful security footage from around the club where they met. I sat with a sketch artist earlier though, and he made this."

She pulled out a picture of a blonde woman and passed it over to the director. He nodded and gave her a genuine smile. "Good thinking."

Gunner stood by his desk and looked it over. "Yeah, that was good thinking, Erin," he added quietly.

She felt a trembling in her nether regions as she caught sight of the heat in his eyes. Oh, that was a look that she'd come to recognize and relish over the last few days. *No, down nympho, bad girl!*

"Let's get this out there and see if anyone recognizes her."

The director looked up at the ceiling. "So if Silver was targeted for his heart, who would know that he was compatible with Murphy?"

"It wouldn't be that difficult," piped up Jessie in a surprisingly squeaky voice.

Everyone looked at her as red dusted her cheeks, and she spoke quickly. "I did a bit of research before we came up here, and all you would need is someone of the same species and blood type. Because of shifter healing abilities, organs are never rejected."

"But still," said Wayne, "someone would have to know their blood type. I don't know about anyone else here, but I've never been to a doctor. The only person I've donated blood to is the SEA for their files."

Erin gasped. "Never?"

The tall gator shrugged. "Nah, my congregation had its own healer, and we hardly ever get sick."

"Wow!" breathed Erin. She couldn't count the number of doctors she'd seen over the years. But then, she had grown up in an institute, so she was kind of a special case.

"Me, either," added Cutter, "but then I am a fine specimen of manhood."

"That's debatable," muttered Erin.

She flushed as everyone around her – including Cutter - laughed, even the director had to stifle a smile. *Crud.* Damn shifter hearing. *Oh, well, score one for her.*

Gunner pulled himself together. "That's probably why our un-sub is doing this. The number of shifter transplants must be pretty low. Most shifters die of old age or die in an accident, and their organs aren't viable."

Erin frowned. "So by that logic, the list of shifters actually needing transplants should be very short. Wouldn't most shifters just heal themselves, and if the injury is so bad that they can't, they would most likely die?"

"She has a point," said Jessie. "I can see if I can find a list of shifters needing transplants."

Gunner nodded. "And maybe see who is no longer on the list, see who was recently taken off it. A doctor had to have done the surgery, so let's for now assume that it was a doctor who found the victim. Jessie, check out who was our victim's doctor – who knows, maybe we'll get lucky."

"When do we ever?" grumbled Cutter.

"Avery keep working on the Cinderella aspect and keep up to date with the tip line. Cutter and Wayne, check with local PD about the possibility that someone has started a made-to-order shifter organ business. If we're right about this, someone out there is making a business out of harvesting organs, and one way or another they have to get the word out."

"What about us?" asked Erin, keenly.

"I thought we could go through our victim's things, give you a little break from the blonde hunt."

She nodded. "Sure."

"You get started; I just have to check in with the Zeta team about their missing person investigations. I better let them know that if our suspicions are right, they're all dead and before they died, they lost an organ."

*

Erin braced herself as she held their victims toothbrush and… she got a vision of him brushing his teeth.

Ugh. She'd touched six objects, had six visions, and all she was left with was a headache and mild case of dehydration.

Oh, well. She picked up a shoe and saw him putting it on and… looking at his reflection in a mirror.

"Hey!"

Erin jumped and mashed the heel of her hand into her heart. "You scared me!" she squawked.

Isis grinned widely. "Sorry." *She didn't sound the least sorry.* "What are you doing?"

Erin hesitated, they were colleagues – *technically* - but all Erin could think was that this bitch was trying to steal her polar bear!

"Just touching some of our victim's belongings, I'm trying to get a vision that might help."

Isis nodded her head. A bright lock of red hair escaped from her ponytail. *Jeez, even that looked artful and on purpose.* "How interesting. Enjoying your time here?"

"Yes."

"Enjoying working for Gunner?"

"Yes." *Where was this going? Was she about to admit that she wanted to thrust her catty tongue down his throat?*

"Yeah, he's a great guy, don't you think?" she asked with wide, innocent eyes.

Erin shrugged. "Sure." *Although, she could think of some much better words to describe him.*

"Well, I better get going, busy, busy, busy! By the way, you look really pretty today. That shape of top suits your body type."

"Umm, thanks," she said uncertainly.

Isis gave her a finger wave. "See you around, Erin."

The tigress sauntered away, swinging her perfect hips and leaving a furious Erin to glare after her. *Body type! Read – dumpy!*

Erin was still fuming when Gunner came ambling in a few minutes later.

He stopped short on seeing the thunderous look on her face. "Everything okay?"

"It's nothing, I just had a visit from your ex," she muttered, bitchily.

Gunner raised his eyebrows at her tone. "Yeesh, babe, I'm sorry to say this but you'll have to narrow that down."

Her cheeks heated even more; you could almost fry bacon on her face! "Isis!"

"Oh." His face hardened. "What did she want?"

"Whoa, back up, you mean you've dated women in this building other than her?"

"I wouldn't say dated…"

"I don't want to know," she muttered grouchily.

"C'mon, babe." He gave her his most ingratiating smile, and her ire did start to melt a little. "Don't be like that. What did Isis say to make you all grumpy?"

He came to stand next to her and ran a finger up her arm.

"Nothing, really, she didn't say anything. She was… polite."

Oh, his finger had made its way up to her neck and was now tracing her collarbone.

"Hmmm, you're gorgeous when you're grumpy."

Goose pimples peppered her skin. Mmmm, if only that finger would make its way down to her breasts…

"Don't, not here," she breathed regretfully.

A low growl vibrated through his throat. "Tonight cannot come soon enough."

"Hey, what are you guys up to?"

Jessie cut through the erotic tension as she bounced into the room.

"Nothing!" squeaked Erin as she jumped a foot away from Gunner.

Erin looked at the floor while Gunner stared at Jessie blankly.

The squirrel pouted. "Mmm hmmm. Silver didn't have a regular doctor, but after I went through his credit and bank statements with a fine-tooth comb, I found out that a month ago he was admitted to a clinic to have elective surgery."

"Elective? What did he have done?" asked Gunner.

"Rhinoplasty," replied Jessie.

"Rhinoplasty?"

"Nose job," she clarified. "So the clinic will have taken a blood sample of his, and they'd have known he was a match to our delightful tyrant Tom 'the screwdriver' Murphy."

"Hammer," corrected Gunner.

"Like it matters."

"What do you say, Erin, you up for a field trip?"

"Sure." *Was he kidding? Hell, yes, she was up for getting out of there.*

Jessie waved as she skipped out the room. "I'll text you the address. Have fun, kiddiewinks."

*

"This is a hospital? It looks more like a yoga retreat."

The building was modern and surrounded by a lush garden, and people were actually practicing yoga on the lawn.

Gunner pursed his lips distastefully. "Yeah, it's pretty awful alright. You didn't have to come, you know? I know you're not exactly keen on hospitals."

"It's fine; I was getting a little sick of being in the office."

He pulled the door open for her, and she trotted through, marveling at the cool and serene interior. A blonde goddess pounced on them before the door even closed.

"Welcome to the Blue Lotus Health and Wellbeing Centre," she trilled like a songbird.

The goddess took Erin's hands. "I'm Lara, and I'd be pleased to be your guide on the road to wellbeing."

Gunner held back a snort and Erin just gaped.

"Do you have an appointment?"

"Umm…"

Lara beamed reassuringly. "No matter, I'm sure we can fit you in for a couple's consultation."

"Ahh…"

"We're not here for that," growled Gunner.

"Nonsense," soothed Lara. "We could do both of you the world of good." She tapped a manicured finger against her lips and surveyed Gunner. "Just off the top of my head, we could plump up those thin lips and perhaps smooth out those bags under your eyes. And as for you," she swung her attention to a terrified looking Erin, "we could..."

"She's fine as she is," interjected Gunner in his harshest tone. "We came for information."

"Information?"

Gunner took out his badge and flashed it at her. She deflated a little. "How can I help?"

"We need to talk to the doctor who operated on a former patient of yours. His name was James Silver."

She looked thoroughly disappointed, but she didn't forget her manners. "I'll have to talk to the doctor, please, take a seat and help yourself to a glass of cucumber water or a shot of wheatgrass. And if you change your mind about the consultation, our brochure..."

"Thanks," interrupted Gunner with a tone that didn't invite any comeback.

Lara swept away.

"Would you like a glass of cucumber water or a shot of wheatgrass?" asked Erin, trying to hide a smile.

He grimaced. "Can't say that I do."

"Me either, give me soda any day of the week. Although, being around all these toned women is kind of making me rethink the way I eat."

Erin eyed a couple more blonde goddesses who walked through the lobby and gave Gunner appreciative glances. She was pleased that he didn't even look at them; his focus was directed exclusively at her.

"I wasn't just trying to shut up that airhead woman, you are fine as you are. Better than fine, you know what you do to me."

He gave her a lascivious smile and her eyes automatically flicked down to his crotch. *Was he always hard?*

"You know, if you are worried, you could always work out with me."

He watched her closely, gauging her reaction. She almost sniggered at his look of concern. *He probably thought she might explode into tears and accuse him of calling her fat.*

"How often do you work out?"

Actually, she was interested in that. Over the past few days, she'd pretty much been privy to his entire schedule, so unless he was working out in his sleep, the only exercise he was getting was with her – the horizontal kind. *Not that it was always horizontal…*

"Usually every day. Of course, I've been a little too tired these last few days."

"Oh?" *Judging by the twinkle in his eye, she knew where this was going.*

"Yeah, I've been kept up every night by this hot brunette who keeps throwing herself at me and begging me to ravish her. She's insatiable."

Erin licked her lips. "Well, if you're too tired to accommodate her, then next time she throws herself at you – duck."

Gunner looked affronted. "And deprive her of this body? I would never be so cruel."

"Mmm, you're all heart." *No, he was all arousal.* "So what do you normally do when you workout?"

He pursed his lips at her for ruining his flirty fun. "Usually weights or the punching bag, but when I can get a good partner, I like to spar."

He chuckled as her eyes widened. "Don't worry, I'm not expecting you to spar with me. We'll restrict our wrestling to the bedroom. But maybe you could think about spinning or using a treadmill. Not that I think you need to! It's just if you want to."

"Take it easy, big guy, I think it's a good idea. But I was kind of thinking that maybe I should take some more self-defense classes."

"Really?"

Erin pinched the skin on her hand self-consciously. "Yeah, I mean I know I'll never be a match for a shifter, but it would make me feel a little less helpless, and I was kind of starting to enjoy the lessons Avery gave me."

"I think it's a good idea. One of the trainers at my gym gives lessons; she's really good. I'll introduce you."

She bit her lip as an unexpected flicker of jealousy nipped at her. *Don't ask, don't ask, don't ask!* "An ex of yours?" *Oh, lord, why did she ask?* Her mouth really wasn't connected to her brain.

Gunner gave her a hard look. "No, Erin, in spite of what you clearly think, I haven't slept with every woman on the planet."

"I don't think that… just a large proportion of the women in Los Lobos."

He narrowed his eyes, and she was about to get a blast of his annoyance when she was happily saved by Lara.

"The doctor will see you now."

Erin scurried after the goddess, ignoring the dark look on his face. Why couldn't she control her damn mouth? *Why couldn't she control her jealousy?* She couldn't really blame him for all the women he'd been with before he met her, but she couldn't help but feel intimidated about them either. Especially when they were wandering round the SEA offices throwing the fact that they slept with him in her face.

The doctor was a small, slim man with dark hair and green eyes. If Erin had to guess by the plastic quality of his smile, he was no stranger to going under the knife himself. That seemed a little odd. He couldn't have been more than about thirty, and yet he seemed to have had extensive work done. Well, maybe he'd been in an accident or something, or maybe he just really hated the way he looked before. *Or maybe he was trying to hide…*

"Welcome to the Blue Lotus…" he began.

Gunner was in no mood for bullshit. "I'm Agent Christiansen, and this is Agent Jameson, and you are?"

Erin perched on one of the chairs opposite the doctor's desk, and, stiffly, Gunner sat down next to her. His eyes were rigidly set on the doctor.

"I'm Doctor Philip Ross, how can I…"

"You operated on this man."

Gunner passed him a picture of James Silver. Philip picked it up, and his eyes widened a little; he looked between Erin and Gunner.

"Ah…"

"He's dead," announced Gunner, brusquely. "Doctor-patient confidentiality is at an end."

Philip sighed and passed the photo back. "How sad," he commented automatically. It was hard to tell what his emotions were, his face hardly moved. "I performed a routine rhinoplasty operation on him about a month ago. I don't recall his name, Lara mentioned the name James Silver, so I assume that is it, but of course, I remember the face."

Gunner glared at him, and the doctor shifted uneasily in his seat, although sadly it wasn't enough motivation to make him confess anything.

"How many people work here?" asked Erin, cutting through the tension.

Philip looked at her startled, like he'd forgotten she was even there. "Oh, me, three nurses, a receptionist and a cleaner. We're a small operation. We share our garden with the yoga school next door."

Erin nodded encouragingly, and the doctor's wariness abated a little. "How long have you worked here?"

He smiled his tight smile. "Well, I actually own the place. I founded it about two years ago."

"Is it common to take a blood sample of your patients before performing surgery?"

"Of course," he said in his most patronizing voice. "We need to know that in case we need to give the patient a blood transfusion for any reason."

"And what did you do before you opened this clinic?"

Philip blanched at the question. "I worked at a hospital overseas," he mumbled unconvincingly.

Erin shot Gunner a curious look, and it was clear that the bear was just as suspicious as she was.

The doctor stood abruptly. "Sorry to cut this short, but I have another meeting to prepare for. If you have any more questions, please do come back. Or," he pulled a card out of his desk and handed it to Erin, "here's a coupon for a free consultation if you're ever that way inclined."

"Consultation?" she repeated, gulping.

First Lara, now him, were they trying to tell her something?

"Yes, we do everything here – face lifts, liposuction, botox, breast enlargement." His eyes raked up and down Erin. "We can turn the ordinary into extraordinary."

Erin felt rather than saw the fury rolling off Gunner. She said a hurried thank you to the doctor and hustled Gunner out the clinic to the car. *Thankfully, he didn't put up a fight.*

The headlines really wouldn't have looked good – 'obnoxious plastic surgeon beaten to pulp by angry polar bear after calling his girlfriend ugly.' *Yep, not good at all.*

*

Philip watched them through the slats in his window blind. Tension poured out of the polar bear. *Fuck, that had been a bad move.* All he'd wanted to do was fluster the woman into leaving, fluster her into thinking he thought she needed plastic surgery. Human women were easy to manipulate that way. They were always so uncertain about their bodies; he could easily get them to pay for numerous procedures they didn't need. But he hadn't realized that the two agents were an item, and bears were notoriously possessive of their females. He felt lucky to still have all his teeth intact.

He prayed the polar bear didn't come back; bears weren't known for seeing the funny side of things, and the brute might not be so restrained next time.

The bear helped the female into the car, ghosting a large paw over her ass as he did. Hmmm, it was a little big for his taste. He had trouble imagining any man going for a woman like that when someone like Lara was available. She'd been nipped and tucked so many times that she was almost perfect. *Almost.* It was just a shame that he couldn't perform a brain transplant.

Fuck. *Speaking of which…*

He grabbed his cell phone and made a call.

"Hey, I was just about to call you…"

"The SEA were just here," interrupted Philip.

A breath was exhaled down the phone. "Shit, who?"

"A polar bear and a human."

"Gunner Christiansen and Erin Jameson. What did they want?"

Philip rubbed his forehead. "They were just asking about James Silver, about his nose job. But she asked whether we take blood samples, and she also wanted to know what I was doing before I came here."

His friend laughed down the phone. "Perhaps she's not as useless as everyone thought," he said ruefully.

"What am I supposed to do? What about tonight?" whined Philip.

"Nothing, don't do anything. Just act normally. Go about your schedule as you would any day, and when I need you, I'll call you."

Philip frowned into the phone. "But won't they be watching me?"

"They will, but it will be fine, we prepared for this kind of thing, remember? For now, I'm making arrangements for our new customer. Time is of the essence."

CHAPTER SIXTEEN

"Are you mad?"

Erin looked at his handsome profile as he drove. His mouth was set in a grim line, and his eyes were the dark brown of his bear.

"No," he growled. "Yes," he amended a second later. "I don't know."

"Mad at me?"

"A little," he admitted. "I can't change the fact that I've been with other women before I met you, and it pisses me off that you're trying to make me feel bad about it."

Erin pursed her lips and folded her arms crossly. "I'm not trying to make you feel bad. If you feel bad maybe it's because you realize that it's not okay to be a manwhore."

Gunner flicked her a surprised glance. She hid her smirk as his eyes quickly traveled down to her jutting breasts. *Ha, horny bear.*

He softened ever so slightly. "Manwhore, huh? I don't think I've ever been called that."

"Not to your face," she said tartly.

"You got me there; I guess no one's ever been brave enough."

"Or suicidal enough," she muttered under her breath.

Gunner grunted. "Well, you're just going to have to get over it."

"Excuse me?" she scoffed.

His jaw ticked with the effort of maintaining his temper. "I can't change my past, so you'll have to get over it. And that's all it is – the past – it's not like I'm seeing any other women. I'm with you. I thought I made that clear."

Yes! She knew that, and she did trust him. She didn't actually think he was the kind of guy to cheat, but her concerns were more based on the fact that he could easily get bored of her and pick up with one of the perfect women he'd been with before he met her. Feeling masochistic, she'd managed to corner Avery before they left and found out just how long the list of women he'd been with really was. *And those were only the ones who worked at the SEA!*

Erin placed a cool hand on her burning cheeks. "But can't you see that it's difficult for me, though?

"It shouldn't be," he snapped before letting out a ragged breath. "I'm only interested in you; I'm not going to be with another woman."

"But you're you and I'm me!" *Could he not see the distinction?!*

"What the hell does that mean?" he exploded. *It was a wonder he managed to concentrate on the road at all.*

And, apparently he really couldn't see the distinction. Well, to put it mildly, he had the appeal of a nice, big slab of chocolate cake, and she had the appeal of a cheese Danish. Sure the Danish was okay, but come on; it was barely palatable compared to chocolate cake!

Erin sniffed. "You're hotter than I am."

"Tell that to all the men we work with," he said, with more than a little bitterness.

"What?" she giggled. *He was not serious!*

Gunner cut his eyes to her. "Can you not honestly see all the men panting after you?"

She looked at him blankly, mouth open in surprise.

He let out a short, hollow chuckle. "There's Diaz, Wes, Lake from tactical, Emerson from the tech division, Wiley from archives – they're all after you. They all bet on who would get to fuck you first."

"You knew about this and didn't tell me?"

"Uh…" He had the grace to look a little sheepish at that

"They made me into a bet?" *What was this? High school?*

Gunner reached over and placed a hand on her thigh. He relaxed when she didn't move to slap him away. She was tempted, but his touch was welcome. *Even if she was pissed off with him.*

"Well, yeah, but on the plus side, I already technically won."

He beamed at her – smugly! *That was what he was focusing on?* She did slap his hand away for that. He let out a whine as he pulled his hand back.

"Ugh, you're all disgusting."

"Hey, I didn't place a bet."

"And you're changing the subject. It doesn't matter how many men are interested in me," *although she still didn't believe any of them were,* "the point is I have to work with dozens of women you've actually slept with."

"Not dozens, exactly," he interjected, although she could see that he was trying to calculate the number in his head. *She didn't give him chance to finish.*

"I have to see your exes parading around everywhere. How would you feel if you had to deal with the men I'd slept with every day?"

His knuckles turned white on the steering wheel, and his muscles seemed to grow and expand even more. "I'd be fine with it," he said tightly.

"Yeah, sure, I can tell. And, you know what? It bothers me that your number is so much higher than mine. You have so much more experience than me."

Gunner really did laugh at that. "Experience doesn't matter."

"Humph, maybe I should have a few flings to even it up a bit."

Hell, she regretted *that* the moment she said it. It was half said in joking, but half in spite and she hated herself for thinking it, never mind saying it. She cringed, waiting for his outrage, but instead, he remained calm, in fact, he might have even relaxed a little at her words.

"You wouldn't be so cruel," he said simply.

Erin leaned back in her seat, deflating a little. "I'm sorry, you're right, I wouldn't do that to you."

His lips curled up, and he displayed a sharp row of teeth. "No, I mean you wouldn't be cruel enough to even flirt with another man knowing that I'd rip him apart."

"You wouldn't," she whispered, disturbed by the malice in his soft tone.

"I would. I know you haven't been with a shifter before, and this is a steep learning curve for you, so let me make it clear. You're mine, Erin. You belong to me and me alone. No one else is allowed to touch you. You're the only woman I want to be with. You believe me, right?"

Yes she actually did believe that he would hurt someone – badly – over her. There was no doubt in her mind that he could be moved to acts of extreme violence, but it didn't scare her. It might have been messed up, but it was oddly comforting to know how possessive he was of her. It had been a long time since anyone had felt anything so strong for her. *If ever.*

She placed a hand on his cheek. He gasped but quickly nuzzled into her touch, rubbing his stubble over her palm.

"I do believe you, and I don't want anyone else to touch me. Just like I don't want anyone else to touch you, either. You believe me, right?"

"I do, babe, I do."

Impulsively, Erin unbuckled her seat belt and leaned over to plant kisses on his neck before pulling his earlobe between her teeth.

His large frame shuddered as he let out an almost painful groan. "Fuck, you drive me crazy."

She slipped back over to her own seat. "I wish I could say the feeling was mutual, but I was already crazy. Must be why I'm so hot for you."

"Hmmm. So what did you think of the badger?"

Wow, talk about a 180! She frowned in confusion. "What badger?"

"The plastic surgeon, Doctor Ross."

"He's a badger shifter?" *She did not see that one coming!*

"Sorry, I forgot you can't scent shifters… uh, but you have so many other talents."

Aww, he looked so apologetic! Damn, she must come across as being so needy.

"Alright, I think you can stop pandering to my ego, let's just get down to business. So, okay, the badger, do you think he could perform a heart transplant?"

"I don't know. But he does have a surgery all ready to go. I'll get Jessie to do a background check; he acted funny when you asked him about his life before Los Lobos."

"At least we have this."

Erin pulled out the card the doctor had given her, and Gunner scowled.

"You should have thrown that in his fucking face. Ordinary to extraordinary my ass!"

"You don't need to go Incredible Hulk about it; I only took it so we'd have his fingerprints. I didn't get any visions from him, but my guess is he has a past he wants to hide."

"Huh, good thinking. I should have thought of that. I was ready to punch his teeth out for what he said."

"No kidding," she remarked dryly.

Gunner blew her a kiss before calling Jessie and asking her to get cracking on a background check, and to get the rest of the team to make discreet inquiries about what goes on at the surgery, and whether they did any unscheduled procedures. If the doctor were performing the transplants, he would need people to assist with the transplant, so his accomplices might be his nurses. He also asked Jessie to get tactical to start following him.

"Jeez, does Jessie ever sleep? She always seems to be doing a hundred things at once," said Erin, wonderingly after he finished his call.

"Yeah, we're lucky to have her. Squirrels tend to be kind of hyper though."

Erin sucked in a breath and opened her mouth to speak before hesitating.

Gunner grinned. "That's such a cute tic you have. Did you know your eyes shine when you do that?"

"I just wanted to ask you whether you'd ever dated a squirrel shifter, but I was afraid to ruin the good mood, especially since we'd just started speaking again."

"We were always speaking... but, no, actually I haven't. At the risk of getting my ass kicked by a five-foot-five human, I have to admit that I generally used to go for large shifters, you know, bears and wolves."

"First of all, I'm five-foot-six," she told him haughtily, "second of all, I'm not mad, I was actually interested. And thirdly, you missed cats off your list."

Gunner harrumphed. "There was only one cat; I'm not dumb enough to make that mistake twice."

Erin clucked her tongue. "Come on, you were with her more than once, I know you were together in your apartment, in your car, at a gym... let's be honest with one another. You know my embarrassing sexual secrets, so I should know yours too."

He was surprisingly quiet until he pulled into the SEA parking lot. He shut off the engine and turned to her with narrowed eyes. "How do you know those details about me and Isis? I never told anyone all that."

"Ummm..." she bit her lip and desperately wished she were invisible.

Well, she was so embarrassed at that moment that there was a possibility that she might just burst into flames. *She could only hope.*

"Did Isis tell you all that?" His voice had turned downright arctic.

Erin hid her face in her hands. "No, I got a vision of you two together when Isis bumped into me at the coffee shop."

"A vision?" he repeated slowly.

"More like a montage," she explained in a muffled voice, not wanting to see his face at that moment. *Wasn't it bad enough that the images of him and Isis together would be with her forever?* "The memories must have been close to the surface when she touched me."

"Erin, fuck, I'm sorry."

She looked up in surprise to see pain etched across his face. *Okay, not the response she was expecting.*

"A few minutes ago you were telling me I had to get over your past, and now you're sorry. Jeez, and you can't even blame PMS on your mood swings."

Gunner took both of her hands in his and rubbed his thumbs over her knuckles. He tried to twist his face into a smile, not very successfully. His mouth looked like it was being pulled by elastic bands.

"Knowing about my past is one thing, having to see it is another. I couldn't cope if I had to... if I could see another man..." He swallowed with difficulty, "touching you. I hate that you have visions; I hate all the things you have to see, and hell, I really wish you didn't have to see that."

Erin clambered over and sat on his lap, briefly pressing her ass into the horn. She giggled as the loud toot diffused the tension settling into his hard body.

"I've seen worse. Although, only just…"

She squealed as he nipped her buttock.

"But, I think Isis did it on purpose. I think she was deliberately thinking about it and then bumped into me. I'm not sure why though, maybe she knows about us."

"Fuck!" he roared, jerking her body.

"Oh! Right in my ear!" she grumbled.

"I'm sorry, I'm so sorry, babe," he crooned, rocking her body lightly. "But I think I know why she did it. She wanted to piss you off."

"But, why?"

Gunner didn't answer, and she patted his arm.

"To steal your gun."

Her horror mounted as he told her about Isis finding it and then her attempted at blackmail.

"Oh, crap, I didn't even realize. My gun was in my bag this morning."

"I put it back."

Erin tried to scramble out of his lap, but he clung onto her.

"Why didn't you tell me when it happened?" she grouched.

Gunner snorted and looked at her like she was crazy. "And upset you before we had sex last night? Are you kidding me? I'm not that dumb."

She ignored that and instead focused on what the situation meant for her. She'd be fired; she was sure of it. *There was only so much bumbling the agency could put up with, and she'd reached her quota.*

"Oh, this is really bad."

"I'm going to deal with it; I'm going to talk to Isis."

"I should be the one..."

"No, don't, you stay away from her, she's not reasonable," he told her firmly.

"So how are you going to reason with her?"

His face hardened. "I'm not, I'm going to threaten her."

"Gunner! You can't do that!" *He cannot be serious!*

"She needs to back off. Look, I'll deal with it – end of discussion."

*

A couple of hours later, Erin was sitting outside Isis' apartment building. Yeah, as terrific as Gunner's plan to threaten Isis into leaving her alone was, Erin had decided to take matters into her own hands.

After cajoling Jessie into giving her Isis' address, she took Gunner's car – which he insisted she use in spite of her many objections – and decided to drive to Isis' place and wait for her. She really didn't want to talk to her at the office.

Erin lucked out. She'd only been waiting for ten minutes when she saw Isis pull into the parking spot behind her. She watched in the mirror as Isis got out and looked at Gunner's car for a couple of beats.

Crud, she must recognize it. Well, here goes nothing.

Erin hopped out and actually managed to startle the smug tigress.

"What are you doing here?" blustered Isis, genuinely shocked to see Erin walking toward her.

Erin squared her shoulders, and tried to look as fierce as possible. Which was probably about as much as a stuffed panda bear. "We need to talk."

Isis snorted and started walking to the door of her building. "No, we don't."

"You tricked me into losing my gun," accused Erin.

"I didn't make you do anything," said Isis, coolly.

"Why are you trying to blackmail Gunner? Are you pissed at him because he's not interested in you anymore?"

Isis turned toward her, eyes flashing. "No, it's because you have my job. You're a joke; you're not capable of doing this job. You should be an analyst or a consultant and leave the hard stuff up to the rest of us. Do us all a favor and just request a transfer. There's no shame in failure."

"Then you shouldn't feel ashamed of the fact that you failed to get my spot on the Alpha team."

Isis bared her fangs and hissed. "Watch your mouth, human."

"Don't bother threatening me. I've spent my whole life seeing visions of people beating each other, torture, rapes, murders... I've seen the worst that the world has to offer and you don't scare me. Leave Gunner alone. If you want to tell the director what I did, then stop yapping about it and do it. I made a mistake. I know you manipulated me into doing it, but it was still my error and I will deal with the consequences. Just don't involve Gunner, he's not to blame for this."

Isis watched her through hooded eyes. "You're very protective of Gunner."

Oh, she didn't like the happy expression dawning on Isis' pretty face. Uh-oh, a flush started creeping over her body. Had she just managed to give Isis even more fodder against her?

"And you're driving his car, and his scent is on you." The tigress' face lit up like a firework display. "Oh, my god! You and Gunner! Oh, this is too good."

"I don't know what you're talking about..." began Erin, limply.

Isis grinned horribly. "Well, that's settled then, if you two are together, you definitely can't work together. I'll tell the director in the morning and he can arrange your transfer. And since I'm in such a good mood, I'll agree not to mention the gun incident."

Erin sagged. Well, that was kind of what she wanted. At least she hadn't made the situation worse; this was kind of a step up from the way things had been ten minutes ago.

"Look, Isis…"

"Quiet!" snarled the tigress as she took a step toward her.

Erin prickled in indignation. "There's no need to be…"

"I said quiet!" hissed Isis as he clamped a hand over Erin's mouth.

Erin was about to struggle when she noted Isis' eyes had turned yellow and were widened. The tigress sniffed the air a couple of times before she sucked in a breath.

"Fuck, Erin, run!"

Isis pushed her toward her car – Gunner's car – but before she made it, she ran straight into a very hard set of muscles. Not the achingly familiar muscles she had come to know and love, no, these were an altogether different and unfriendly set.

She looked up to find the owner of the muscles, but a sharp smack to her face sent everything black. Vaguely, as she fell into unconsciousness, she was aware of the sounds of a tigress roaring.

CHAPTER SEVENTEEN

Gunner squeezed the receiver in his hand as, once again, Erin's answer machine cut through the call.

"Erin, it's Gunner, call me!" he hissed before slamming it down.

That may have seemed harsh, but it was the tenth call he'd made and the fifth message he'd left. His bear was prowling furiously. *Where the fuck was she?*

Earlier, she'd been a little standoffish about his plan of action where Isis was concerned, and then even more so when he'd made her promise to use his car. She said it was too much, and that he needed it, but he suspected another objection was the fact that he'd had sex with Isis in it. *Not his finest or most enjoyable hour.* He was already considering getting a new car to replace it. Not just for that reason, it was getting a bit old, and the strain of having to transport his more than ample frame gave it a shorter life expectancy than usual.

But still, she'd taken the keys and after trying to get some more visions from their victim's belongings, her nerves had been fraught and she was pale and shaky. Gunner insisted she leave to go home and relax. *Surprisingly, she did without argument.* That was now over an hour ago, and he hadn't heard from her since.

His bear was riding him to go to her, and to see what she was doing that was so damn urgent that she couldn't answer her freaking phone! But the man tried to rationalize the situation. If she were asleep, she couldn't answer the phone, and he certainly didn't want to interrupt that. Likewise, if she was trying to take a relaxing bath.

But what if neither of those scenarios was true? What if she'd got in a car accident on the way home? *What if she was now covered in blood, being crushed to death by his car just waiting for him to come rescue her?!*

His bear howled in despair and Gunner tensed, gripping the edge of his desk, as he felt his bones cracking, trying to realign themselves. *No, not now.* The bear grunted and turned his back. Yeah, he got it; the hairy asshole wasn't happy. *Controlling his beast seemed to be a full-time occupation.*

Perhaps he would calm a little once Erin was bonded to him. That couldn't come soon enough; he just wasn't sure how to broach the subject. *Oh, by the way, you're my soulmate, now hold still while I take a chunk out of your neck with my razor sharp teeth.* He chuckled imagining the look on her face if he dared to say that. He wondered how she would feel about the prospect of being bitten. Absently, his hand stroked over the patch of skin where she had dug her blunt teeth into him when they were making love. Even without her breaking the skin, it had felt phenomenal. Maybe she wouldn't be so averse to a little nip after all.

Gunner sighed and scrubbed his hands down his face. He needed to go see the director. *Again.* The director wouldn't admit it, but he was on edge about this case and getting pressure to close it quickly. Nobody liked the idea of shifters being harvested for their organs, which meant around the clock updates on their progress. *Or their lack of progress.*

He lumbered to his feet, stretched out his limbs, as far as his tiny office would allow, and made his way to the elevator. His fingers itched over his cell phone in his pocket. Maybe he should just try her again. There were plenty of rational explanations as to why she wasn't picking up or returning his calls, but he just had a bad feeling.

He gave in and fumbled for his phone just as the elevator dinged at his floor. He composed himself when he saw Rory, the undeniably creepy medical examiner, inside.

Rory gave him a slimy smile. "Going up?"

Gunner grunted that he was and, with a heavy heart, he stowed the phone in his pocket and got in.

"How's the case going?" asked Rory simply.

"Fine," he muttered not wanting to be drawn into a conversation.

Although, it wasn't really fine. They thought they'd find a link to the other missing shifters at the plastic surgery clinic. But other than their victim, none of them appeared to have undergone any procedures there. The only way to be sure would be to get a warrant to see the clinics records, but given that they're medical records, any judge would be hesitant to do anything given how little evidence they had.

They were just hoping that the doctor would incriminate himself.

"How's your new recruit, Erin, working out?"

His jaw tightened as his sullen bear perked up again. *Erin was none of this fucking rabbit's business.* "Fine," he said through gritted teeth.

To Gunner's chagrin, Rory got off at the same floor and walked with him down the corridor. Would it be too rude just to say, oh fuck off! *Yeah, probably.* His bear grumbled an objection.

The rabbit brought it on himself. He was dismissive and rude to just about everyone in the building. Not to mention, he was kind of misogynistic and made inappropriate remarks to the female agents about them being inferior to males. The last time he told Isis that she ought to quit and find a mate to raise cubs with, he ended up with a fractured wrist and twin black eyes. And, he tried to stir up trouble between teammates. A wolf in tactical had been kind of sweet on Avery until Rory managed to convince the idiot that she was sleeping with Cutter. *As if!* The two of them were more likely to punch each other than kiss each other. But the wolf didn't believe it, and Avery had been a little subdued since then.

So the last thing he wanted was this poisonous rabbit getting his claws into Erin. *Whoever said rabbits were harmless was clearly talking out of their ass!*

"I heard there was a bet going on about who'd be the first to get Erin in bed."

"You heard right," murmured Gunner, blandly.

"Although I heard the bet was over already."

Gunner sucked in a breath and sped up a little, trying to shake the smaller man. Unfortunately, Rory refused to take the hint and was almost running to keep up with him.

"I mean, given that Diaz already sealed the deal."

His bear roared in outrage. *Lies! All lies!* He knew for a fact that she hadn't been anywhere near that smarmy jaguar shifter. It was the only thing that did allow him to keep his temper – the fact that he knew it wasn't true.

The rabbit chuckled. "Two and a half weeks she's been here. She didn't keep her legs closed for long."

That was it! Gunner grabbed the rabbit by the throat and slammed him against the wall. Rory's eyes bulged as the bear roared in his face.

"You are never to talk about her again! Do you understand me?!"

"Gunner!" snarled the director, "put him down."

He flicked his eyes between the snake and the rabbit shifter, torn between doing the right thing and doing what he wanted. *Namely to rip the inferior shifter's throat out!*

"Gunner!" hissed the director.

With a huff, he dropped Rory to the floor and stepped over him to get to the director's office, ignoring the look of thunder on the snake shifter's face.

All he could think was that Erin better call him back soon.

*

Large, warm hands clutched her arms. She looked up expecting to see her polar bear, but screamed at the monster staring back at her…

"Erin, wake up."

Erin blinked and groaned as pain wrenched across her face. She couldn't help the strangled yowl that escaped her lips. *She felt like she'd been side-swiped by a freaking bulldozer!*

"At least you're alive," said the disagreeable voice. *Ugh, Isis.*

At that moment, Erin wasn't sure being alive was such a good thing.

She found herself sitting up but leaning her head on Isis' shoulder. Her hands and feet were bound with rope.

"What happened?" she gurgled as she tried to soothe her wooly mouth.

"Some assholes abducted us. After they knocked you out, they injected me with some kind of drug. I've no idea where we are. How's your head?"

Erin looked up to find Isis staring at her with a mixture of concern and anger. *Isis, concerned about her? Damn, how hard was she hit?*

"It's not that bad; I've had worse headaches."

She used to suffer migraines from her visions, so she was accustomed to a little pain in the head department.

"Still, we need to be careful in case you have a concussion."

Erin pulled back as far as the ropes would allow and gazed at Isis doubtfully.

Isis rolled her eyes. "Look, I'm a bitch, but I'm not evil. I don't want you dead any more than you want me dead."

Wellll… Okay, fine, no, Erin didn't want to wish her any particular harm.

They were in a plain room; there was no window and just one solid looking door. The room was illuminated by a single, flickering bulb. While Erin was bound with rope, Isis was in shackles.

Isis saw her looking at them. "Silver, they stop shifters from, you know, shifting. Plus, it's fucking painful."

"Did you see who took us?"

"Four shifters altogether: a wolf, two bears, and a cougar. Fuck, I should have scented them coming earlier. My tiger's livid."

"It's going to be okay," said Erin automatically.

Isis smirked. "Spare me, let me guess, you were a cheerleader in high school?"

"More like the weird kid that no one wanted to talk to because she heard voices, and freaked out and had visions during gym class," admitted Erin sadly, "although, I would have done pretty much anything to get out of gym."

"Jeez, maybe you are perfect for Gunner."

"This from the tiger who was trying to hook up with him yesterday," scoffed Erin.

"I only said that to annoy you…"

"Mission accomplished."

"I'm not interested in him; he's a bit too serious for my taste. Given all your issues though, you make a great couple."

She couldn't help the bubble of laughter that escaped. "Wow, almost a compliment, I'm flattered."

Isis pouted. "You should be; I don't give them out lightly. I don't suppose you told Gunner where you were going tonight?"

Erin blushed. "No, he told me to stay away from you."

The tigress smiled toothily. "Good advice. But given that no one will think to check on me until tomorrow, I would say we are screwed."

She bit her lip. "What about your neighbors? Surely they heard what happened and called the cops."

"They're used to hearing a lot of screaming from me and my guests. Although, that's usually only with my male guests."

Erin narrowed her eyes, and Isis rolled hers in return. "I didn't mean Gunner."

"It doesn't matter if you did, Gunner already told me about the two of you. He said it was just *functional* sex." She emphasized the word for effect.

The tigress barked out a laugh; her eyes danced with flecks of yellow. "Yep, that sounds about right for Gunner. Old, romantic bear."

Erin frowned as a wave of protectiveness assailed her. *Gunner was perfect just as he was!* "He doesn't need to use flowery language, he says what he means, and that's what's important."

"Wow, you've got it bad. I can see why you like him, most women are attracted to the power he radiates, but I gotta say, I'm surprised he would go for a human."

"You didn't have to say that," replied Erin, primly. "Just because you don't think I'm pretty enough…"

"It's nothing to do with looks. I mean, I'm not saying this from a personal point of view, but most shifters want to be with other shifters. Humans are so… breakable."

She made humans sound like eggs. "Not that breakable…"

"A guy in the tech division – a moose shifter - mated with a human, and they got a little rough in bed one night and he broke her arm by accident."

Erin shook her head. "I trust Gunner not to hurt me."

And she did. She knew he was a hell of a lot stronger than her – *he was like twice her size!* But, she trusted him to keep her safe. Although she'd be interested to know just how rough was a little rough.

"It's not personal, Erin. But shifters are animals, do you really think he'll be satisfied with gentle sex with a human, making sure he doesn't sneeze too hard and break your ribs? When he could be having wild, animalistic sex with a shifter?"

Now that was something that bothered her. If six months – or even one month – down the line Gunner did decide she was too 'breakable,' and took off to be with someone more suitable, what would she do? She'd already fallen for him, hook, line and sinker. *Hell, she already loved him!* How would she cope if he left her?

"Ladies!"

Erin let out a very undignified squeal as a huge man burst through the door. She would guess he was a bear shifter, given that he had height and muscles to rival Gunner. She wasn't proud of herself, but she pressed herself as far against the tigress as she could. Isis, in turn, tried to shield Erin.

Alright, so the tigress wasn't as bad as she seemed!

He gave them a horrible grin, and Erin almost gagged at his scent. He smelled like a wild, unwashed animal; even she could tell it was bad.

"So glad you've decided to gossip instead of trying to break out. I suppose that's the benefit of kidnapping women, too busy flapping their big, fat mouths to be of any use."

Isis snarled and bared her teeth.

"Careful, kitty cat," he crowed, "we need you alive for now, but I'm not above punching you in the face."

"What do you want with us?" demanded Erin, with bravado she definitely didn't feel at that moment.

The big guy squatted down next to Erin and ugh, his breath was as bad as his scent. *It's called mouthwash…*

"You? Nothing, we just want the tiger."

"Let her go then!" snapped Isis as she helplessly tried to kick him.

"Can't do that now. She's seen our faces." He ran a finger down her cheek. "What are we going to do with you? Me and the boys have never been with a human; it might be an interesting new experience."

Isis snorted. "I wouldn't bother, they just lay there like wet fishes. Do you ever wonder why human males look so miserable all the time?"

Wet fish indeed! Erin held back her pique; she knew Isis was just trying to help.

Sadly, it didn't seem to be working. His leer intensified. "Only one way to find out."

He began roughly pulling at Erin's clothes.

Erin remained still, and glassy-eyed, but Isis struggled against her bonds. "Don't you dare!" she screeched.

"It's okay, button, everything's okay…" whispered Erin calmly.

He stopped and stared at her with frightened eyes. 'Wha… what did you just say?"

"It's okay, button; I forgive you, button."

The shifter shot across the room as if scolded. He gulped and looked between Erin's dreamy expression and Isis' look of bewilderment. He opened his mouth as if to say something, but changed his mind and fumbled with the door, escaping the room as quickly as he could.

"What the fuck was that?" exclaimed Isis.

Erin shrugged. "His mom told me what to say. Her ghost follows him around."

Isis looked around the room suspiciously. "She does?"

"Yeah, he killed her, so she's following him until he dies, and they can be reunited."

"Shit. Why'd he kill her?"

"I think he loved her too much, and if he couldn't have her..."

Isis curled her lips and let out a growl. "Ugh, disturbing. And I'm disturbed by how calm you are about the whole ghost thing, but at least it got rid of him."

"And he didn't lock the door on the way out..."

Isis looked to the door, hope sparking in her eyes. She wriggled against her chains. "I need to get out of these."

"Can you cut through my ropes?"

Erin twisted until her hands were hovering over Isis'.

"Just, it's hard to shift with this silver."

The tigress flicked out a claw and began sawing through the thick rope. Soon enough, her hands were free, and Isis then worked her way through the rope around Erin's ankles.

"Now what?"

Erin stood up and stretched. "Now, I need to find the key to your chains."

"Be careful," ordered Isis.

"Sit tight," quipped Erin.

"I promise not to leave this room," she replied scornfully. "If you can't find the key just look for a door and get out of here, call for help when you can, just make sure you get out. No reason we both have to die."

"Don't be so quick to sacrifice yourself, you're not Bruce Willis and this isn't Armageddon. I'm not leaving you here."

"Yeah, well don't be so quick to go down with me. He said they wanted me, remember? You need to protect yourself. We're not Thelma and Louise."

"Well, if we were, I'd be Susan Sarandon."

*

Gunner paced Jessie's office. The squirrel shifter surreptitiously started hiding all the stationery and paraphernalia on her desk. *He was in a throwing kind of mood.*

"I've called her over and over but I can't get a reply. Cutter even drove by her place on the way back from talking to Los Lobos PD, no lights were on, and she didn't answer her door. Jessie, track her phone. Now."

Jessie hopped to it. *He was not in the mood for an argument.*

"It's outside, oh…."

"What?" he growled.

"Well, she wanted to know where Isis lived, and I sort of told her…"

He full on roared. "What?!"

Jessie shrank just the teensiest bit into her seat. "Her phone's at Isis' apartment."

Gunner gritted his teeth and called Isis. *No answer.*

He panted with the effort of controlling himself. The bad feeling he'd been having was growing to epic proportions. Something was wrong. Deep down he could feel it. "Something's going on; I'm going to find Erin."

"Wait… I know you're worried about Erin, but it's about the case…"

He stared at her coldly for a few seconds. "What have you found?" he asked quietly.

She couldn't help the sigh of relief that popped out. "I couldn't find any record of our doctor anywhere before two years ago when he opened his clinic."

Gunner grunted. "Fake ID?"

"Yes, I'm trying to find out who he used to be. I'm trying to find out if he actually did train as a doctor. All I can say is that the clinic is doing well –

as far as I can tell – and they've never been sued or anything like that. So if he is an amateur surgeon he appears to be doing a good job."

"Hmmm, okay, keep digging."

"I hope Erin's okay," she added softly. "I don't think Isis would hurt her."

"No, I don't either."

He just had a very bad feeling, and his restless beast was no help.

He dialed Lake from tactical as he ran out to one of the agency SUVs.

"You still on the doctor?" he demanded as soon as the call was answered.

"Hasn't left the clinic in four hours; car's still here."

That was the great thing about Lake. *Direct, to the point, no bullshit.*

"Go in and check," ordered Gunner.

A few minutes later, Lake called back.

"Fuck, he's not here, how the fuck could he have gotten away?"

Good question, but however he did it, the reason why he needed to was not going to be a good one.

CHAPTER EIGHTEEN

Erin made an undignified scuttling motion across the floor. She was very thankful no one was there to watch her. Getting around the building was actually as easy as she expected. It looked like an old hospital, ugh, more like a mental institute. Most of the rooms had glass panels in their walls, and she found walking upright wasn't possible.

She held still as she heard a squeak. What was that? Her heart pounded in her chest, and she could swear that her breaths were louder than an industrial fan. *Lord, this was so much more nerve wracking than they made it look on Mission Impossible.*

Her lip trembled as she heard gruff voices up ahead and the sound of a door opening. She plastered herself against the wall, hoping for the best. No way could they fail to see her there, unless the building was graced with a lot of exceedingly bumpy walls.

Erin blew out a breath as the voices retreated in the opposite direction.

Stop stalling! She admonished herself. She needed to get a wriggle on. Isis was in danger, and panting up against a wall was not helping. No way was she leaving without Isis.

She tried the first door she came to and slowly pushed it open. It was a hospital room. Thankfully, an empty one. The next couple of rooms were the same, but the room at the end looked more like a surgery.

Razor-tip winged butterflies fluttered in her stomach. *This was bad...*

Erin trembled as she slunk towards the voices. If the key to Isis' manacles was anywhere, it would be near them.

She peeked around the corner into what looked like a hospital waiting room. Four brawny men, including the shifter who had tried to maul her earlier, were watching the TV. With distaste, she noticed it was a porno, and, ugh, the men were actually rubbing their crotches.

Focus!

She glanced around the room and saw the ghost again. The specter smiled and pointed at a table close to the door. Erin frowned and looked in that direction. A cell phone. Yes, she could call for help. *Perfect.*

She sidled into the room and reached her arm out. The ghost shook her head quickly, and Erin froze. One of the males stood up and walked to the window. Erin held her breath as he looked outside, scratched his rear and then settled back into his seat.

Erin snatched the phone and then scrambled back out the room and in the direction she came from. Her fingers floundered over the keys as she typed in Gunner's cell number.

She almost shrieked in despair as it went straight to voicemail. She tried his home, his office, and then his home again – but no answer. *Gunner, where are you?*

She fought back the frustrated tears that wanted to spill and instead called Jessie's number.

"Hello?" came the voice of the curious squirrel.

"Jessie!" cried Erin in the loudest whisper she dared.

"Erin! Where the heck are you? Where are you calling from?"

"Jessie, I can't talk, please just track this cell phone I'm using. Isis and I have been abducted..."

"Wha…"

"We're in danger, please track this number and come get us, hurry! Shit, I think someone's coming."

The squirrel was suddenly all business. "Don't hang up, I'm tracking you, and don't worry, help is coming."

Erin switched the phone to silent and slipped it into her pocket. She could hear the rumblings of movements echoing down the corridor. She bolted for the room where they were keeping Isis and sat back down, trying to artfully drape the rope back over her ankles and wrists.

Isis glared at her. Her expression spoke volumes, or rather it said, 'what the hell do you think you're doing, you moron?'

But before Isis could let rip at Erin, the men she saw watching the porno walked into the room.

"Shit, Hank, you didn't even lock the door."

The man who'd tried to put his paws on Erin – Hank apparently – sneered and gave Erin a disagreeable look. "Fucking bitches didn't even notice."

Hank and two of the others grabbed hold of Isis' struggling body. The tigress was strong, but she was no match for three male shifters. Although, Erin was pleased when Isis managed to head-butt one of them. *She drew blood and everything!* The guy just grunted and tried to restrain her with more gusto.

The fourth guy plunged a syringe into Isis' neck and eventually she went limp. They took off her bonds and carried her out the room. Hank eyed Erin warily before closing the door, and this time he made sure he locked it.

Crap. She had a really bad feeling that the case they were working was hitting a little too close to home for Isis.

Erin grabbed the phone out of her pocket and was dismayed to find it was dead. *Frak.* She tried the door, and she even tried putting her shoulder to it – that only resulted in giving her shooting pains. She inspected every inch of the room, but it was pretty pointless – it was just a room, oddly enough it had no secret passages.

If only she were a shifter! She would just bust through the door and go beastly on all their asses! But, no, she had to be a human, didn't she?

Hell, how much time had passed? If they really were plundering one of her organs, how long would it take? Maybe they'd already taken her heart!

In distress, she tried the door again. Still locked. *Oh, why wasn't she more capable?*

Erin stared at the door, willing it to open. She almost climbed the wall when it did just that.

The smell of Hank wafted into the room, quickly followed by the man himself, and his ghostly mother, shaking her head sadly.

He shut the door behind him and placed himself in front of it, glowering at her. *Okay, clearly Isis wasn't the only one in danger.* At least he seemed to be ignoring the fact that she'd made her way out of the ropes.

"How did you know what my mama called me?" he growled.

Yep, definite bear. She stared at him blankly, refusing to answer. Quick as a flash, his hand swiped at her head, knocking her to the ground. Stars danced in front of her eyes, and she felt the blood from a split lip, but she refused to cry out. Shakily, she got up and stood before him, shoulders back.

"How did you know?" he ground out through gritted teeth.

"I'm psychic," she replied petulantly.

He lifted his paw to smack her again, and, lord help her, she flinched. Her ears were already ringing, and her brain felt scrambled, a few more blows like that might kill her.

"I'm psychic," she said more forcefully, "I can see your mom's ghost. She follows you around and has done so ever since you killed her."

His hand hovered in the air, menacingly waiting to strike her.

"Nobody knows about that."

"You strangled her with your bare hands because you were angry and jealous that she was going to get married," blurted Erin.

Fury lanced across his face as his muscles twitched and seemed to grow. *Maybe she went too far...* Surprisingly, though, he chuckled and rubbed his jaw.

"Huh, maybe you really are psychic. The boss said you were, but I didn't believe him."

"The boss? Who's the boss?"

He snorted. "This ain't some James Bond movie. You really think I'm gonna tell you?"

"What does it matter if you're going to kill me anyway?" she asked innocently.

"Good point, but I'm done talking."

His face darkened as he took a step toward her, and latching onto all the bravery she could muster, she stood her ground, and didn't even yak at the smell.

"Because you don't know?"

"I know well enough," he spat.

Oh, well, time to push a few buttons... "Yeah, right, you're just a hired thug; the guys doing this wouldn't tell you anything important."

Hank grabbed hold of her shirt, pulling her toward him until their faces were inches apart. "Shut your fucking mouth."

She'd never felt so scared before; she'd never felt like she was in so much physical danger. Not even when the young wolf shifter attacked her. But from that fear, she felt a rush of adrenaline, and no way was she going to let that go to waste.

"Why, you're going to kill me, aren't you? What does it matter what I say?

You really care so little about your fellow shifters that you're allowing this Frankenfreak doctor to cut them open and fish out their organs?"

His eye twitched. *She was right.* Through some awful twist of fate, Isis had become the next victim of the guy they were looking for. *Oh lord, poor Isis.* Erin was all too aware of the fate awaiting her - if she hadn't already met it.

"People die every day; they might as well donate a few organs so that people can live."

"But the people who are dying are fit and healthy, this is murder, and kidnap and... and..."

The brute pushed her against a wall. "Well, since I'm already going to hell, I might as well enjoy myself."

He licked her cheek and Erin gagged. Ugh, the feel of his rough tongue over her cheeks was the most horrible, most repellant thing she had ever felt, and she'd endured electro-shock therapy!

Hank stiffened and looked up. "Fuck."

He grabbed her arm and pulled her out the room; Erin allowed herself to be physically dragged by him.

As he pulled her along corridors, she soon realized what had him so riled. Gunfire and shouts were echoing all around them. And if she wasn't mistaken, there was a roar of one very pissed off bear. *Oh, she hoped that was her bear.*

His fingers dug into her arm in a punishingly tight grip. She dared a glance at him and found him snarling at her.

"You bitch; you did this!"

She couldn't deny it.

"If you think you're getting out of here alive..."

He stilled and pulled Erin in front of him, trying fruitlessly to hide his large bulk behind her body. Erin spied a huge wolf creeping toward them. The creature was growling and snapping his jaws at them. It could only be Cutter; *even in wolf form he could sneer at her disdainfully.*

"One step closer, wolf, and I'll snap her neck."

The animal stopped but huffed his annoyance.

Hank started pulling Erin backward. Crud, if she didn't do something he was going to get her out of the building and take her as a hostage.

Erin looked to his mom for help and nodded her head as the ghost imparted a tidbit of information. Erin braced herself, and with all the force she could muster, stamped her foot down on his.

He howled and let go of her. She heard the warning howl from Cutter and dropped to the floor. The guy screamed as the enormous wolf pounced on him, and Erin covered her ears and closed her eyes to drown out the screams.

After a few minutes, she opened her eyes as something cold nudged her cheek. She blinked as she found herself faced with the head of an enormous polar bear.

A smile swept over her face, and she winced at her split lip. She ran her fingers though his fur, and he nuzzled her hands. Lord, he was magnificent. So majestic, so beauteous, so *big!*

"Hey, beautiful," she murmured, and if she wasn't very much mistaken she heard a wolf laughing. She didn't care, and the bear didn't seem too either. She would have been more than happy just to curl up in his fur, except...

Oh, crap. "Isis!" she exclaimed.

She scrambled and jumped to her feet, ignoring the angry rumblings of the polar bear. Her feet padded down the corridor, and she jumped over the fallen goons' bodies as she went. She burst into the room she saw earlier - the surgery.

"Stop!" she screamed.

Three people in surgical gowns and masks looked up in surprise, and Erin was relieved to see that their patient – Isis – still appeared to be intact.

The polar bear and wolf shifter came careening into the room behind her and swiftly changed to their human forms, barking out orders. They took control of the medics who had been trying to relieve Isis of one of her organs, and Erin rushed over to check on the unconscious tiger shifter.

Isis had a long cut on her chest, but otherwise she was okay. Erin sagged in relief and was pleased when warm, strong hands caught her. *She'd never tire of the feeling of being caught by him.*

CHAPTER NINETEEN

Isis sat up in bed, abruptly. "What's happening? Where are they?"

Erin rushed over and placed a hand on her shoulder. "It's okay; it's over. We're safe; we're both safe."

Isis looked around the hospital room wildly, breathing in and out deeply. "What the fuck happened?"

Succinctly, because it had been a long day and Isis was still groggy from all the drugs she'd been injected with, Erin explained that she had been targeted to donate one of her organs - *unwillingly*.

Isis was suitably outraged. "One of my organs? Those fuckers were trying to steal one of my organs?"

"Specifically, your heart," clarified Erin.

"My heart?"

"Yeah, turns out you do actually have one."

Isis gave her a sour look before shaking with laughter and clutching her chest. "Don't make me laugh, I'm still tender."

In body only, thought Erin. She didn't say it out loud though; it would just lead to more painful laughter.

"When I got out of the room, I managed to find a phone and I called for help. Jessie tracked the phone, and she sent the cavalry. Turns out they are the people we were looking for. The guy who was about to operate on you was the doctor we'd been following."

"So you've caught them, then? Case closed."

Erin sighed. "Not exactly; we caught the doctor who was performing the transplants. It was the badger plastic surgeon like we thought. And we caught two nurses who were assisting him, but they were just paid to be there. They knew it was illegal, but they thought it was just black market stuff, they didn't realize people were just being snatched off the street and killed for their organs. And we got the woman who was waiting to take your heart."

Isis gingerly ran her finger up and down her chest, feeling where the cut had been. It was healing, but as it was made by a silver knife, it would take longer than usual and would, in Gunner's words, hurt like a bitch. Apparently, all surgery on shifters has to be done with silver instruments, otherwise the shifters would heal the incisions too quickly. *Another reason why shifters avoided hospitals.*

"Why'd she need a new heart?"

Erin slumped into a chair. "A witch's curse, apparently, although she won't say why. In Cutter's words, 'the bitch probably had it coming.'"

Isis pursed her lips. "That Cutter, what a charmer."

"We didn't get the guy who was arranging everything. All the goons are dead – they went out fighting, and just about all of them got ripped apart. The badger doctor broke down and admitted to doing the transplants, but he can't explain how all the victims were found – a couple had been to his clinic – one we didn't find out about. But he wasn't the one orchestrating it, and he wasn't the one who dumped the bodies either."

Erin hadn't really had a chance to talk to Gunner since her unfortunate incarceration, he'd given her a death-squeeze hug back at the prison/hospital of doom, but they hadn't talked. She imagined he was less than calm about the fact that the 'mastermind' of the whole organ stealing endeavor was still on the loose.

"At least, though, we can give death notifications to the families of the other victims. That's where the rest of the team is at the moment, apart from Cutter who's still shouting obscenities at the doctor, hoping he'll give in and admit to his partner in crime."

In a weary voice, Isis said, "I guess I should apologize for being such a bitch, given that you, you know, saved my life and everything."

Erin smirked. "Hmmm, being saved by a human, how humiliating."

Isis gave her a look of admiration. "Well, this human has skills; I'll give her that. I already said I won't tell the director about the gun... uh, incident, and I'll keep to that, and I won't tell him about you and Gunner either. But, maybe you should."

She let out an inward sigh of relief. "Thank you."

"And I'll kill you if you ever tell anyone I said this, but Gunner's lucky to have you."

Erin raised her eyebrows. "You think?"

Isis fidgeted awkwardly. *Clearly she wasn't used to, or comfortable, with being this friendly.* "Yeah, and like I said if you..."

"I know, I know, my lips are zipped."

Erin made a zipping motion over her lips, and Isis nodded, appeased. She stood as a tall, handsome, blonde doctor came into the room. As tired as Isis was, she perked up a little at his presence, and Erin noted her surreptitiously smelling him. *Ah, he was probably a shifter too.* Which, given his physique and attractiveness, really wasn't a shock.

"I better get going," said Erin, diplomatically trying to ignore the heat in Isis' eyes. "Will you be okay?"

"As long as this guy doesn't try to rip out my heart, I'll be fine."

The doctor blinked a couple of times as Isis licked her tongue over her teeth. *Ugh, did Gunner really fall for this, too?* She was amazed that she didn't actually feel jealous of that fact; it was more a mixture of humor and pity. *Silly bear.*

The doctor graced them with a dazzling smile; his eyes twinkled under long lashes. "With women, it's usually the other way round."

In spite of how tired she was, Isis gave him a feral smile, and Erin quickly slipped from the room. *A minute longer in there and she would definitely see some things that would haunt her.*

She slammed straight into a very familiar set of muscles, and felt herself warm as those strong arms cradled her body. Oh, all her troubles just packed up their bags and went on vacation when she was in his arms.

"Hey, how long have you been here?" she mumbled into his chest.

Gunner tangled his fingers in her hair and carefully lifted her head to look at him. "Just a few minutes," he murmured.

His eyes bore into her, almost devouring her. His lips twitched, and his body tensed as he studied her face. Gently, he ran a finger over her bruises. *Ah, yes, they'd take a while to heal.* To say he didn't look pleased was an understatement. Fighting the urge to not howl and punch every wall in sight was more like it. *Quick, distract him!*

She ran her hands up his chest, and his eyes widened a little in lust. *Hmm, good start.* "Why didn't you come in to see Isis?"

"It didn't seem appropriate." The big bear actually looked a little awkward. Dang, she'd made him feel that way with all her jealousy over the tigress. That didn't sit right with her. She guessed after what happened she was just feeling a little more charitable towards the tigress, and a little ashamed of how she had tried to make him feel guilty over being with Isis before he met her.

"Is she okay?"

A loud peal of feminine laughter ripped out of Isis' room.

"She'll be fine," deadpanned Erin.

He smiled tightly as his thumb lingered over her lip. "Have you had someone check out your bruises?"

"Yes, and I'm fine." Well, she was actually incredibly achy, and her head felt like it wanted to explode – but she wasn't about to admit that. She knew what she wanted to make her pains go away, and she knew Gunner wouldn't give it to her if she admitted to just how shaky and sore she was.

Without warning, Gunner swooped her up and started marching out of the hospital, carrying her princess style. "I'm taking you home," he told her gruffly.

Goody. *Her nympho was very pleased to hear it.*

*

When Gunner said home, he actually meant his apartment. Any objections she might have had were shot down before she had a chance to voice them. He wanted her in his apartment, in his bed, surrounded by his scent, and he wasn't open to argument. He did relent a little, and, grudgingly, asked her if it was okay, and asked her if she would do this for him. *He said he needed it.* Of course, she couldn't say no to that. *Not when he needed her.* Just that fact sent her heart fluttering and her arousal surging, and that sure wasn't helped by the shower he made her take, *with him in the shower with her, naturally.* He washed every inch of her, massaging her tired limbs and cataloging her bruises. Erin could see the disapproval on his face, but was thankful he kept it to himself. Particularly about the bruises on her shoulder earned from the very ill-advised attempt at breaking down the door...

He gave her an oversized t-shirt to wear in bed. Well, oversized on her, probably tight on him. It had a picture of a cartoon polar bear and proudly proclaimed that 'polar bears can go all night.' *Yes, she could attest to that.*

Gunner gave her a half-embarrassed smile when she saw it. "Gift from my brother," he explained. "I have others if you don't like it."

"No, I like it." She pulled it over her head and found it was more like a dress.

"Hmmm, it might be a good idea for you to keep some clothes here." He looked at his closet thoughtfully.

"Are you envisioning more sleepovers?" she asked, hopefully.

"I sure hope so, although you won't be doing much sleeping." His hand ghosted over her ass, and she shivered.

Gunner took her hand and led her back out to the living room. He was only wearing a pair of sweatpants that hung precariously from his waist; his chest was deliciously displayed. She had an urge to lick and kiss her way over the smooth skin. Instead, she settled for curling up in his lap.

"I guess the usual game of truth or dare is off the table? I heard it's something kids do at sleepovers."

His fingers danced over the bare skin of her thigh. "Can't say I ever played it."

"No, me either, I never had sleepovers though, the other kids thought I was weird... they weren't wrong."

"Their loss, I didn't have sleepovers either. The other cubs kind of thought I was scary," he admitted, completely uncaring.

"You? The only scary thing about you is your aftershave."

Gunner snickered. "True. But I might have been a bit rowdy when I was a kid; I had my brother anyway, so I was never alone."

"He's older, right?"

"Only by thirty-seven minutes," he grouched.

Erin sat up and looked at him. "Wait, you two are twins?"

"Yeah, fraternal though, not identical. Multiple births are really common in my clan. My brother and his mate have twins."

"How common?" she asked uneasily.

Over the last few days, she couldn't deny that she had considered her future with Gunner. She'd envisioned a house, a minivan and yep, a little blonde boy and girl running around causing mayhem. Although, she had to admit she was a little apprehensive about the thought of giving birth to polar bears. *They came out human, right?* Having twins suddenly made the future a little more daunting.

"Uh, let's save that discussion for another day." He quickly changed the subject. "Hungry?"

She traced a finger over his collarbone. "Would you be mad if I said no?"

Gunner let out a long breath. "No, but I'll insist on feeding you in the morning."

"Deal," she agreed in relief. She was hungry, just not for food.

"Now, how about that game of truth or dare?"

"Really?" *What was next, hide and go seek?*

His chest vibrated with laughter. "Sure."

Hmmm, maybe this would be fun. "Okay, truth or dare?"

"Truth."

She considered all the things she could ask, mostly pertaining to their own relationship and the possibility of a future together. But it had been a long day, and she wanted to keep the atmosphere light

"Who was your first kiss?"

"Ha, Cindy Larsen. We were thirteen; she kissed my brother and then me in the janitor's closet at school. Turns out she was kissing all the boys in our class and rating them out of ten. She ended up mating with a walrus."

"Really? What was your score?"

"Three," he muttered reluctantly.

"Bummer."

"My turn," he growled, and she could sense he was keen to move on from that. "Truth or dare?"

"Oh! Truth." She wasn't really up to dares at that moment.

Gunner looked at her thoughtfully for a few beats. "Did you mean what you said earlier?"

"Hmmm? About what?"

"When you said I was beautiful."

Erin burst into laughter.

"It's not that funny," he grumbled.

"Of course I did, you have a very beautiful beast."

He leaned his head back and closed his eyes; a ragged breath of relief escaped his lips. "Thank god, I thought you'd freak when you saw him."

"Why?"

"Well, you hadn't seen him before; I was planning to introduce you to him gently."

"I've been around shifters before, maybe not this up close and personally, but I know what happens when you change. And I mean it; you've got a gorgeous beast, maybe even more gorgeous than you."

His bear preened, and Gunner gave her a rueful smile. "Don't, you'll give him a big head."

Erin traced a thumb over his lips. "Well deserved, I shouldn't wonder."

"Erin, stop."

She pressed closer to him. "I'm not doing anything."

"You've had a long day; you need to rest."

Erin carefully rubbed her breasts against his chest.

"Erin…"

"I'm not doing anything," she breathed.

She brought her lips up to his, a mere whisper apart, but not actually touching.

"Oh, my psychic princess, you don't play fair."

"All's fair in…"

She blushed before she said love and instead pushed her lips against his roughly, ignoring the twinge of pain from her cut. His tongue plunged into her mouth, tangling and massaging with her own. *Three, indeed! Cindy Larsen was a fool.*

She slithered on his lap until she was straddling him; her hands smoothed down his chest until she reached the waistband of his pants. Her hand delved inside, and she gripped his swelling manhood. He moaned into her mouth, half-heartedly trying to protest what was happening, but there was no way in Hades that she was going to stop.

His moans became guttural as she massaged his member. Panting, he drew his mouth away and leaned his forehead against hers. "We shouldn't be doing this…" he rasped, his eyes swimming with the brown of his bear.

Her hand froze on him, and with a little amount of satisfaction on her part, he whimpered. "Would you like me to stop?" she asked wickedly.

Gunner bucked his thighs up, needing her to move, needing her to caress him. She took that as a no, but instead of picking up where she left off, she grabbed hold of his pants and tried to pull them over his hips. She giggled, and he growled as his erection caught in the waistband. With tender care, she freed him and settled her body over his, their sexes touching. She rolled her hips, rubbing her nether lips against him, rubbing the honey weeping from her over his member.

He placed his hands on her face. "Erin, I can't be gentle, my bear, he's… he's too close to the surface. He's still angry about almost losing you. If we do this, it will be hard and fast. I won't be able to hold back."

"I trust you. I want you. I need you." Erin pulled the t-shirt off her head and delighted in the hungry look on his face. "Mine," she cooed.

Gunner let out a savage growl. His hands found her hips and within seconds he lifted her up and forced her down his length. She cried out in pleasured shock and dug her nails into his shoulders as he started thrusting in and out of her. She gasped each time he filled her and mewled each time he withdrew.

His eyes were wild, and his face was etched with fierce lust as he mercilessly gave her pleasure and took his pleasure in her body. With some alarm, she saw that dark, black claws pushed out of his fingertips. *Was he changing into his bear?!*

No, no he wouldn't. He wouldn't hurt her. No matter what, she was sure of that. With him was the one place that she was safe. In such a short time, he had become everything to her. *Her life, her lover, her family.* Yes, she loved him more than she thought possible, and he loved her, she was sure of it. She was his, and he was hers. *Forever.*

The thrill of knowing that sent her over the edge. She tumbled into her release and screamed his name as her body clenched around him. Seconds later, he ground her down on him and howled as he sought his own climax. Feeling him erupt inside her sent a second mini-orgasm shooting through her, and she collapsed over him, sprawling her tired, sweaty limbs over his body as the tremors of their lovemaking shivered through her.

"Mine," he rumbled, wrapping his arms around her.

"Yes, yours."

CHAPTER TWENTY

Erin blushed as Gunner ushered her into the conference room. He bit back a chuckle at all the concerned, yet smiling faces staring at her. Yep, they were all proud yet worried about her after the adventure she had the previous day. To say he had been worried was an understatement. *It was like saying space was big.*

The director came forward and placed a hand on her shoulder, squeezing it lightly. His bear sucked in a breath. *Fucking snake should keep his hands to himself!* There was the slightest possibility that he was still on edge about what happened, and liable to overreact. Roaring at Tony, the coffee shop barista, because they had run out of blueberry muffins, and Erin had wanted one, was probably a testament to that.

"How are you feeling?" asked the director.

"She's fine," snapped Gunner. "We need to get on."

He directed Erin to a chair and sat in the one next to her, of course, all while ignoring the coldly suspicious look his boss was throwing him. *Well, the snake was being overly familiar – it was his own fault.* He'd never shown so much interest in any of the other teammates before, except maybe for Jessie, but then she was one hardworking squirrel.

"Is Isis okay?" asked Erin, with genuine feeling.

Gunner beamed at her proudly. Just yesterday Isis had been trying to sabotage Erin's career, and here was his little human all concerned and worried about the tigress. *She was something else.*

Avery snickered. "Sure, just pissed about being in hospital, although she's getting her claws into that dishy doctor, so she's not complaining too loudly."

Erin frowned. "You went to see her?"

The lioness waved a hand. "Sure, we've been friends for years."

"Oh, I just thought…"

"They're typical female cats," interjected Cutter, gleefully, "they're always fighting and making up. They fight like a cat and a… well, another cat."

"We're not that bad," grumbled Avery.

"Getting back to the task in hand," said the director, smoothly, "I take it we still don't have any further information from our doctor?"

Wayne clicked a control, and the security camera image of Doctor Ross flicked up on the large screen at the end of the conference room. "No, Cutter pretty much destroyed every item of furniture he could find and screamed at the guy repeatedly, but nothing."

The doctor was lying on the floor, presumably because Cutter had systematically destroyed all the other furniture that used to be in that room. He was huddled in the fetal position and muttering to himself. Jeez, the guy already looked broken.

Jessie chose that moment to burst into the room, making Erin jump. Gunner hid his grin. She was so easy to startle. He placed a hand on her thigh under the table and squeezed gently. His bear felt a twinge of satisfaction as she quivered, and a sliver of her arousal could be scented.

The squirrel shifter waved some pieces of paper around. "Hot off the presses… hey, how are you, Erin?"

Erin smiled. "I'm good, thanks."

"Stroke of luck you being kidnapped by these guys, huh?"

Gunner's eyes were hooded as he regarded the squirrel peevishly. *Oh, sure, let's hope all our cases end with Erin being taken hostage – wouldn't that be fabulous!*

"Get to the point, Jessie," he rasped.

"Right, I found out who our guy is, his fingerprints and DNA are in the system. He is actually a trained surgeon – apparently he was a damned good one – but there is a warrant out for his arrest for killing his ex-wife."

"Jeez," muttered Wayne.

"Yeah, it was pretty brutal murder too. Doctor Melvin Hague was arrested and disappeared while he was out on bail. Then, six months later Doctor Philip Ross suddenly turns up in Los Lobos and opens up a plastic surgery clinic."

Jessie passed around pictures of the man Doctor Ross used to be. There were vague similarities, but honestly, no one would think they were same person if they didn't already know.

"He must have had plastic surgery himself," said Avery.

"Yeah, a lot," agreed Cutter.

"It seems like he had a lot of money to open up the clinic," Jessie informed them, "but according to the reports of his disappearance, he didn't take anything with him."

Gunner stared at the picture. "So he must have had help. Help to get a fake ID, help to get money to set up his practice, help to have his own procedures done."

"Someone who he felt indebted to, maybe someone he'd be willing to risk helping…" suggested Erin.

"We can't see a way that the good doctor, or whoever he is, picked his victims," added Wayne, "maybe he isn't the only doctor running the show. Maybe someone else actually found the victims."

"I spoke to Isis," said Avery "and she has literally never visited a doctor or given blood other than for her physical to join the SEA. According to her, the only place anyone could find out her blood type would be through her record with the SEA."

Erin snapped her fingers. "The goon!"

Gunner arched an eyebrow. "The goon?"

"The one that, ah, that was talking to me in the room," she hadn't quite been able to admit to Gunner about Hank's darker designs on her. "He said that his boss told him I was psychic, but he didn't believe it. I don't think they knew who I was when they took me, but someone must have recognized me, someone who knows about my abilities."

"Are we really thinking that it's someone within?" asked Avery uneasily.

"It could easily be someone who hacked our files," said the director.

Jessie bristled. "Hacked our files? Puh-lease."

"Alright, let's just take it easy for now," said Gunner calmly. "Given that we have the doctor under arrest, it's time we started going through his life to try and find out who his mystery partner is. Jessie, background, financials, find out who he was before he changed his name. Avery, Cutter and Wayne, I want his house, his clinic searched, I want you to go through all his friends, co-workers, girlfriends, boyfriends, whatever, find out what you can. He must have been in contact with this mystery guy so there must be some record somewhere. Erin, you're with me."

Her eyes sparkled. "Oh?"

"We're interviewing the good doctor."

The director frowned. "Erin needs to write up her report about what happened yesterday."

She nodded. "I will."

"She will," agreed Gunner, gruffly.

The director ignored the glower Gunner was leveling at him. "And are you sure you're up to interviewing after your ordeal?"

"I am."

"She is," hissed Gunner.

The director rolled his eyes at them. "Okay."

As everyone left, the director held up a hand for Gunner to stay behind. He waited until Cutter had closed the door. "So things are working out okay with Erin?"

His bear prowled uneasily. He didn't like any man talking about his mate, even if the words were innocuous. "Sure, good, great even."

"Even though she's human?"

"Even though."

He already felt inordinately ashamed of himself for his uncharitable thoughts towards Erin; he didn't need the damn snake to rub it in!

The director stifled a smile. "So, your hissy fits were all for nothing, then?"

Gunner narrowed his eyes. Ah, the director was just trying to rile him. *Humph.* "If you'll excuse me, I need to get going."

*

Erin leaned against the wall, waiting for Gunner to finish with the director.

"Thank you," she squeaked as Cutter sauntered past her.

He froze, startled by her words.

"For saving me yesterday," she clarified, thoroughly embarrassed.

Awkwardly, he mumbled that she was welcome. He made as if to move away, clearly uncomfortable with sharing any finer sentiments with her.

However, he stopped and looked at her curiously. "That guy who had hold of you yesterday…"

She tensed. "Yeah…"

"How did you know to stamp on his foot? He was a bear shifter; you shouldn't have been able to hurt him."

Erin laughed nervously. "Oh, that! The ghost of his mom told me he had a painful ingrown toenail."

He stared at her in disbelief for a few moments before laughing and shaking his head. "I'm kind of sorry I asked."

She shrugged. Welcome to her world.

Cutter winked at her. "Catch you later."

"What did he want?" asked Gunner tetchily.

She actually managed to refrain from jumping a foot in the air as he startled her. "Nothing important, what did the director want?"

"Nothing important, c'mon."

The corridor was empty so he took her hand in his, and they walked together, hand in hand. She flushed happily. It felt so normal, such a 'boyfriendy' type thing to do. She almost wished they could just keep walking. *But no, they had something to do.*

"Why do you want me in this interview?"

He squeezed her hand. "I want you to see if you can get any visions from him, plus, you do pretty up a room."

Erin snorted. "You sweet-talker, you."

*

Gunner pulled out a chair for her, and she gave him a shy smile before sitting. Huh, either they had brought in new furniture or he'd been moved to a new room.

The doctor, sitting opposite her, regarded them both warily. Erin placed both palms on the top of the table and considered him, dispassionately.

Gunner prowled around the room like a caged beast. It took all of Erin's self-control not to ogle him like a teenager. *Oh, he should be arrested for being so sexy*. But, getting back to the man who actually had been arrested…

His face was guarded, and his eyes were big and frightened. Erin imagined she'd be pretty wary too if she'd been arrested for multiple murders, and had spent the better part of a night being shouted at by Cutter. Admittedly, she would have broken down and confessed to everything the moment Cutter opened his mouth though.

Erin continued to look at him while Gunner huffed, grunted, snorted, growled, and strode around the room, his long legs easily eating up the small space. The doctor tried to keep his eyes on both her and Gunner, but he seemed to be getting a little dizzy.

"Shouldn't you be asking me questions?" asked the doctor, hesitantly.

"Why?" snapped Gunner. "Do you plan on answering them?"

"Ugh…"

The bear shifter sneered. "That's what I thought." He spoke softly to Erin, "Take your time."

Erin spread out her fingers over the table, and the doctor studied her at first in amusement, but then worry as her face took on a blank look. Even Gunner stopped pacing to watch what was happening. She closed her eyes, and her body jerked as a vision flashed before her.

Her eyes snapped open, and she hugged her arms around herself. Gunner ran his hands through his hair as he tried to quell the scared look on his face. Somehow she doubted he'd ever become accustomed to her visions. They were kind of a hard sell in a relationship, although he definitely wasn't limbering up for a run to any nearby hills.

Erin shook her head. The vision she had wasn't useful – or at least it wasn't useful to their case. She focused for another ten minutes trying to grasp at another vision, well aware of Gunner's fidgeting unease. But she got nothing. *Nada. Zip. Bupkis.*

Gunner inclined his head to the door, and she silently agreed. The doctor watched them leave, even more alarmed than before. Well, if anything, maybe their strange actions would get him to say something.

As soon as they were out of the room, Erin apologized and started pinching the skin on her hand. "Sorry, nothing about the guy we're looking for, but I saw him killing his wife - it was not pretty, maybe I can try again…"

He caught her hand and frowned over the raw skin before bringing it to his lips. "Babe, it's okay. Why do you do that to your hand?"

Erin laughed; she hadn't even realized she had been doing that. "It's just a coping mechanism for when I'm anxious. I used to use rubber bands around my wrists, and I'd snap them whenever I felt overwhelmed. This hurts less."

"If you feel overwhelmed then punch me in the shoulder – punching things is very cathartic."

She wrinkled her nose. "Won't that hurt?"

Gunner gave her a proudly condescending smile. "You wouldn't hurt me."

Oh, lord. "Not you, big head, I meant me. I could easily break some bones trying to hit your rock-hard muscles."

"Hmmm, good point. Try punching Cutter, he's much doughier than me."

Erin ran her free hand over his belt buckle. "How about every time I feel anxious I kiss you instead?"

He placed a kiss on her palm. "Sounds like a plan. For now, I'm gonna talk to the New York SEA, and see what they want to do. I'm feeling generous, if they want him, they can have him."

"I saw him put the murder weapon – an ax," she shuddered, "in a building site. He dropped it into some drying concrete. I could describe the buildings, and maybe they can still find it."

"I'll let them know. You're amazing, by the way."

She flushed, but she felt joy at hearing that. Amazing was a word he kept using to describe her, and she loved it. *It made such a change from weird, odd, crazy and nuts.*

"You have to say that because you're my boyfriend."

"No, I have to say that because it's true."

Erin pouted. "Kiss ass."

He leaned down to whisper in her ear. "You mock but I seem to recall you really enjoyed that last night."

"Not funny!" she scolded him playfully as her cheeks burned bright red.

"Look, I'm gonna go talk to New York; you stay out of trouble."

"I'll go and see if I can help Jessie."

He nodded in approval before kissing her hand one more time and walking away. After eyeballing his butt for a few seconds – *it really was spectacular –* she shuffled from foot to foot.

Okay, she could go and see if Jessie needed any help, but, from experience, she knew that Jessie would just get frustrated with how slow Erin was with a computer. When the squirrel got going, she had tunnel vision, and anyone else trying to interfere in her work was not a welcome distraction.

On the other hand, she could actually try to make herself useful and use one of the gifts that actually got her promoted to this team. While she wasn't getting anything from the doctor, and their victim's belongings had yielded nothing helpful, there was one last avenue she could mosey on down. *Yep, it was time to feel up a dead body.*

James Silver's body was still in their morgue. She could go down and see if she got anything useful. She felt vaguely uneasy about her plan of action, as she knew that Gunner was opposed to it. But, whether he liked it or not, there were going to be times when she had to do things that he found unsavory. *That's just the way it was.* She knew her abilities freaked him out, but he was strong enough to deal with it.

With determination, she strode over to the elevator and punched the down button. Of course, she'd tell him what she'd done after she did it. *Telling him beforehand was just downright dumb!*

CHAPTER TWENTY-ONE

Erin tapped on the door to the morgue. "Hello…"

No answer. She pushed the door opened and shivered immediately. Darn, it was cold down there.

She was surprised no one was about. She recalled, from the tour Avery had given her, that there was a medical examiner, and he had several assistants.

She crept through the room, feeling like an intruder. She was deliriously glad that all the cold, metal tables were empty. Yeah, she was depressingly familiar with dead bodies, but that didn't mean that she blasé about seeing them.

Hmmm, now where would James Silver be?

"Hey."

Erin squeaked and clutched at one of the tables. Images of the bodies that had lain there flickered before her eyes and with a yelp, she snatched her hand back. She whirled to find an average looking man watching her detachedly.

"Hey, Erin, right?"

Ah, of course, he was the medical examiner. She knew they'd met but for the life of her, she couldn't remember his name. On the tour, Avery hadn't been keen to spend much time down in the basement, or in his company.

"Yeah, and you're... ah..."

His lips twitched ever so slightly. "Doctor Roark Maitland, but you can call me Rory. I'm the medical examiner."

"Right, sorry."

"You're Gunner's newest girl, right?"

"Oh, ah..."

"Don't worry, I won't tell anyone. You've nothing to be embarrassed about. You're just going where countless other women in this building have gone before."

Rory smirked, and Erin decided she hated him. *Perhaps he thought he was paying her back for not remembering his name.*

"What are you doing down here?"

"Well, I..."

He didn't bother to wait for an answer. "I heard Isis Martin was in hospital."

"Yes."

Rory gave her a scornful look. "Another of Gunner's girls."

"You make it sound like he has a harem of women," she grumbled folding her arms over her chest.

"They just flock to him," he said with a small trace of bitterness.

Well, Erin couldn't honestly blame them – she didn't exactly play hard to get. He was watching her closely, and Erin realized he was trying to upset her. Not in the bitchy, spiteful way Isis did – that Erin could handle and almost excuse because she now realized that Isis actually did have a heart. No, this was just malevolence for the sake of being malevolent, and it kind of scared her.

She decided to ignore him and tried to act professionally. "I actually just came down to see if I could get some kind of vision from James Silver's body."

It was quick, but she could have sworn that she saw a look of abject hatred flutter through his face. She almost thought that she'd imagined it, but she was getting a very bad vibe from this guy.

"Yes, I heard that you were psychic, I didn't believe it though," he said, almost casually.

"It's hit and miss," she admitted hedging.

"So how can I help you?" he asked condescendingly.

"I'd like to see James Silver's body," she declared, ignoring the jitters in her stomach.

"Oh, I'm sorry, the body has already been released to the family," he told her smugly.

Crud. "But, on whose authority?"

"Mine," he hissed.

"Shouldn't you have checked with the director or Gunner?"

"That bear is not my boss!" snapped Rory as he absently rubbed his neck.

"But…"

"I've told you that the body isn't here so you should go."

Rory stomped to the door and held it open for her. She bit her lip. *Well, if the body really isn't there, there was no point in hanging around.* She sighed and was about to leave when a flicker caught her eye.

A ghost materialized next to Rory. The specter ignored her and instead stared at Rory, *for all the good it did.* Erin almost gasped as she recognized him as James Silver. Their victim's ghost was hanging around the morgue and he did seem to be focusing on the medical examiner.

Rory tapped his foot impatiently. "I don't have all day."

It was this moment that James noticed that Erin was staring straight at him. "You can see me?"

Erin parted her lips and inclined her head ever so slightly to say yes.

James looked between her and the increasingly short-tempered Rory. "You need to leave."

Oh, she desperately wanted to ask why, she desperately wanted to ask him some questions, but for some reason, she felt afraid of doing it in front of Rory.

Slowly, as his lips curled upward, Rory closed the door. "What's wrong, Erin? Have you seen something you shouldn't have?"

Oh, crap.

She didn't need James' ghost to tell her. She already knew. "You're the one who's been kidnapping shifters and taking their organs."

Rory cocked his head on one side. "Yes," he replied simply.

Erin edged backward slightly. *Alone in a morgue with a murderer was a very bad place to be.* "But, why?"

He locked the door. The snick of the lock echoed sickeningly throughout the room. "Money, of course. Why else?"

"But I don't understand…"

"There's nothing to understand. The idea came to me when I was working on a dead body about a year ago. All of the guy's organs were intact, and he would have been a perfect donor, except for the fact that he was a murder victim, and therefore none of his organs could be touched. It seemed like such a waste. So then I started thinking about how much people would be willing to pay to get organs they needed. I looked into what the donor market was like – and for shifters it was pretty much non-existent. It was kind of sad."

He looked at her as if he truly wanted her to believe that he had feelings. *Please! He was a monster!*

233

"At first, I was trying to match people up with dead bodies, but the timing was never right. I could never find the right donor and get their organ quickly enough. So, it became clear that I had to use live donors."

"So you just killed whoever you felt like?" murmured Erin.

"Well, it's not like any of them were exactly setting the world on fire. They were no great loss. I mean, James Silver was a womanizing hippo shifter – who gives a fuck about him? And as for Isis, wouldn't you have felt better with that whore cat out of the way?"

"No!" she exclaimed.

He snorted in disbelief. "Right, sure. It was a surprisingly easy endeavor. All I needed was an empty hospital wing – I had the old mental institution that was closed for giving its patients lobotomies renovated. Then, I just needed muscle to grab the victims, and my old friend, Melvin was willing to do anything for me, given how much help I'd provided in escaping the little matter of going to jail for killing his wife."

"That guy tortured and killed his ex-wife, you should have let him go to jail."

"She had it coming," he said nastily.

She suspected he felt that way about most women…

"How did you get rid of the bodies?"

Yes, keep him talking.

"Easy, I just got that Cinderella company to pick them up when they collected the rest of SEA's trash. The camera in the loading bay is broken, and they never look too closely at what they're collecting, so it was perfect. It was a shame that Silver's body wasn't disposed of, but no matter, now."

"How did you choose your victims?"

Someone – Gunner at least – was bound to notice she was missing soon.

"I had to degrade myself to do that – don't think I haven't suffered in this whole thing! I was going to take everyone from the SEA roster, but I thought that would be too obvious. So I had to volunteer at a free clinic every Saturday to find the correct matches, plus Melvin found a couple through his clinic. Now, have you any more questions?"

"I, ummm…"

Oh hell, think of something!

"No? Well, thank you for listening; you know it's actually been quite beneficial to admit this to you. It's been like a weight off my chest."

"Oh, my pleasure, I'll just let myself out…"

Rory took a step closer to her. "I don't think so."

Unbeknown to him, James Silver's ghost took that moment to throw himself in front of Erin, trying to protect her. "Stay back from her," he commanded.

Sadly, only Erin could hear him.

"I appreciate the sentiment, but that's not going to help," she whispered frantically.

"What?" snapped Rory.

She inched her way around one of the tables, putting it firmly between the two of them.

"Whatever drove you to do this…"

Rory hooted with laughter. "I wouldn't bother."

"What?"

"Trying to figure me out. There is no sad, pathetic childhood story behind what I do. I wasn't abused, I wasn't unwanted or unloved, and I wasn't a nerd who harbored unrequited love for the head cheerleader who wouldn't give me the time of day. I had a normal, healthy life. I'm a normal person. I just did this for the money, which I will now be taking with me when I retire to a nice Caribbean island with no extradition to the US."

"Normal people don't kidnap others and harvest their organs," Erin scoffed.

Maybe it wasn't a good idea to goad him, but Rory seemed unperturbed.

He shrugged. "Because they're not smart enough and don't have the requisite skills to do it. Ordinary, idiotic criminals rob stores and pick the pockets of old women. No, no one else could have pulled this off. You think your idiot bear boyfriend could have done all this?"

"He wouldn't want to," she cried indignantly.

Rory snickered. "Oh, I'm just sorry that you're not going to live long enough to have your heart broken by that idiot. He'd have gotten tired of you and thrown you over as soon as something more interesting came along."

He sobered a little and actually smiled a little sadly. "I'm sorry I have to do this to you; I'd prefer it if Gunner were here instead. You seem so nice, but I can't change that now."

Rory made a lunge for her, and she shrieked, running away as quickly as she could. She was extremely thankful that he wasn't exactly graceful, or fast. *Because she was neither of those things either.*

She ran out of the room, slamming the door behind her, pleased when she heard a thump and a scream. Yep, she got him. She ran through a series of interconnecting offices. *Oh, why couldn't she remember the way back to the elevators?* The basement was like a maze, and her navigation skills were questionable at best.

She needed a phone or an exit. Her eyes darted around but she couldn't see anything. No, but she did hear Rory's feet pounding after her.

Erin ducked into a room and swiftly closed the door. She backed up slowly, praying he just went past.

"Hi."

She slapped her hands over her mouth to muffle her scream. James Silver's ghost had chosen that moment to reappear.

"Don't do that!" she whispered furiously.

The ghost shrugged. "You need to get out of here; he's a bad man."

"Yes, I had noticed!"

Why had she come down here without her gun or her phone? *It was like she was determined to get herself into trouble!*

James disappeared for a few seconds before reappearing again. "He's gone back to the morgue, go now."

"Thanks," she breathed, yanking the door open.

She got a jolt as James appeared in front of her again and pointed in the direction she should go. She nodded and pelted that way.

"Erin!"

A familiar roar echoed throughout the basement, making everything shake.

Gunner! Yes, he was here - he was coming for her!

Erin stopped and tried to listen for his voice. Suddenly the door to her left burst open, and a manic-looking Rory flew at her. He knocked her to the ground, and they grappled with one another as he tried to pin her down.

Crap, he was strong! He was soon restraining her, and he wrapped his hands around her neck.

"I'm going to fucking kill you, you bitch!" he snarled.

She gasped and scratched at his hands. "And when I'm done, maybe I'll kill that fucking polar bear, too!"

That was it! No one threatened her polar bear. She grabbed one of his fingers and sharply tugged it, bending it back at an abnormal angle. He yelped and loosened his grasp. She took that moment to hit him where it hurts. *Yep, she punched him in the crotch.*

Rory went limp; his face went green, and she pushed him off her body. He made a desultory grab for her, and she sucker punched him in the face. He tumbled to the ground like a sack of potatoes.

"Erin!"

They were quickly surrounded by other SEA agents. Gunner swept her up into his arms and gave a swift kick to Rory.

"Ugh, you're crushing me!" she gasped, although she wasn't all that unhappy about it.

He relaxed his grip a little, but there was no way that he was about to put her down. He nuzzled her neck. "Sorry, babe."

She curled her body around his; one eye watched as other agents led Rory away. She smiled as James Silver gave her a thumbs up and disappeared. *Poor guy, but at least he would have justice now.*

"How did you know to find me?"

Gunner sighed. "I was already worried when I realized you weren't with Jessie, and when you weren't answering your phone," he told her with a fair amount of disapproval. "Then when Jessie found out that Melvin Hague went to med school with Rory… and knowing your propensity for being in the wrong place at the wrong time, I just had a really bad feeling."

"Thank the heavens for your bad feelings!"

He chuckled. "Oh, I don't know, you seemed to be handling him just fine."

"Yeah?"

He pulled back to look at her. "Yeah, you continue to amaze me. I love you, you know that, right?"

Erin's eyes became wet with tears. "I strongly suspected. Did you know that I love you?"

"Well, you're only human."

She rolled her eyes. "Idiot."

"Your idiot."

"Yes, mine."

CHAPTER TWENTY-TWO

Three weeks later

Erin kicked off her shoes and stretched her arms over her head. She smiled as Gunner kissed the back of her neck.

"I like your hair up like this," he whispered into her skin, "easier access."

She spun and startled him by crashing her mouth against his. Although he didn't stay inactive for long; soon enough, his hands were snaking their way around her body and heaving her up his own.

It had been three weeks since 'the incident that we will not talk about again.' After it had happened, Erin had been pumped up and just about ready to take on anything. Gunner, on the other hand, had been almost a nervous wreck. He claimed that the incident had taken ten years off his life and tensed every time it was mentioned. *Melodramatic bear.*

Rory was being charged with eight counts of kidnapping and murder. The money he had amassed from the transplants was being given to the families of the victims. Doctor Philip Ross, aka Doctor Melvin Hague, had been sent back to New York to stand trial for his wife's murder. Depending on how that went, after he had served whatever sentence he was given there, he would then be expected to stand trial for numerous counts of accessory to kidnap, murder and organ trafficking. It was a fair bet that he wouldn't see the outside of a prison cell for the rest of his life.

The blonde woman who had lured more than a few of their victims to their deaths was actually a call girl. She had no idea what was going on, and had thought it was just a series of elaborate pranks for a new hidden camera TV show. She was very disappointed when she realized she wouldn't actually be on TV.

To the annoyance of the SEA, Tom 'the hammer' Murphy was not being charged with anything. Neither Rory nor Doctor Ross or Hague – whatever, would admit to operating on Murphy – they were far too terrified of the hippo shifter. So, short of repossessing his heart, they had no evidence to arrest Murphy. And no judge would allow them to do that, they knew because they'd asked. Murphy would have to wait for another day.

Erin had virtually moved into Gunner's apartment, in that whenever she made noises about needing to go home to her place he found some way to distract her. *And boy was he distracting.*

Instead, they'd settled into a routine that now actually involved the beginnings of a weekly tradition of having a family dinner at Erin's parents' house. It was awkward; her parents were too afraid to say much, they focused more on their disgust about how much food Gunner actually ate. Her family was used to dainty portions. *Gunner had once cleared out an all you can eat buffet.* But, she knew he suffered the meals for her, and it made her love him even more.

They'd just come home from one such dinner. Although they disapproved of him, her parents were a little less frosty after Gunner terrified the cable repair guy into paying them a visit. The guy's first offer was a visit within the next six to eight weeks. After one conversation with Gunner, he said he'd be there on Sunday. *See, having your very own polar bear came in very handy.*

"You tired?" he rumbled.

"Nuh-uh."

"You wanna watch TV?"

"Nuh-uh."

"What do you wanna do?"

Erin smiled prettily and fluttered her eyelashes.

"Erin Margaret Jameson, you are insatiable," he crooned in mock admonishment as he carried her to the bedroom.

"What can I say? I was seduced by this polar bear, and now I'm a nymphomaniac."

"Wow, he really does sound like a keeper."

"I agree." She nibbled on his earlobe.

His big body shuddered. "Erin, there's something I need to say."

He placed her on the bed, and she watched him wonderingly as he paced up and down the room.

"Is something wrong?"

Gunner shook his head and knelt on the floor in front of her. "No, not since I met you. I love you Erin, more than anything, and I want you to be mine forever. I want you to mate with me, and I want you to bond with me. I want us to move in together. I want you to come up to Alaska to meet my family. I want to marry you, and I want you to have my cubs. I want you to be with me, forever."

He was almost panting by the end. His speech had become increasingly loud and frenzied, and not at all like the logical arguments he had prepared and had wanted to put forward. *But, in the heat of the moment, logic had no place in his heart.*

Erin blinked at him and gulped a few times. "Wow, you don't want much, do you?"

He looked away, shamefaced. "I'm sorry; I shouldn't…"

"Yes."

Gunner looked at her sharply. "Yes?"

"Yes to all of the above."

"You're saying yes," he said slowly as if he couldn't believe his ears.

"I want everything you want. I love you, Gunner."

"You... you mean that?" he breathed incredulously.

"Yes, yes, yes!" she cried in exasperation. "Do I have to shout it from the rooftops?!"

He rolled his shoulders. "Couldn't hurt."

"Good lord, maybe you should come and make love to me before I change my mind."

Gunner graced her with a lascivious growl. "Now there's an offer I can't refuse."

Within moments, just in case there was a chance she might change her mind, Gunner was nude and had managed to wrangle Erin out of her clothes. Honestly, she suspected he was a magician in training. *And now for my next trick, I will make all of Erin's clothes disappear!*

She squirmed, and giggled as he pushed a digit inside her needy core. He raised it to his lips and licked her honey.

"Oh, babe, you're already so wet. Wet for me."

His eyes flashed dark brown, and she bit her lip, excited at what was coming. She leaned back on the bed as he kneeled between her legs and ran his fingers over her thighs, enjoying the feel of her skin.

"Do you understand what it means to bond with me?" he asked roughly, as his bear fought for control.

"I do; it means that we'll be joined, and we'll be able to sense each other's emotions."

She'd been reading up on the subject; she wanted Gunner, and she was prepared to do whatever it took to keep him. *And the thought of being bound to the rugged shifter was a total turn on.*

"So you understand I will bite you when we make love? You'll have a permanent scar. Are you prepared for that?" Her heart swelled with love as he gave her such a vulnerable look.

"Yes, I want this as much as you do."

"Not possible…"

Gunner pulled her hips against him, smoothly impaling her on his hard length. She moaned in utter satisfaction and grasped at the bed covers as he filled her over and over, touching and caressing every sweet spot she had. He took her with leisurely, long thrusts, slowly building the kindling fire within her.

Her body started tingling as she felt the stirrings of her release. She started bucking her hips back at him and squeezing her inner muscles. He threw his head back and let out a sensual snarl. His movements became more urgent, and she felt his claws graze her skin.

With breathtaking speed, he flipped her onto her stomach and began pounding inside her. She squeaked and pushed back against him with carnal glee as his flesh slapped against hers. Without missing a delicious beat, he lifted her body up until she was sitting over him. He braced one arm against her chest, his hand kneading her breast. His tongue lapped at the juncture between her shoulder and neck as his other hand sought her clit, strumming that oh-so-sensitive little collections of nerves. *All the sensations were just too much for her…*

She pressed her hands over his and pushed her body against him as fireworks exploded through her. She screamed his name as his fangs sank into her shoulder, and they both reached their releases together. The wrench of pain on feeling his bite fled, and she was overwhelmed by pleasure, desire, love and need. She trembled in awe as his feelings for her poured into her body, and she gladly returned them.

"You're mine, now, Erin. All mine," he crooned into her shoulder.

"I always was," she breathed. *From the very first moment.*

How long they sat there, entwined so intimately, she couldn't say. She dozed, enjoying the gentle pulses of his manhood softening inside her, the feel of his tongue laving her bite mark and relishing in sharing his emotions.

"Do you have a lot of turtlenecks?" he asked, out of the blue.

"Hmmm?" she replied dreamily.

Slowly, he lifted her up and laid her down on the bed. She whimpered as he slipped from inside her, but moaned when he lay behind her, spooning her and rubbing the soft flesh of her breasts and stomach.

"I'm thinking you're going to want to cover up this bad boy for a while," he said referring to the bite. His voice was half way between joking and anxious.

Erin frowned and reached out into their newly shared bond. *Whoa, head rush!* It was very strange to have someone else's emotions vying for attention, yet it was oddly intimate. Of course, it also meant they couldn't hide anything from one another, like his worry over the mark he had given her.

"Nuh-uh, I'm not hiding this." She proudly stroked her tender skin, pleased he couldn't see the slight wince on her face. *Well, come on! She'd just been bitten by a freaking polar bear; of course it was going to hurt!*

"I want everyone to see it, to prove to them that we've bonded. I'm proud to be your mate."

Gunner let out an audible sigh of relief, and she knew it had been the right thing to say. *Aww, he was so cute when he was needy.*

"Thank you," he rasped, his voice full of emotion. "Now about all those other things I want…"

EPILOGUE

Six months later

Erin snuggled into Gunner's chest, completely unperturbed that they were in the middle of the busy bar.

Gunner ran his hands down her back. "C'mon babe, let's get out of here and have our own celebration."

"Gunner," she chided softly, "we can't blow off our own bachelor and bachelorette parties."

"Sure we can, our boneheaded friends can celebrate without us."

"Charmed, I'm sure," grumbled Wayne.

Erin tried to stifle her laugh as she looked around at the mixture of amused and annoyed faces surrounding them. Yeah, Gunner could be really tactless at times, but at that moment she could care less. It was official; she and Gunner were getting married. They were having a small ceremony in Los Lobos with their friends, and a few of Erin's family, and then they were travelling up north to Gunner's bear clan to have a big celebration.

Over the last six months they had moved in together, visited his bear clan twice – *he and his brother acted like teenagers whenever they were together* - and now they had gotten engaged. At work, she had applied for a transfer to a different team. Gunner hadn't liked it, nor had the rest of the team who blamed losing her on Gunner seducing her. The director agreed with that in spite of her trying to tell him otherwise. *Please, she practically threw herself at Gunner!* Plus, Gunner had been even more furious when she was transferred to Diaz's team. But, they were making it work.

Although her desk was further away from him, she still had mementoes of him. Namely the slightly large picture he'd given her for her desk of the two of them kissing – everyone who stopped by her desk noted how big it was - it was kind of embarrassing! And, he had bought her a small, cuddly polar bear for her desk. Now, that she did love; little Gunner had pride of place next to Waldo. Although whenever big Gunner came by for a visit, strangely enough, Waldo somehow managed to find his way inside one of her drawers. *Strange that.* Her mate just couldn't abide any male cats in her life at all. As for her new boss, Diaz, Gunner was keeping the jaguar on his toes. *Mainly by constantly reiterating that if he even thought about touching Erin, the bear would beat the hell out of him.*

Erin had surprised herself by becoming close friends with not only Jessie and Avery, but also Isis and a nurse who worked for the SEA called Lucie - who also had an enormous crush on a very embarrassed Cutter. Yes, for once Erin actually found herself with friends who cared for her! Even Isis did! Moving to Los Lobos was the best thing she ever did. *Of course, most of her time was taken up by her very possessive and very needy bear mate…*

She blushed pink as his hand swept over her ass. "Gunner!"

"Maybe you should get a room," suggested Avery, unfazed by their groping.

"Sound advice," agreed Gunner. "Let's go get a room, babe."

"But we have plans…"

Gunner gestured to the assembled group. "Who cares about these idiots? They can entertain themselves."

"Remind me again why we're friends with this guy?" Cutter jerked his head at Gunner.

Jessie shrugged. "Well, I like Erin."

"And Gunner just seems to be attached to her... one way or the other," supplied Isis with a mischievous smile.

Gunner let out a low warning growl, and Wayne slapped him on the back. "Cheer up, it's gonna be fun. It's not every day you get married..."

"Tomorrow will be the only day I ever get married; we'll be together forever," corrected Gunner.

This was met with awws by the female members of the group, although Erin suspected Isis' aww might have been sarcastic.

Cutter clucked his tongue in irritation. "Who else is coming tonight?"

"We're meeting the rest of the guys downtown at a club a cousin of mine owns," said Wayne. "Pretty much half of the Los Lobos SEA will be there. I think even Diaz is coming."

"Fucking cat," muttered Gunner and Wes gave him a sour look that he completely ignored.

"Well, we're going uptown," Avery informed them, "and the other half of the Los Lobos SEA will be at the bachelorette party. We're just waiting for Lucie to arrive. No, wait there she is."

Cutter paled, and his face took on a hunted look. "Fuck, I'm going out the back. Don't tell her I'm here."

Wes nodded sagely. "Got your back, Jack, bitches be crazy."

Cutter thanked him and took off as Avery slapped Wes around the back of his head.

Lucie, a sweet hedgehog shifter bounded over, her eyes gleaming excitedly. "Hi guys! Was that Cutter just leaving?"

Wes nodded. "Yeah, he ducked out into the alley, said he wasn't feeling too good. Maybe you should go check on him."

"I will."

Lucie bustled away.

"You're so cruel," Jessie scolded.

Wes held up his hands in surrender. "He's a grown wolf hiding from a hedgehog shifter for hell's sake; he needs to man up."

Jessie pursed her lips. "No, I meant you're being cruel to her, encouraging her to chase after him like that when it's clear he's not interested."

Isis agreed wholeheartedly, or with as much heart as she could muster. "Yeah, given her crush on that mangy wolf, it's obvious she's suffering from some kind of severe head injury – cut her some slack!"

Gunner groaned and clutched Erin to him. "You really want to spend the night with these lunatics when you could spend the night with me?"

"We can all hear you, you know?" muttered Wayne.

"Go and have fun with your friends," said Erin, soothingly, "and just know that I'll be waiting for you when you get home."

"Fine! You have fun too, just not too much fun."

Isis tapped her chin thoughtfully. "How many male strippers are too many? Six? Ten? Twenty?"

Erin rolled her eyes. "Ignore her. There will be no strippers. I love you."

Gunner huffed. "Yeah, I love you, too - more, in fact, given that I'd be happy to blow these guys off to be with you."

"Okay, he's seriously starting to hurt my feelings now," griped Wayne.

Lucie came back frowning. "He wasn't in the alley; I'm sure I could scent he'd been there though. Do you think he had to go home because he was sick? Maybe there's something seriously wrong with him!"

Jessie slipped an arm around Lucie's shoulders. "Honey, let's go enjoy Erin's bachelorette party, and while we do that we will be more than happy to catalogue the list of things that are seriously wrong with Cutter."

"I second that," purred Isis.

Gunner let out a martyred sigh. "Since I can't change your mind about tonight, right?"

He looked at Erin hopefully who just shook her head.

His shoulders slumped. "Then I guess we better get going and get it over with."

"That's the spirit!" cried Wayne giving him another hearty slap on the back.

As they stepped out into the cool night air and prepared to part, Gunner ignored the fact that he could see Cutter lurking in the shadows and pulled his mate in for a lingering kiss.

"I love you," he murmured.

"I love you, too," she cooed. "I'm yours and you're mine forever, polar bear."

She was right; he was.

*

The stranger watched as the SEA agents poured out of the bar. He sneered as the brutish polar bear shifter fawned over the human woman. It was enough to make him sick. Mixed species matings should be illegal. The half-breed children those two would make should be drowned at birth.

But he was getting off track. He wasn't there for them. He was there for one reason – the wolf shifter currently skulking in the shadows like the coward he was.

Yes, the wolf would pay for what he had done, and when he was through, Cutter was going to wish he'd never been born.

To be continued...

The author is an obsessive reader of cozy mysteries and supernatural stories – in particular she loves supernatural cozy mysteries, and has watched every single episode of Psych at least twenty times. She spends far too much time reading or watching TV and

firmly believes that you can never have too many books, handbags or brooches. When she isn't writing supernatural stories she is at her day job, daydreaming about writing supernatural stories.

www.elizabethannprice.com

Printed in Great Britain
by Amazon

37307081R00156